Killing Virginia Crowe

A Novel

By Tyler Tullis

Cover art and interior layout by Mieko Takeshita

ISBN-10: 0692513558
ISBN-13: 978-0692513552

For my editor, colleague and friend, Jessica Wade.
(Which is a terrific western name in its own right.)

KILLING VIRGINIA CROWE

A Novel

TYLER TULLIS

1. Mud, Blood and Fine Fabric.

ART MADDOX HAD WISHED FOR SONS but received daughters. Three of them, before the doctor told his wife, Sadie, enough was enough.

The first girl arrived unexpectedly. Folks noticed Sadie's bump shortly after her beau marched south to fight Johnny Rebel in 1861. Art didn't lay eyes on his daughter until the war's end, when she was four years old. He came up with the name though. Paula, after Sadie's brother Paul, who lost an arm in the Battle of Bull Run. Art figured the gesture would help earn his way back into the good graces of Sadie's family once the news of her pregnancy broke.

Sadie's father, Reginald, a well-to-do banker out of Chicago, was hesitant to marry his youngest daughter to a soldier with no education, but when Art returned home a father and war hero, Reginald was left with little choice. Shortly after the marriage, Art determined fortune lay west along the new transcontinental railroad. With a few acres in Wyoming, he could be a bona fide cattle baron in less time than he'd been at war.

Reginald gave his blessing to the marriage—on the condition Art give up any damn fool idea of Wyoming. "Savage natives, slums of immigrants, bloodthirsty outlaws," he said one evening over cigars from the balcony of his Chicago townhouse. "Each more riddled with disease than the last, no doubt. Hardly country to raise a daughter, yes?"

Sadie took more offence than Art to the notion her veteran husband couldn't protect them. So, she and Art ran out one night with little more than their clothes and Paula.

Art worked for the Union Pacific mining coal outside of Rock Springs for a time. The pay was steady and Art hadn't spotted the right area to homestead yet. It was said too many Sioux roamed the plains, the land still too raw.

Elizabeth, the second daughter, arrived shortly after their escape west.

Months of waiting, mining, saving, working other ranches, holding out for the best land, turned to years. Six of them. Sadie had enough. The confrontation was ugly. She asked if he ever planned to make her a rancher's wife, threatened to go back to her father with the girls.

So, Art purchased the Maddox family homestead. Four acres in the southern Laramie Plains outside the mining town of Carbon. The soil wasn't particularly rich, but it was practically free. With a ranch hand and at least one son surely on the way, it would be profitable soon enough. What money they had left went toward the first head of cattle with the hope ten would multiply to fifty in a matter of years.

Sadie worried the complications of Elizabeth's birth had left her barren, but five years later came Hannah. Paula and Elizabeth seemed the only ones who took joy holding their baby sister for the first time. Paula would never forget the vacant expression in her mother's eyes as she stared at the baby.

After seven years with no sons, three years of drought, a ranch hand who'd disappeared after robbing them blind, and the continual threat of the Sioux, Art Maddox's long-awaited profit remained elusive. Farming crops sustained them for a time, but the drought left them near bereft. Pressure mounted to sell to bigger ranches nearby. By Paula's fifteenth birthday it was all the Maddox family could do to survive season to season, down to seven cows and four hogs.

Which brought Paula to the task at hand.

She found Brownie dead around noon, collapsed in a corner of the sty. The other hogs appeared healthy at first, but Henrietta was running a fever, likely taken by whatever had killed Brownie. If she wasn't separated within the hour the infection would surely spread.

Paula knew Pa could ill afford any more livestock falling dead. Unfortunately, he wasn't there, still up at the Alvord ranch trying to speak with Cliff Ritter about the water flow. Like many tasks on the ranch, this one fell to her. She stood on the sty's railing for several long minutes, wondering what she would do once she got a hold of the old girl.

Paula's delay came from two factors. Elizabeth, standing behind her, reminded her of the first. "You've never been in there without Pa before," she said, her little voice almost lost in the prairie wind.

"I know," Paula replied.

"Pa says you aren't strong enough to wrestle them," Elizabeth went on.

"Beth."

"Pa says you aren't supposed to go in there without him."

"Pa ain't here."

Elizabeth was quiet a moment, captivated watching Henrietta root through the trough the way 10-year-olds are captivated by everything. "So are you going in?" she asked at last.

Paula's grunt seemed loud as a hog's. "Go back in to Ma," she nearly shouted.

Elizabeth pouted some but turned to march back toward the house.

Paula performed another inspection of the road to town as her sister retreated. Pa had called for Sheriff Blanchfield yesterday to complain about the water flow. Blanchfield hadn't shown up, but if he did, he'd surely have his deputy in training with him. His son, Bo, went almost everywhere with his father. And he was the same age as Paula.

This was the second factor deterring her leap into the hog pit.

Henrietta's squeal summoned Paula's attention back to the sty. Ma told her it wasn't right to pray for selfish things, but she did anyway, asking that if Blanchfield and Bo showed up it wouldn't be in the next few minutes.

Climbing over the railing, Paula eased herself into the sty so as not to upset the hogs. She trudged through the mud to open the adjacent pen's gate, then positioned herself between Henrietta and the others. She'd watched Pa do it enough to know how it worked. Giving Henrietta a gentle rub, Paula began nudging then tugging at her middle to turn her away from the trough. It was near empty, but that hardly disinterested the hogs.

Henrietta squealed loudly once Paula shoved with all her might, working the animal toward the gate while trying to block the others. It had rained just enough that morning to churn the mud, and Paula slipped when

Henrietta scampered back to the trough. Paula cursed as she picked herself up, wiping the mud from her backside. Elizabeth, having only withdrawn to the back of the barn, broke out in laughter.

Paula ignored her sister and channeled her frustration to strength. Heaving on the pig as Pa had warned against, the hog twisted violently and toppled Paula again. This time her forehead struck a wrung in the fence on her way down. Wincing, Paula rose dizzily to make her exit. Elizabeth stopped laughing, rushing forward to ask if her sister was alright and to stare at the blood. Again Paula ignored her, marching for the barn and a heated cattle brand from its furnace.

Henrietta's selling price, if not her life expectancy, would probably fall with the hulking brand on her side, but she fled into the gate as predicted when the smoldering iron seared her flesh. The other hogs screamed just as wildly but kept their distance from Paula.

Hearing the commotion, Sadie exited the house with Hannah crying in her arms. "What's going on out here?"

"It's fine," Paula shouted back, not in the mood to elaborate.

Handing Hannah to Elizabeth with instruction to return to the house, Sadie hurried to Paula's side, taking the iron from her. "Out with it. What's this about?"

"Henrietta is sick, I had to separate her."

"And slice your forehead while you were at it?" Ma returned, dabbing the blood on Paula's brown with shawl. "Your father told you not to—"

"I wouldn't have to if he was here!" Paula yelled, pulling away. "You sure as hell weren't going to climb in there!" Paula grunted loudly and marched to the house, ensuring no one was on the road from town.

Sadie let her go, hands on her hips, standing alone with the odor of hog shit on the breeze.

Paula cleaned herself as best she could, hurriedly stripping off the muddy clothes and drawing herself a bath. Elizabeth reminded her she still had chores outside, but Paula didn't care. To her mother's chagrin, Paula emerged from her room thirty minutes later wearing a dress and a small white bandage on her forehead.

Sadie let her impatience known through a loud huff. "Young lady, what are you wearing that for? And that bandage is so small it barely covers your cut, you're lucky you don't need stitches."

"I'm fine," Paula said, striding outside to the porch. She planted herself on Pa's stool.

"That's your best dress, Paula," Ma pressed. "You—"

"It's my *only* dress," Paula corrected. "Margaret Vance in town has eight."

Ma walked in front of her daughter with downcast eyes. "You aren't Margaret Vance. And you would never talk to Pa this way."

"She wants to wear it for Bo Blanchfield," Elizabeth teased from the doorway, her smile goading.

Paula rose in a tower of fury. "Shut your mouth, Beth!"

"I've had my fill of this obstinance," Ma said, hefting Hannah in one hand while she pointed the other at Paula. "You will not behave like this. You'll either go to your room in that dress or put your clothes back on and get to your other chores. When your father hears how you're—"

"What makes you think Alvord didn't shoot him?" Paula shouted, turning to run back into the house for her room.

Sadie flinched as the bedroom door slammed. She didn't say anything until Elizabeth emerged from the front door. "Don't listen to her, she's just flustered from hitting her head," Sadie said, rocking Hannah to stop the crying. "Your Pa will be back this afternoon."

Neither Pa nor the Blanchfields came that afternoon. Paula hid in her room until sundown, content to sulk. She resumed her chores only to distract herself from worries of Pa. Before leaving the house, she removed her dress and laid it on her shelf as if handling baby Hannah.

They'd sold Ma's dresser with the mirror last winter, so Paula had to judge the bump along her brow with her fingers. It felt as big as Henrietta, though the pig probably looked more attractive. Paula had little to thank the Almighty for but offered a modest glance of acknowledgement to the heavens for keeping the Blanchfields away.

Paula ignored the dinner plate waiting for her with potatoes and beans on the kitchen table, the same as she ignored Ma and Elizabeth. She had no interest in sitting with them. The uneasy silence would only invite more drastic thoughts of Pa. Instead, she strode outside to the orange-washed prairie to feed the livestock.

Afterward, she climbed the barn and watched the horizon. He'd been gone since sunrise, but his ride should have taken a few hours at most. The Alvord ranch was just four miles northeast along the creek. The creek that had been dry for three days.

Paula knew there would be trouble when he went. She'd warned him, but the bump on her head reminded her that her stubbornness came from him. As the last of the sun vanished behind the hill, Paula slinked down from the roof. She wondered what they'd do if he never came back—if Alvord had buried him somewhere out in the prairie. Brushing their horse Jessamine in the barn, Paula considered saddling the old girl and riding up the creek to look for Pa. She knew both her parents would forbid it, especially at this hour.

Then she caught sight of a figure approaching from the north.

Paula ran from the barn with Pa's rifle in hand. The failing light shadowed the figure. She trained the rifle on him and called out, then relaxed at the familiar voice returning to her. "Watch your muzzle, sharpshooter, it's only me," said Pa.

Paula sprinted to him when he stumbled and collapsed. He took the rifle from her as she helped him back up, using both it and his daughter to aid his steps. Art wasn't a big man. If anything, he looked outright fragile these days. He'd lost considerable weight through years of drought.

Paula's hand dampened when she touched his back. There was just enough light to see the red stains in his shirt. Her teeth clenched. "Alvord did this?"

Pa shook his head and gently squeezed her shoulder. "Calm down and get me inside, daughter," he said.

"Where are you shot?"

"I'm not. Just took a tumble from Jake."

"Where is he?"

"Shot," Pa returned, his voice sagging.

Paula called for her mother at the porch. They both helped Art up the few stairs and into his bedroom. In the light they made out cuts along his right side and a swollen right ankle underneath his boot. "What happened?"

Paula asked after they dressed his cuts with their remaining bandages.

"Let me see to your father," Ma said, "your sisters need you."

"What happened?" Paula insisted, planting her feet.

Her mother fiercely pointed to the door, but Art waived a disarming gesture to his wife. "It's fine, mother, Paula is getting older," he said. "Sure enough, Alvord dammed up the creek on his land. I was going to head for the ranch to talk with Ritter but he found me at the dam, shot Jake from under me. Took a tumble into the creek bed."

"That's murder, now Blanchfield will have to do something," Paula exclaimed, as excited as she was angry.

"Murder charges don't exactly extend to horses, daughter," Pa said. "Maybe property theft. Ritter said he thought I was a rustler."

"What did he think you were there to steal, the dam?" Sadie asked. "You weren't even on Alvord's ranch."

"Well, he claimed he had the right to shoot since I was trespassing. It'll be his word against mine."

"That's our water!" Paula exclaimed.

"That may be, Paula, but before it flows here it resides there."

"This is horseshit," Paula returned, shaking where she stood.

"I won't hear such language from my daughter," Pa said, though his tone was anything but imposing.

"So what are we gonna do?" she pressed.

"I'm going to handle it," Pa insisted. "Tomorrow."

"Blanchfield isn't going to lift a finger for us, he's bought and paid for like you said."

"I'm going to talk to Alvord. Ritter said he was out in Cheyenne on business, he'll be back in Carbon tomorrow on the train."

"The only talk Alvord wants with us is to hear we're leaving, Pa."

"This is an adult matter, Paula Maddox, your father knows best. Now see to Hannah."

Paula nearly continued but her father gave a subtle shake of his head. He'd talk to her later. She stormed to the girls' bedroom. Talking was all he ever did.

✦ ✦ ✦

"What would you do if you were me, Paula?" Art asked later than night when tucking her in.

There was no accusation or challenge in his voice. He never spoke to belittle or shame. He never even spoke to discipline, leaving that task to Sadie. Even when Paula drove a cow too hard, lost a tool in the barn or made some other mistake that cost time or money, he never raised his voice. He only observed the mistake and corrected it. The man couldn't bring himself to show anger or weakness in front of his daughters. Paula saw plenty of each all the same.

She hesitated and looked out her window. "I'd shoot him," she returned quietly.

Art sighed and shook his head. "What would that accomplish?" he asked patiently.

"What else can we do?"

"We can think ahead to consequences," he told her. "If I kill one of the richest, most influential men in the territory, even with good legal standing, which I don't have, then I go to jail, if not the noose. Where would that leave you and your sisters? Your mother?"

"We don't have water," Paula reminded him. "We barely have the cows. He's gonna boot us off the land. Where will that leave us?"

Art missed a beat, trying to hold onto his smile. The special one he saved just for her. "I won't let that happen," he said with his most reassuring voice.

The way Paula looked at him drained the confidence from his face. She hated to do it, to make her father feel low, but she didn't know how to make her eyes lie like his did.

"Sometimes... sometimes a dream is all you have, daughter. Do you understand that?"

She didn't say anything.

"That's what this land is, Paula. The chance to do anything. With enough hard work, we..." He sighed, then finished tucking her in and told her not to worry.

She listened to him limp out of the house to the barn where he kept his bottle of whisky.

2. Line of Credit.

PAULA WOKE TO HANNAH'S CRIES IN the morning. They came before the rooster's call more often than not. The baby didn't sleep well, sometimes struggling to breathe. The doc had warned Sadie a third child would be risky after the complicated cesarean with Elizabeth. There were almost 13 years between Paula and the toddler bawling in the next room. Proof of her parents' desperation for a boy.

Paula did her best to fill the role of strong lad. She rose alongside Pa most mornings, herding cattle between fields to graze, seeding, repairing fences, checking irrigation. Paula took care of the calves with Sadie or on her own. She enjoyed feeding in the winter and spring, though Art reminded her not to get attached. Branding and castration were never easy for Paula. None of it was easy.

Certainly not for a spindly 15-year-old shy of 110 pounds at five feet and three inches.

As a child she'd been happy working outside with Pa. The joy of fresh air and freedom had since diminished, especially on mornings when Pa was… indisposed. He'd picked up the bottle in recent years. They never spoke of it. Once Paula heard Pa tell Louis Vance at the general store that the drink helped ease his old war wounds, but he hadn't been wounded so far as she knew.

Pa didn't emerge from the barn until mid-morning, a new record by Paula's reckoning.

Paula paused from her work digging new rows for her mother's bean stalks when she saw Pa leaning on the barn door. He looked as off-kilter as he had rambling back from Alvord's, his face pale and sweaty. She wanted to look away as he rambled to the water barrel to wash off but couldn't. She could still smell it on him when he walked by. Paula didn't say anything but found her knuckles white gripping the shovel.

"I'll handle that," Ma said a few minutes later, emerging from the house in her trousers. She reached for the shovel in her daughter's hands. "You're bound for town. Pa needs help with the supplies."

"Do we have money for supplies?"

Ma repeated the command with her eyes.

As much as Paula usually liked trips to town, she didn't feel like riding anywhere with Pa that morning. "Is he not feeling well?" Paula asked. She regretted the cheap shot when Ma paused with the shovel, swallowing whatever she might have said in her defense.

"Go fix Jessamine to the wagon," Ma said. "Then clean up."

"Can I—"

"No dress, you'll ruin it lifting goods into the wagon."

"At least town would finally know I'm a girl," Paula said, turning to make for the barn.

Pa climbed onto the wagon a few minutes after Paula finished the hitch. He tried a smile, complimenting her on how fast she could get Jessamine ready. Paula didn't say anything.

The ride to town was an hour over Simpson Ridge, a gradient so steep the railroad often needed double engines to cross. Carbon was a small but bustling little town along the rails. A chief coal mining site for the Union Pacific halfway between Rawlings to the west and Cheyenne to the east, Carbon coal ended up in locomotives across the country. Last year the railroad established new mines under the Wyoming Coal and Mining Company. Since then, the town had seen an influx in Finnish and Scandinavian miners. They worked for less than the old Brit crews. Railroad men kept much of the town's order through labor disputes, leaving Blanchfield's office to handle matters specific to longtime residents.

Which meant Alvord policed things outside the railroad, Paula thought.

Ma often said she didn't like what the town had become since the railroad bought the mines. With all the foreigners it could get rowdy in a hurry, and it wasn't the cleanest town along the tracks. Sickness like typhoid, diphtheria and cholera were commonplace among the miners. Still, there were good folks who depended on the beef industry that Alvord had brought with him from Texas years ago. There were plenty like Art whom he'd run afoul, but with all the influence Alvord waved in the capital and the money he brought into town, he was well liked by most.

From what Paula knew, Alvord had started as a Texas cowboy who made some of the first cattle drives north when the beef bonanza started. He brought the industry to Wyoming with ranches in the Laramie Plains, outside Cheyenne and further east into Nebraska.

He was a family man, a Christian first and foremost, as he described himself. Folks liked him because he was down to earth. He paid his men fair wages for fair work.

The problem was Alvord's notion of fair wasn't on the level with Pa's.

Paula glanced at her father as he halted the wagon outside the Vance general store. He still looked hungover. More than that, he looked exhausted. It wasn't just from being thrown from his horse or the extra work the dry creek had created.

Perhaps Pa used up all his luck surviving the war because he had none left. Years keeping unhealthy cows alive on disputed land wore him down, not to mention always looking over his shoulder for Alvord, Carbon's seedy element and the Sioux. Paula knew protecting so much, his girls included, weighed heavy. She felt more and more of the weight as his strength and tenacity waned.

Art's haggard frame matched his malnourished spirit. Unrealized dreams deteriorated a man far more than an honest day's labor. His eyes alone gave off enough vulnerability to attract vultures, and he knew they were circling.

But still he wore a smile when he looked at her.

Whatever faults Art Maddox's possessed, a shortage of love for his daughters wasn't among them. He rarely spoke of hardship in front of the girls, as eager to protect their peace of mind as their home. That had changed recently, of course, but only with Paula. She was brighter than most girls her age, and she'd matured quickly—too quickly—thanks to three son's worth of responsibility heaped on her.

Paula knew he loved her, perhaps more than Elizabeth and Hannah, but to see him fraying at the edges this way, giving in to the bottle, up against the inevitability of destruction... She wasn't sure what to say to him, so she didn't say anything. All she could do was all she'd ever done—trust when he said he'd take care of it.

"Suppose I'd better go see if he's back yet," Pa said with a long breath, looking toward Alvord's Real Estate Company. He turned to Paula with a raised eyebrow. "Unless you want to go chew on him first."

His smile told Paula he was trying to make her laugh. It faded when she folded her arms.

He dismounted and helped her down as well. "Why don't you pay the Professor a visit, I'm sure he'd like that. I'll just be a bit."

"You ain't going to find Blanchfield first?" Paula questioned. "He never even showed yesterday."

"Might as well go straight to the source if I can," Art said. "And I doubt the Professor would be inclined to hear 'ain't' uttered from those pretty lips."

Paula held her frown, turning for Bob Jack's Boarding House beside the store.

Paula once came to town weekly for a lesson from Atticus Roland. The former college professor had made the trip west when he took to coughing. Originally bound for the dry climate of Arizona, he settled on the then quiet town of Carbon when he discovered the unpleasantness of heat further south. He'd taken an immediate liking to Paula when he encountered her at the Vance store one afternoon. He'd never agreed to any formal tutelage, but he told her stories whenever she was in town. Stories of magnitude, of course, not the dime novels the boys read.

The Professor was a Western Civilization buff. From Socrates to Augustus, from Thermopylae to Hadrian's Wall, Paula found it all fascinating. Sadie loved the idea of a classical education for her daughter, piecemeal though it be, and allowed the lessons. Roland was harmless enough. Particularly since he'd become bedridden altogether last autumn. Red said he probably wouldn't make it another year.

Speaking of Red, Paula heard his thick accent call out as she leaned on the door to the Boarding House. "Top o' the mornin', Miss Maddox," he said, trying not to sneak up on her.

She jumped anyway, wheeling about to face him. Red was the town doc, his name earned for his flaming Irish hair. His real name was something outlandish, at least to Paula. Flanners or Flannery, something like that.

"Didn't mean ta' frighten ya, Miss. Whatar ya doin' standin' about?" Before Paula could answer, Red glanced down the street and noticed Art walking into Alvord's. "Ah, in town for a bit of business, oi see. Keepin' watch?"

"I was just…"

"Don't fret, Miss," he assured, patting her head. She liked Red but hated when he petted her. "Oi'm sure it'all be fine." Red pushed up his spectacles and went into the store.

Paula was too anxious for one of the Professor's stories. She waited outside for Pa to emerge from Alvord's, biting her cheeks despite Ma's admonishments. Pa hadn't even taken his gun from the wagon. She found herself hating him for not hating Alvord.

She released a long breath when Pa emerged from Alvord's, making for the Railroad Depot. He spoke to a man for only a moment before trudging back through the dust, hands in his pockets. His limp was more prominent now.

"His train won't be in until after three o'clock, there was a delay," Art said when he returned to the wagon. "No sense in riding back only to turn around the second we get home. Why don't we supply ourselves and visit for a spell?" Paula wordlessly trailed him to the general store.

✦ ✦ ✦

Louis Vance was a portly man. Business had been good for him with the influx of miners and Alvord's investments to town. Construction was already underway to expand his current store into departments by winter. Word was Alvord would help him open a second store at the Cullen Mine within a year.

A line commonly ran from Vance's door in the mornings, but he'd been holding shorter hours during construction. He wouldn't be open for business until the late afternoon but unlocked the door when he heard tapping on the glass. The look he gave Pa at the door flushed Paula red with anger. It wouldn't make what her father had to do any easier.

"Maddox," was his greeting from behind the half open door. "Come to make payments?"

"I need to speak with you," Pa returned.

Vance managed a smile for Paula when he noticed her behind her father. "Hello, young lady. You're looking pretty as ever."

It was a lie. Paula knew she wasn't pretty, least not dressed as a ranch hand with a shortened braid.

Vance sighed but waved them in.

Paula immediately sneezed once inside, kicking up sawdust. Vance locked up behind them and set to covering more of the counter with a sheet to protect from the dust. "Apologies, I'm not really fit for customers yet."

"And yet here we be, Mr. Vance," Red said from down an aisle.

Paula found the doc collecting bottles of chloroform from a wooden crate recently arrived. Red often forced stores to open early under the pretense of a medical emergency. Even Paula had been in town enough to witness it on more than one occasion. She decided to wander his way while Pa spoke to Vance, not sure if she had the constitution to endure the discussion.

"Morning," Art called to Red. He knew the doc's fondness for Paula, having lost a daughter of his own to snakebite, it was said. When Art turned, he found the shopkeep behind his counter. "Certainly warm for this time in May. Apt days for construction."

"They are," Vance echoed, folding his arms. Waiting.

Pa forced a meek smile and looked to his boots.

Paula hated when he did that.

"Looks like Mr. Alvord decided to dam up Carbon Creek on me," Art began. "I intend to talk to him about it this afternoon upon his return."

"Don't expect he'll be inclined to do much talking, Maddox. Not unless you decided to sell."

"No cause for that. Just need him to be a bit more neighborly."

"Well that sounds like a fine plan, Maddox. Though it doesn't inspire much confidence on my part. Certainly not as the good Samaritan who floated you for that flour and iron last month. I expected you last week for payment."

"And you'll have it with interest, I just need that water back to turn the corner with the ripe cows I got in the wings."

Vance noticed Red glowering his way and sighed, leaning closer. "Maddox, do you know what Alvord would say if he knew I was getting you by month to month?"

"It's been one month," Art said in a stiff whisper.

"Why do I get the feeling it's about to be two?"

Art stared at him hard before glancing back to his feet, swallowing hard. "Because you're a good man," he said just loud enough Paula could hear. "And good as he's been to you, you know what he's offering me ain't right." Art's voice broke. "Shot my damn horse out from under me yesterday, Louis. How am I supposed to get square with anyone if I can't get a fair take?"

Still Vance was silent.

"You have a girl too, Louis. I have three."

"That's why I keep her here, where it's safe," Vance snapped in a whisper. "I don't put her at risk chasin' dreams out of reach."

Art swallowed hard again, his shoulders sinking. As he backed from the counter, Vance rolled his eyes. He turned to shout into the next room. "Mother! Find Margaret, little Paula is here." He gave a small nod to Art, handing him a crate to fill. "Our daughters are friends. Not many girls around here their age, after all."

"Thank you," Art said, extending his hand.

Vance hesitated before taking it, looking around to make sure Red was the sole witness.

Paula braced, waiting for the inevitable spatter of footsteps to burst into the room. Margaret wore a pink dress, a matching ribbon in her blond hair. Likely a new outfit her father had ordered from back east, which Margaret confirmed within a few moments of conversation.

Paula knew it was wrong to hate anyone, so between Alvord and Margaret Vance she'd have plenty of prayers to say before bed that night. Margaret had everything Paula didn't. The latest fashions from the city, dainty jewelry, her own bedroom, a secure future and weekly (if not daily) conversations with Bo Blanchfield.

Not to mention prettier hair and a cuter face. Margaret was a girl becoming a lady. Envy set Paula off bad enough as it was, but the way Margaret gloated…

"Mother is taking me on the train to Nebraska to see our Aunt Eliza next week," she started. "It's been so sunny I'm going to ask for a new parasol before we go. I want to keep my skin white as porcelain. Boys like that."

"Where in Nebraska?" Paula asked to shift the subject.

"Lavender Station. I'm much more interested in the cities further east, though. They're more sophisticated. Weren't you born in Chicago?"

Paula had answered Margaret's question twice before. It was all that interested Margaret, despite Paula's inability to remember anything about the city. "I was only a baby," she reminded Margaret.

"But you still have family there?"

"My grandfather, I think. Maybe an aunt. Ma and Pa don't keep in touch with them."

"A pity. Do you get to travel with your father much?"

"Not much. I'm busy helping him at the ranch."

Busy rolling in cow shit, Margaret must have thought. Ma would have slapped Paula for even thinking the word, but Paula found obscenities top of mind around Margaret Vance. It would be easy enough to ignore her, to shove her into the dust and tell her what a spoiled brat she was, but ending the false friendship wouldn't do Pa any favors. Not after what Margaret's father had just done for him. Instead, she asked Margaret what there was to do in Nebraska and how long she'd be there. She only pretended to listen, focusing on the shifting conversation at the counter while Red rang up his goods.

"Heard about yar horse, Maddox," the doc said, leaning on the counter by one arm. "One a'the boys was laughin' bout it in Jim Ross' place. T'ain't right."

"I'm sure Mr. Alvord will talk to his men," Vance said, playing the middle. "He has to keep on a hard sort for security, but he doesn't stand for wanton action."

"Aye, he's dealin' with worse men at the rail hub, oi reckon," Red said. "Politicians. Been in Cheyenne for a week wranglin' the slipp'ry bastards into sending army here 'gainst the Sioux."

"Nice to have that kind of pull," Pa said, motioning for Paula to help him carry supplies to the wagon. Margaret shadowed her, still talking about her new dress from the catalogue.

"Don't know if it'll do much good at the end of the day," Vance admitted, leaning over the counter. "Word is General Crook has his eyes focused further north. Prospectors are flooding Dakota, and the Sioux don't take kindly to company after their treaty at Fort Laramie. The Black Hills are supposed to be off limits to prospecting."

"Oi don't suppose too many a'the boys siftin' dirt up there know about the treaty, fresh in from Missouri to New Mexico," Red offered.

"And Crook doesn't seem too intent on educating them," Vance said. "Looking for an excuse to tear that treaty up, I expect. Root the Sioux out once and for all. Lord knows the railroad wants it. And in the meantime, they still run amok on the plains. How many men have you treated with arrows to the back in the last year, Red?"

"T'ings aren't usually as dramatic as all that, Vance. But yes, there've been injuries. Fatalities."

"Even with all his hired guns, I'm amazed Alvord has done this well keeping his cattle safe through the raids. Hard to imagine how you've warded the savages off this long, Maddox."

"I reckon a hundred head paint a bigger target on your back than seven," Art offered with a humble smile. He carried a crate out the door. "Not all doom and gloom though, Vance—I hear Blanchfield and the town threw you quite the party after they hauled in the Sibling Gang."

From the way Vance blushed, Paula guessed he either didn't know or didn't care that her father was only buttering him up.

"I didn't have all that much of a hand in it," Vance gushed. "I just mentioned to the marshal that I heard one say where they were headed. They held up that train I was on. And they only nabbed the sister, not the whole gang. Virginia Crowe."

"She was the worst though, from what I heard tell," Art said. "You cut off the snake's head."

"It was the marshal who brought her in. Just glad to have one less menace out there. How many times did the Sibling Gang hold up payroll to the miners? Alvord's men had to help Blanchfield put down a riot the last time."

"Must've been somethin' to be under the gun of Virginia Crowe, though," Red mused.

"Wasn't an experience I'd care to repeat," Vance said after a loud huff. "She gunned down men for breathing wrong on that train. Scars on her face, burns on her arm… Who knows how a woman gets like that. Don't expect her trial at the Fort will be long after all the blood she—"

"Father, not in front of the girls," Mrs. Vance chided as she stepped into the store. Margaret had tuned out but Paula looked away in a hurry, blushing.

"Yes, well, we need to be running out to the Alvord ranch with supplies anyway," Vance said. "When Alvord returns, they're set to drive a herd northeast. Mother and I saw a soldier headed through town that way this morning. A scout, perhaps. Maybe Alvord has at least brought some fresh attention to our plight on the plains. Suppose we'll see."

Red helped Art and Paula finish loading their wagon as Vance mounted up in his. Paula paused at the store's door when she saw Blanchfield come around the corner, walking with a scattershot over his shoulder as he was accustomed. She supposed it made him feel big since he clearly didn't do all that much.

The sheriff sighed when he saw Art, but the rancher wouldn't let him by without an explanation for the lack of help the day prior. Paula set a heated glare Blanchfield's way but rescinded it when she caught sight of Bo trailing his father. Margaret left a sentence about Nebraska hanging, beelining for Bo. Half embarrassed to be seen doing boys' work and half surrendering to the prettier girl, Paula kept her head down and continued lifting supplies to the wagon.

As predicted, Blanchfield offered no help or advice to Pa other than to reconsider Alvord's offer for the Maddox ranch. "I can't make it out to every homestead upon request, Maddox," the lawman said. "I have to give priority to issues pertaining to the city proper when they boil up."

"It's a matter of jurisdiction," Bo chimed beside his father.

Blanchfield might have looked proud had Red not seized on the boy's comment. "And might Curtis Alvord's ranch be in yer jurisdiction, Sheriff?" The Irishman's wide smile diffused what would have been an incendiary question from Art.

Blanchfield frowned nonetheless. "Several of his businesses are," he answered, "and I'll thank you not to presume where I allocate my time."

"Just observing where it wasn't spent," Art said as he helped Paula with supplies. "Ritter shot my horse with me on it."

"While trespassing on private property," Blanchfield finished. "Heard about that. Not an ideal situation to press charges. Best you reconsider Mr. Alvord's offer before this spat boils over. Like Bo said, my jurisdiction only goes so far."

Paula watched her father flinch, biting back whatever she wished he would say. Not paying attention to her footing in her fluster, she stepped too quickly off the porch and dropped a crate of sugar and corn feed. The bags scattered along the road but mercifully the contents did not. Unmercifully, Paula landed square on her backside with a sharp yip. All eyes turned to her. Pa and Red scurried to help but she pushed herself up in a hurry, pretending the pain away.

Collecting their goods with cheeks as red as the doc's hair, Paula noticed why her father had scuttled so quickly to the scene. A previously hidden bottle of whisky lay by the crate. Paula left it for him to pick up. She set the crate into the wagon and took the reins to Jessamine. "I want to go," she said while Margaret struggled to keep a laugh to herself.

3. Carbon Café Donuts.

OBSERVING HIS DAUGHTER AS EMBARRASSED as she was frustrated, Art led the wagon down to the town café. "What say we enjoy a treat while we wait for the train?" he asked. "Lord knows you've earned one, putting in so much work lately."

Paula didn't say anything, dismounting the wagon but checking the ties over the blanket hiding their supplies. Her father had been looted before by miners with idle time.

She followed Pa into Carbon Café, the latest addition to the town largely financed by Alvord. He had his own table in the back, Paula heard tell. A slender woman in a flowery red dress beamed at Pa as he batted dust from his coat. Ms. Ladeaux. Alvord had hired her to run the place, though she insisted folks call her Rebecca.

She had an accent and plugged the occasional French word into her sentences. Paula wasn't sure if she did it because she was French or wanted people to think she was. "Bonjour, you can have a seat at the bar if you would like," she called, filling up a woman's coffee at a booth.

"Reckon a cushioned seat would be appreciated," Art returned, placing a hand on his daughter's shoulder.

Paula blushed, this time from the look of realization on Rebecca's face. It wasn't the first time Paula had been mistaken for a boy in town.

"Je suis désolé, just a moment for Mindy to clear a table for you two." They waited for a booth by the window. Art let Paula sit first. Her gaze stayed fixed out the window rather than the menu Mindy handed her. Pa tried another smile.

"On a scale from cowboy to Henrietta, how hungry are you?" he asked.

"Henrietta died this morning," she answered blankly. "Caught the fever from Brownie. He died yesterday. When you were gone."

Pa only blinked. He'd failed to look in on the livestock, and she knew it.

Mindy coughed away her discomfiture.

"Uh, do you need a spell to make up your mind, daughter?" Pa asked.

"I'm not hungry," Paula said.

He fumbled for her menu while mustering a smile for Mindy. "Course you are, been a long day already." He ran his finger down the menu for the first sweet thing he could find. "A doughnut, I hear you glaze 'em these days."

"Sure do," Mindy returned. "One for each?"

"Just coffee for me."

Mindy nodded and took the menus back.

When his daughter kept her gaze on the outside passersby, Art folded his hands on the table and leaned forward. He thought for a moment about what to say but couldn't arrive at anything that mattered. "I appreciate what you did back there," he offered at last. "The Vance girl annoys the blazes out of me too."

She allowed a thin smile, granting him a single nod.

He grinned and took a long breath. "Thank the Lord your mother knows how to raise girls with a sense of decorum. A pretty dress or two doesn't make a lady."

"At least she looks like one," Paula said. Even she was surprised how much bite she put into the words. She looked to her father to measure his reaction. His frame slouched some. So in turn did Paula's.

Pa's eyes darted back and forth as Mindy brought over his coffee and Paula's doughnut. Neither of them moved, just waiting for the other to say something. "When I met your mother, she was wearing a dress a might like the one you have," he said at last.

His eyes glazed over. Paula knew the look. He'd told her this story before.

"She wasn't much older than Elizabeth then. Twelve, maybe. Spunky little thing for a banker's daughter. We wouldn't be married until after the war, but I knew right away. Too adventurous to be hold up in that big house of your granddad's. Had everything in the world, except something of her own. She wanted to build her life. So did I."

Art slowly ran his hand over the tabletop until it reached his mug. He shook his head and smiled before taking a sip, his eyes lost in memory. "The day we stepped onto that train bound west... It was like I'd given her everything she'd ever wanted and more. Like everything we'd ever need was just over the horizon. In that moment I felt bigger than I had driving the rebels back at Bull Run."

He chuckled to himself, swirling his coffee. "A Chicago townhouse probably sounds pretty good to her these days."

Paula softened when his eyes drifted to hers. "Your mother and your sisters deserve better than all this, Paula. You deserve better. You ought to have a closet filled with fine dresses. You should be in school with the likes of the Professor, not out digging ditches and moving beasts through the dirt. At the very least you ought to have a Pa who doesn't leave you to his chores while he... wallows in disappointments."

When a tear collected in his eye, he quickly wiped his it clear, forcing a soft laugh. "Sometimes I wonder if even little Hannah knows the sort of man I am."

Paula had never heard him so exposed. She wasn't sure what to feel. "You're a good sort, Pa," she said.

The silence hung for a long moment. "I'm sorry, Paula. I'm sorry you must worry about all your old man's problems. I'm sorry I can't spoil you like you ought to be."

"I don't care about that," Paula pressed, something heavy rising in her throat. "I just want everything to turn out right."

"It will," he managed, regaining hold of loose emotions. "Of course it will. Things'll be better once we can sell them ripe cows, get them delivered for fifty-five dollars a head back east. We just have to clear this matter up with Alvord and things will be fine. Vance is right, he's a fair man. He'll make it right when we're face to face."

Paula asked the question with her eyes alone. *But what if he doesn't?*

"I'll handle it," he promised again.

She wasn't accustomed to staring at him for so long. She looked away, blushing. "You're making a scene, Pa."

He only grinned wider, pushing his empty mug out for the next time Mindy came by. "You're very bright. You know that, don't you?"

"Pa…"

"You get it from your mother. Maybe your granddad. It's a miracle after all the time you've spent out here with only me and them dumb cows."

She didn't say anything.

He reached across the table to take her hand in his. It was thick with calluses and fresh blisters, but even now she felt safest at his touch. "If all I have to show for myself is you, Paula, I'd still be a proud man."

Whatever Paula was fixing to say scattered upon the blow of the horn from the train pulling into the depot.

Pa withdrew his hand and took a deep breath. "Looks like my train's here," he said. He rose after throwing three bits, possibly his last, on the table. "I'll go catch him before he heads off to his ranch. Stay here and I'll be back shortly, alright?"

When all she offered back was a worried expression, he leaned down to kiss her forehead and gently tugged on her braid as he had when she was a child. "I'll see you soon. Eat that doughnut." Art walked out of the café and threw on his duster. He offered a final reassuring glance through the window.

Once he was across the street, Paula rose without touching her pastry, intent on following him.

4. Civil Discourse.

CURTIS ALVORD WAS A BIG MAN. An abundance of muscle stretched his shirts tight and bulged under his rolled-up sleeves. A normal sized kerchief looked like a child's around his neck, wide as his cheekbones. His wife teased that she couldn't serve him her fine china—his calloused fingers wouldn't fit through the handles.

Alvord might have been mistaken for hired muscle rather than a ranch boss. His ten- gallon Texas wide brim was stained with sweat from days outside with his men and cattle. People like Louis Vance admired him for it. He was one of them, they said. He shared in honest labors.

He stepped off the 3:40 from Cheyenne wearing a brown jacket and mismatched bolo tie. As usual, a veritable congregation had gathered to welcome him, many calling for his attention the moment his oversized boot struck the depot floor.

Mayor Hardwick was the first in line, extending a hand. "Glad to see you, Mr. Alvord," he began. "I trust the proceedings…" Hardwick trailed off once he realized he'd been bypassed.

Alvord pushed past Cliff Ritter and his lawyer as well, the clamor of little importance until his lips found his wife's cheek. Beaming, he then lowered himself to a knee in front of his son Jacob. "How's m'boy?" Alvord asked as the eight-year-old leapt at him.

Jacob returned the hug. "Dunlap taught me to make jammers!" he exclaimed.

"Those jelly biscuits of his?" Alvord asked. "You fixin' to end up a slim cowboy or a fat cook?"

"Dunlap says they keep a man goin' on the trail."

"I'll have to remind him jelly corndodgers don't keep on the trail." Alvord swung Jacob around under the arms while the boy laughed, like a doll in his thick hands. "How's the ranch? You protectin' your mother while I'm away?"

"Yes, sir."

Alvord pushed back his son's diminutive hat and ruffled his hair, then rose to kiss his wife again. "How are things?" he asked.

She smiled and nodded toward Ritter. "Best ask your man, I'm sure you're more eager for his report than mine."

"Never," Alvord said with a smile, lifting his boy over his head so he could sit on his shoulders. He took a moment to shake a few hands, make a few jokes, inquire about happenings at the mine. His laugh barreled through the air down the length of main street, more inviting than frightening.

Mayor Hardwick waited patiently. Alvord was more mayor than Hardwick, of course—if the two ever came to odds it was surely Alvord's voice folks would heed. Most everyone knew Mayor of Carbon was a position vetted if not appointed by Alvord.

"Shall we head home?" Alvord asked his wife after thanking a few friends for well wishes. "I much prefer the company of brainless cows to brainless lawmakers."

The mayor's smile dimmed some. "I trust discussions proved somewhat fruitful?" he asked at last.

Alvord shook his head on his way from the depot to the office. "One more moment, Hardwick." He turned to the thin man in black at his side while he lowered Jacob from his shoulders. "Let's have it then, Ritter."

"The third-year lot moved up past the Fort into Nebraska, the rest of the Laramie cows are stuck."

"Sioux?"

"Three raids, eight cows, two men," Ritter said mechanically. "Two raids back-to-back, one in the morning, the other that night. Our scouts aren't doing much good, the Sioux converge before an attack but disappear afterward. Got us blockaded. Short on firepower, shorter on courage. Percy's horse found its way to the ranch three days ago with him tied to it. Wasn't pretty."

"It was disgusting," Jacob said, to which his father shot Ritter a biting glare.

Ritter dipped his head in apology. "We cut him loose soon as we could."

Alvord sighed as they walked down the dirty street. Most of the crowd had dispersed, aware he was busy with business. Only his wife, lawyer, Mayor Hardwick and Ritter followed. "I'll see what I can do about the courage problem. My new friends ought to help with the firepower." Alvord pointed back to the train.

The mayor turned to see nine men exiting the main car. All appeared armed, none wore uniforms. "Is the army sending troops to the plains?" Hardwick asked, unguarded despair in his voice. "How did your meetings go?"

Alvord shot him an annoyed glance. "Cover your ears, son," he said, and the boy obeyed. "I wouldn't trade a bucket of shit for every politician in Cheyenne."

"Curtis," Mrs. Alvord admonished.

"I'm sorry, dear, but they're all worthless. They're more focused on Dakota than Wyoming with the gold rush in the Black Hills. General Crook wasn't even there, they didn't know if he was at Fort Laramie or still down in Arizona killing Apache."

"They aren't willing to help secure the plains?" Mrs. Alvord asked so the Mayor wouldn't have to again.

"We're entirely on our own for now. President Grant has the army focused on the northern Sioux in the Black Hills, they don't give a good goddamn about the plains as long as the railroads survive. I hired another nine guns in the city to help on the drives. I'm going myself as soon as possible, every day those cows don't make it East their value decreases. I want to hit the trail immediately. We—"

Alvord stopped when he noticed the lone figure standing in front of the real estate shop. Art Maddox.

Ritter's hand moved to his hilt, but Alvord motioned for him to hold.

"Maddox," Alvord said. "Something I can help you with?"

"I need my water back, Mr. Alvord," he said.

Alvord asked his wife to take Jacob to the wagon waiting behind the store. The lawyer accompanied them, but Ritter remained at Alvord's side.

"I only have a minute, Maddox," Alvord said, walking past him up the steps to his store. "Can you walk while you talk?"

"As long as you're willing to listen, sir," Art said, following him up the steps. "I need my water. You dammed the creek that flows onto my land."

Alvord strode into his front office, grabbing an operation ledger. "I needed to build a reservoir for my cattle, Maddox. Got plenty up there, as I'm sure you know. Getting them to the creek jams things up for me."

"With respect, sir, what do you think it does for me?"

"That land of yours isn't good for a ranch, Maddox, I've told you that. Half that plot is rock and—"

"It would do fine if it had water."

"Before that creek hits your land it flows through mine, and I have to do with it what's best for business. That's all this is, Maddox, business."

"You're not just destroying my business, Mr. Alvord, you're destroying my family," Art returned.

Alvord stopped flipping through his ledger. "You know that ain't my intention, Maddox. But I warned you when you bought that land, I had plans to expand. And frankly, I didn't appreciate competition encroaching. You had plenty of other land you could have bought just as cheap without stickin' in my craw."

"Further into the plains, sure," Art returned. "Might as well pitch a tent next to a Sioux camp."

Alvord took his book and a cashbox from the back counter, then walked out past Art. Ritter hung close behind.

"Doesn't help that your man here shot the horse out from under me either, sir," Art said, trailing.

Alvord glanced to Ritter, who nodded.

"You've been warned about trespassing before, Maddox," Ritter said, hiding a thin smile.

"Do you shoot at any man who rides up to the front door too?" Art shouted.

Alvord turned, making a disarming gesture with his free hand. "I'm sorry about your mount, but if you rode up to the reservoir out of nowhere, I'm sure Mr. Ritter had cause for alarm."

"Why do you want it?" Art asked, the desperation in his voice emerging. "My land. If it's so worthless—"

"Because you don't deserve it, Maddox." Alvord didn't shout but he might as well have from the shock on Art's face. Alvord sighed. "I'm sorry, Maddox, but you're a mess. You may have been a decent soldier but you ain't no rancher, you got no business takin' up space if you can't turn it around in six years. I need it for my own. Things might have been different if you'd gotten your drinking under control but—"

"That's what this is about?" Art exclaimed. "You'll drive me and my family off because I drank too much at your damn Christmas bonfire?"

"It's best for business *and* best for your family. None of you can last out there. Leavin's the best thing for y'all. Now good day, Maddox."

Hardwick waited out back by the wagon with Mrs. Alvord and Jacob, eager to continue the discussion about Cheyenne. The group tensed when Art followed Alvord out the back, his volume rising. "Those seven cows are all I got for a wife and three children," he said, his face flushing. "You're a family man. Please. Just give me a chance to sell healthy and we can try something new."

Alvord turned, shaking his head. "You think you're going to persuade me by hounding me in front of my family after you've been drinking, Maddox?" he asked, his voice hushed.

The red on Art's face intensified with embarrassment.

"I think it's time you left, Mr. Maddox," Hardwick said, grabbing his shoulder to turn him.

"I'm begging you, Alvord, please," Art said, reaching into his jacket. "Don't make me—"

Everyone jumped at the shot. It was followed by a scream from Mrs. Alvord, ducking away in the wagon with her son pulled close.

Art stood motionless, his gaze shifting from Alvord to Ritter. A few dollar bills wafted down from Art's jacket. He pressed his hand on the blood soaking his middle. Then he dropped onto his back.

"Pa!"

Alvord wheeled around when he heard the small shout from the corner of his shop. A girl he recognized ran to Art's side, sliding beside him as her face tightened and tears ran free.

"Pa! Are you…" Paula's voice choked.

Art slowly reached for her cheek but didn't touch her when he saw his hand bloodied.

Alvord frowned at Ritter, who holstered his pistol and took a defensive step back. "He was reaching for something," Ritter said, looking between his boss and the mayor. "And getting delirious. You said yourself he'd been drinking. I wasn't going to let him pull on you or your family."

Alvord's frown told Ritter he remained unconvinced. "Fetch the doc," he commanded, taking off his coat and pulling his neckerchief free.

Paula recoiled as Alvord knelt beside her.

"I need to put pressure on the wound," he told her gently.

Paula was too distraught to say anything but grabbed his kerchief and did the job herself. She hurt Art at first but Alvord encouraged her to keep holding.

Ritter returned a few moments later with Blanchfield and his deputy, Alan Gregory. "What happened?" the sheriff asked.

"Where's Red?" Alvord countered.

"Doc was riding out for the Cullen Mine to see to some folks, Ritter sent a man to get him back. Shouldn't be long."

"He needs help *now*!" Paula bellowed. "They shot him!"

Blanchfield looked to Alvord, still at the girl's side.

"He accosted me," Alvord said. "He'd been drinking. Ritter thought he was pulling on me, he had no choice."

"He was reaching for this!" Paula said, grabbing the few dollars Art had scraped together. She threw them at Alvord along with a handful of dirt.

Alvord rose slowly, dusting himself off. "I'm sorry this happened, Miss Maddox," he said.

"He didn't even bring a gun!" Paula shouted at Blanchfield. "They knew he wasn't carrying, they had to!"

"Now isn't the time for this," the sheriff said. "He's still alive but we need to get him to Red's." The deputy brought over a board from Alvord's office and pulled Art over it.

"That's it?" Paula yelled as the deputy and Blanchfield started away. She prepared to follow them but Alvord touched her shoulder. She spun around and threw his hand off.

"Wait," he told her. He went for the cashbox he'd set at his side and opened it, rifling through for a stack of bills. He handed her what looked like a large amount.

"I'm sorry about this, truly. Whatever happens… give this to your parents for… whatever they decide."

Paula wasn't sure how much she held, maybe fifty dollars. She heard Blanchfield call for her. Paula threw the money at Alvord's chest, then spit at his boots. She ran after her father past the office.

Alvord stood there a moment, motioning for Ritter to pick up the money. He climbed into the wagon and took the reins from his wife. They started back toward the ranch.

5. The Dutiful Brother.

TEN MINUTES PASSED WITH NO SIGN of Red. The Cullen Mine was only four miles outside town but it might take time find him there. Paula questioned if Ritter had actually even sent a man for Red, but Blanchfield assured her he'd seen the rider leave a trail of dust toward the mine. In the end it was Mrs. Flannigan who kept Paula from bolting. She saw how angry the girl was—the last thing Sadie Maddox needed now was her daughter riding off alone and getting herself hurt.

"The metal is still in there," Mrs. Flannigan said, gently probing around Pa's side with her sleeves rolled up. Red's wife wasn't a doctor but had picked up enough from her husband to observe the lack of an exit wound in Pa's back. "I'd reach in there for it myself but I worry it could have struck a kidney. If so, we'll need Red's hands to... sort things out."

Paula winced along with her father. Fresh tears streamed down her cheek as he groaned for breath. It was all they could do to slow his bleeding.

Though Blanchfield wanted Paula in sight, Mrs. Flannigan convinced him to let her wait by the front door. Keeping an eye out for Red would do her more good than watching her father bleed out, she whispered. Blanchfield ordered his son to keep Paula company. Bo asked if she was alright once Mrs. Flannigan shut the door to Red's procedural room, but Paula ignored him. She wasn't in the mood for talking to anyone while covered in her father's blood.

After another few minutes Paula strode for her wagon and Jessamine. "The hell with this," she declared. Bo ran after her but when he grabbed her arm she spun and wordlessly punched him in the stomach. He staggered back, more surprised at the force than the act.

Jessamine was nearly unhitched when Paula heard the rumble on the horizon. Hoofbeats. She sprinted past the wagon down the length of Carbon's main street, ready to shout for Red the moment she saw him. Pa might only have minutes, seconds left. Every moment would count. As Paula veered around the side of Bob Jack's Boarding House, she saw eight horsemen galloping into town. Frantically searching their faces for Red's, the strength in her legs nearly gave out when she didn't count his among them.

Only one of the men looked familiar, though she couldn't place his face. He rode at the rear of the group, trotting at a slower pace. She hadn't seen him in town before, but somewhere...

Paula remained in the street as the riders slowed to a canter and spread throughout town. She had seen enough miners to know these men weren't. Maybe more of Alvord's gunmen from Cheyenne, maybe Union Pacific men protecting the railroad from Sioux.

"Are you coming from the mine?" Paula asked one as he rode by. "Did you see a red-headed man in a wagon riding this way?"

The man glanced at her with a frown, more annoyed than anything. He didn't look overly friendly.

"Hey!" Paula shouted again as he rode beside the Vance store and stopped. When Paula heard more hoofsteps behind her, she turned to see the familiar man looking down at her from his horse. He tipped his short-brimmed gambler's hat with a smile, eyeing her from head to toe. He gestured to a pale man in a poncho riding ahead of him. The man in the poncho dismounted.

"Sorry about this, miss," the man in the gambler's hat said, still smiling.

The next thing Paula felt was her braid in someone's grip. The man in the poncho yanked her toward him then fired a shot from his pistol. Paula was certain she was dead until she realized the gun had been angled upward and away. She heard gasps as residents of the boarding house leaned out their windows. The warm touch of metal pressed against her back and cries rang out down the street.

"The sheriff!" the man in the poncho shouted. "If anyone values this girl's life, the sheriff and all his deputies will walk into this street right now! Anyone takes up a position on us, armed or not, this girl dies. You got one minute!"

Paula started shaking as the shock set it, the adrenaline from the past half hour turning toxic. The other men on horses drew rifles and pistols down the length of the street, carefully surveying the townsfolk who looked to each other for any sense of what was happening.

Paula looked to Red's, wondering if Bo was still in the doorway gasping for breath. He'd vanished.

The man in the poncho trailed her gaze and grabbed her by the shirt collar. "Sheriff in there?" he asked softly.

Paula wasn't sure if her silence came from her terror or something else, but the man gave her a violent shake that brought her to her knees. "Is he?"

"Yes," Paula said through a sob, trying not to cry as everyone in Carbon took to their windows to see what was happening.

The man in the poncho pointed to the man beside Vance's store, then to Red's. Another two men converged as well.

"You got thirty seconds before this girl's blood is running down your street, sheriff!" the gunman bellowed. "Come out, hands high!"

Another few seconds passed before a voice echoed from inside Red's. "What are your intentions?" it called.

"My intention is to stare through the hole in this girl's skull if you don't surrender your position!" the man in the poncho shouted.

Still no one moved.

"There's no need to harm the girl, I'm coming out," Blanchfield returned

The men at Red's extended their guns toward the door. Blanchfield emerged slowly, hands held up past his head. "It's just me, I have no deputies in town. Two are at the Cullen Mine and there are men at a ranch nearby, but—"

"Reach for that smoke-wagon and you're a dead man," the man in the poncho said.

Another of the riders dismounted and walked to Blanchfield, taking his gun and leading him to the street.

"Search the place. Start with that building."

The two at Red's dismounted and entered the house. A few minutes later they came out with Bo and Alan, hands up. One of the riders threw a badge at the man in the poncho's feet. He looked up to the man in the gambler's hat, who made a show of sighing.

The man in the gambler's hat trotted to Blanchfield. "I can't abide liars," he said, pulling his pistol.

Paula flinched at the shot but couldn't avert her gaze from the gore splattering from the sheriff's head. Blanchfield collapsed like a bag of bloody potatoes. When Bo cried out, one of the gunmen kicked him silent.

The man in the gambler's hat holstered his pistol and looked down the length of the street, shaking his head. He dismounted at the hitching post beside Red's, then walked to the center of the street. He took a long moment to remove his hat and sweep a hand through stringy brown hair.

"I think we've gotten off on the wrong foot here, so let's try this again," he said, smiling. "My name is Roderick Crowe. The men up and down your main street here are my associates. Saw some posters back in Rock Springs that called us the Sibling Gang. Probably on account of me and my sister, Virginia, robbing a train or two. I have no doubt armed deposits of that nature place an undue hardship on you fine folks of Carbon. I'd offer an apology for that, but I make it a point to never apologize for anything."

Paula heard the stifled laugh of the man holding her at gunpoint.

"Anyway, I'm here in your bustling mining town for a family matter. You may have noticed we're one loud-mouthed vixen short of a full gang. That's because the government picked up my dear sister in Evanston a week back. By now they've shipped her to Fort Laramie for a trial which, given our aforementioned disagreements with the railroad, is sure to end in a hanging.

"Now folks, I may be the younger sibling, but my mamma implored I always take care of my sister. Virginia is a crass, overbearing cunt, I'll grant you that. But folks, that cunt is my sister. That's why I need to offer something to the boys in blue to trade her back. Which brings me here.

"We heard tell from Marshal Boyle, who I'm sure y'all know, that there was a Sioux raid along the tracks of Rawlings about the same time Virginia got herself hauled in. Supposedly the Cavalry nabbed a survivor they intend to sweat for information on Red Cloud. And if I know the army these days, they'd give just about anything for a shot to smoke out Red Cloud.

"So, there we were in the western plains, running down the army brigade until we found them encamped last night. At least one of them riders got away with the Sioux prisoner while we were pinned down in the fight. Found tracks leading right here to sweet lil' Carbon.

"This is where all of you fine folks come in. Someone here has to have seen, if not supplied, that soldier. He will have had an Indian with him, probably beat to hell, definitely bound. Hard to miss a spectacle of that nature, I'm sure."

Crowe swept his gaze along the street again, still smiling. "So. Where are they?"

No answer came.

"I'll settle for when you saw them, where they were headed and what they were outfitted with."

Still no answer.

Crowe smacked his lips. "I should also mention that good Marshal Boyle let us in on this nugget about the Sioux prisoner while he was begging for his life being pulled apart by horses on either end," he said, still managing to project charm. "He was the one who nabbed my sister out of a saloon in Evanston, you see, so I found him right quick to express my displeasure. I don't share this to give anyone bad dreams, of course, only to remind you, if your sheriff wasn't proof enough, that my sister is very dear to me, and I will do just shy of anything to get her back."

Crowe turned for the man in the poncho and gave a small nod.

The gunman kicked Paula's back and drove her into the dirt, cocking his gun as he pointed it to her head.

"So I'll ask again," Crowe said over the gasps. "Where are the solider and the Indian?"

The silence persisted until the sound of hoofbeats drew near from the west side of town. Three of the Sibling Gang turned with weapons raised as a lone horse tore around the corner onto main street. The rider pulled to a halt immediately, nearly falling off from the sight of three guns pointed his way.

"Red!" Paula shouted when she saw him.

The doc saw the girl flayed out on the dirt and tried to dismount.

"Hands high if you want to live, Irishman," one of the men called.

Red did as he was told, recognizing the familiar face from the wanted posters. Red called out to him. "Let the lass go!"

"We're just getting to that," Crowe returned. "I—"

"You're a goddamned coward hurtin' a wee lass, whatever you're doin' here!"

Paula saw one of the men tensing.

"Shut up, Red!" she snapped, then looked to Crowe. "Please don't shoot him. I need him to save my Pa."

Crowe turned her way. He seemed to notice the blood covering her hands for the first time. "What happened to your Pa?" he asked to everyone's surprise.

"He's shot," Paula said. "He's been bleeding out this whole time, waiting for the doc. Please, let Red go to him."

Crowe turned back to Red. "You're the doc?" he asked.

"Aye."

Crowe shrugged, as if the delay had been a minor hindrance. "This hasn't been the girl's day. Don't let her Pa die."

Red hesitated for a moment but sprinted for Paula. When he leaned down, the man in the poncho trained his gun on him. "Boss said you could see to her old man, not her," he said flatly.

Red looked to Crowe for an appeal but found none.

"Go to my Pa!" Paula shouted.

The doc reluctantly left her, sprinting to his door.

Crowe let out a huff and turned back to the town. "Unless there are any other life or death issues we interrupted," he began again, his smile fading, "let me say this a final time. I'm sure you folks aren't all that inclined to extend a neighborly hand to either my sister or me, but I'm not asking so much as telling. We know the soldier came through here, if he isn't holed up inside one of these shacks right now."

Crowe opened a pocket watch and glanced at it. "You've got 'til sunset to make up your minds then bring the Sioux to me at the saloon. If he or viable information about him are with me by the time I'm through with a little frivolity, then we shake hands, and my boys ride out of here.

"If I don't get what I want," he said, pulling free his side arm, "then I'm going to start killin' people. One. By. One. Then burn this town. I don't normally harass innocent folk, but like I said, this is a family matter and I don't have all that much time. So. I'll be waiting in the saloon with my new friend…" He glanced to Paula.

When she didn't say anything the man in the poncho drove a boot into her back. "Your name," he grilled.

"Paula," she managed, spitting dirt from her mouth.

"It's a pleasure, Paula," Crowe said with another tip of his hat. "Without further ado, why don't y'all get to—"

"Wait!" Red said, emerging from the door of his place.

Crowe turned with an inquisitive look, as if he'd never been interrupted, certainly not twice by one man.

Red flicked his glanced between Crowe and Paula. "Her father… Now's her only chance."

Crowe saw the doc's bloody hands and shirt. The girl started to cry. He sighed again, gesturing to the man in the poncho.

Paula felt the boot rise from her back. She didn't look to Crowe for permission, scuffling off the dirt and running past Red into the building.

Crowe's charming smile dissipated some as he watched her go. "Too bad," he said. "A father is a terrible thing to lose." He turned, carefully stepping around Bo Blanchfield and the pool of blood running from Sheriff Blanchfield's head. The man in the poncho seized Bo and followed Crowe into the saloon.

6. All We Really Have.

PA WAS PALE AS A GHOST when Paula finally returned to his side. His skin looked thin as paper. The pain had subsided, at least. He looked peaceful enough. Calm. He smiled when his lethargic eyes caught sight of hers.

"He's lost too much blood, lass," Red told her before letting her into the room. "Even if oi'd been here sooner, the…" He stopped, watching the hope drain from her like the blood from her father. "T'ain't nothin' more we can do. Oi'm sorry."

Paula opened her mouth to keep breathing. She wiped the tears from her cheeks before entering the room.

Pa held his smile when he saw her. "So beautiful," he said, his words flowing smoothly. He reached up to graze her dirty cheek, wiping away the salty soot. "I remember when your mother looked this way. When we were children."

"You should just rest, Pa."

"She was always curious," he continued. "She knew she could only ever get in so much trouble no matter what she did. I had to get her out of that city. She wanted more. We both…"

He trailed off as if he'd been driving to a point he'd lost. "This country," he started again. "It was too much for us. We should have seen it. But you were happy when you were a child. You liked running through the grass, watching the animals. Gave us hope. That this could be home."

Pa shook his head on the procedural table. "It isn't. I couldn't protect you from this place. I couldn't...

"I can take care of them, Pa. You made me strong."

"No," he said. "No, Paula. Your mother will take you back home, east. You'll be safe."

"*This* is my home, Pa," she said. "It's our home."

"You've gotta do what's right for your sisters and your mother, Paula. We're not these kind of people. You're not. You care too much. No room for sentiment out here."

"You told me dreams are all we have, Pa. The ranch is all we have."

A dream is only as good as the dreamer, and I'm lying here shot. He didn't say it, but his eyes did.

"Men like Alvord don't deal in hopes and wishes, only money and blood," he managed, his words stuttering. "I should have known, should have sold. You have to have money, Paula, that's why you have to go be with your granddad. You're responsible for your sisters now. Can't make the mistakes I did. Chasin' foolish dreams. You..."

Pa seemed to run out of breath. He struggled for a moment, his eyes straining, then they drifted. They didn't close, just stared off into a void beyond Paula's sight.

"Pa," she said, tightening her grip on his hand. He was completely still but nothing about him looked peaceful. Paula let his fingers slip from hers while her head drifted to his chest. Her sobs brought in Mrs. Flannigan, but Red held her back a moment, doubtful there was any consolation to be had.

When Red eventually touched Paula's shoulder, she looked up, as if trying to discern some meaning in his expression. "Oi'm so sorry, love," he offered.

Paula offered nothing in return.

After a moment Mrs. Flannigan came in to gently take her by the shoulders while Red closed her father's eyes and pulled a sheet over him. Paula twisted away and pulled the sheet back down.

"Paula..."

The girl's face flushed and her fists balled. Red could see her sorrow shifting to something else entirely. She turned for the door. Red tried to stop her but she pushed him harder than he expected and he tripped over a pail on the floor.

Running out of the building, Paula veered for the Vance store where Jessamine remained half hitched to the wagon. Red and his wife called out but Paula ignored them and unhitched the horse. The man in the poncho confronted her on the road. He'd been in the center of town with the other gunmen. Paula ignored him as she threw a blanket over Jessamine's back, her makeshift saddle.

"Where do you think you're goin'?" the man in the poncho asked.

"Paula, get back here," Red said in a hurry, striding quickly to reach her.

The man raised his hand to Red. "I didn't ask you a damn thing, Irishman," he barked. "Get back inside." He turned to the girl. "Roderick Crowe says there's curfew 'til he gets what he wants."

Paula shot him a biting glance. "I ain't stayin'," she announced flatly.

"The hell you ain't." He reached for her collar again but Paula heaved Pa's rifle free from the wagon. She pointed it at his chest. The man in the poncho went for his pistol but the sound in the air the next moment was laughter rather than gunfire.

"Jimmy Reece!" the shout echoed from the second story window of the saloon. Roderick Crowe took a seat on a windowsill. He'd taken residence in one of the rooms Alvord kept for rent.

Paula kept her aim on the man in the poncho as the other gunmen in town trained their weapons on her. She glanced up at Crowe. Even without his hat and jacket he looked imposing. There looked to be someone moving behind him. Maybe Sarah, the blonde from the railroad who'd moved in. Alvord didn't abide whores but he didn't have time to keep track of every trifle in town.

Crowe's huff of frustration was purely theatrical. "This is why I need Virginia back—somebody's got to babysit y'all. Get those guns down, all of you."

The Sibling Gang gradually backed off though Paula kept her muzzle fixed on the man in the poncho.

"All this commotion over a miner's prepubescent daughter, Jimmy?"

"She was fixin' to leave town, boss. Drew on me."

"Well look at that, boys. Jimmy Reece, quickest hand in outfit, beat to the pull by a miner's girl." The other gunmen laughed.

"My Pa ain't no miner!" Paula shouted, not even sure why she bothered.

Crowe held his laugh and folded his hands. He took a moment to study the girl red with emotion and blood.

"He's dead," he said factually.

Paula returned his stare, her hatred brought to bear.

"Isn't he," Crowe pressed.

She didn't respond.

"And you're set on justice. I can see that clear. You gunnin' for me, Miss… Paula, was it?"

"No," she returned.

Crowe kept his gaze on her, fascinated. "I've seen that look," he mused aloud. "Anger of the righteous brand. Hellfire." He tilted his head. "Only one other girl I've seen wear it before." He glanced into the bedroom for a moment, thinking, then leaned on the windowsill with both arms. "Let Paula here be on her way, Jimmy. We've held her up plenty enough today."

"Boss," Reece began.

Crowe stopped him with a wave of his hand. "You ride for my sister too, Jimmy," he said. "You should know better than anyone to never come between a woman and vengeance. Even when the woman in question is pint-sized. Don't worry, you can still shoot anyone else who tries to mount up."

Paula looked back to Reece as he unhurriedly holstered his gun under the poncho. His smile was smug as he stepped out of the way, giving Paula the road.

She kept her rifle in hand as she mounted.

"Oi'm beggin' ya, Paula, don't do anything rash," Red said from his front door. She ignored him as she kicked Jessamine.

7. Town Meeting.

THE SUN NEARED THE HORIZON when Paula dismounted and threw Jessamine's reins into a shrub outside Alvord's ranch. She'd been there twice before. The first time to celebrate Margaret Vance's eleventh birthday. Paula and two other girls who'd since moved away sat for a tea party inside the house while the boys threw horseshoes outside. One of the few occasions that called for a dress, though she ripped it after abandoning Margaret to beat Bo Blanchfield and Austin Greene at horseshoes.

Her second trip to Alvord's came the day after her fourteenth birthday. To find Pa. He'd wandered from town to curse Alvord in a drunken stupor but earned a beating from two of Ritter's men for the trouble. Red rode out with Paula to collect him and treat the concussion he'd sustained.

Paula wished she had shot Alvord then and there.

The place had grown since then, boasting a new addition to the house, nearly complete. New wood and iron fenced the entryways. Alvord's ranch was nearly a town unto itself, with 30 or more people here most of the time. Sheds that served like barracks sat between the house and barn for all the ranch hands and security. They'd probably need more space with the new men Alvord hired in Cheyenne.

It turned out the fields were as empty of men as they were cows. Paula worried Alvord and his men had already set out on the trail. Alvord couldn't possibly have left so soon, could he? He'd only been back for an hour or so, even he couldn't have outfitted and organized all those cowboys so quickly. Unless his herd was already on the trail and he'd ridden with his reinforcements to catch up.

She knelt beside a boulder near the main road, her father's rifle tightly gripped. If she had the strength, she might have snapped the weapon in two. Alvord might not be back for weeks, maybe longer. He personally oversaw drives into Nebraska where he handed lots to distributors bound for Chicago or further east.

Paula rested her back against the boulder. The image of Pa's lifeless eyes staring into nothing bubbled up, choking her. Somehow it hurt worse than when she'd stood there in front of him. She gritted her teeth at the image of Roderick Crowe grinning. He had slowed Red down. Surely he was complicit in Pa's death. Maybe she should ride back to shoot him instead.

Paula cried, trying not to let her sobs rise above a choked murmur.

She concentrated on her rage to block the tears. Ritter was the one who shot Pa while Alvord stood by. They had it coming first. Even if Alvord was gone, perhaps he'd left Ritter behind in charge of security. Ritter usually held things down when Alvord was away.

Paula steeled herself, bent on action. She might not have this opportunity again—the ranch was practically unguarded. She was sick of waiting, sick of hoping things would get better.

Rage pushed her into a crouched run from the boulder to the fence. She climbed over a top rung and landed silently in the grass. She thought about running for the barracks but noticed the barn. At least five saddled horses waited outside. Someone was in there. Maybe Ritter.

She ran for the barn, taking care to mind her step in the falling darkness. Movement at the house's porch caught her eye. She dropped for what little cover could be found in the brush. The figure looked armed with a rifle, but he hadn't noticed her. When he sat on a rocker and lit a smoke, Paula crawled forward, too afraid to sprint the rest of the way.

It took her nearly six minutes to make it to the barn on all fours. Her reward was the sound of hushed voices inside. At least six or seven from what she could tell. Ritter's voice didn't sound present, but it was hard to tell, too many people talking over each other. The door was firmly shut. She thought about pushing it but couldn't give herself away until she had a shot lined up. She would only get one chance.

Paula ran for the west side of the barn where a ladder stretched up to the loft bay. She made the climb in view of the man on the porch, hopefully concealed by twilight and cigar smoke.

She climbed as quietly as she could with the rifle in hand, taking her time on each step, each new grip. Piles of hay masked her entry into the loft. She'd have plenty of angles to fire into the group below. She made out plenty of familiar faces, though Ritter and Alvord weren't among them.

Mrs. Alvord stood at one side, flanked by three men. One was Michael Dunlap. Alvord had pulled him from the Cullen Mine a stretch back, wanting his cooking skills for men on the trail. He typically rode with the cowboys, but it looked like he'd broken a leg recently. The other two didn't look familiar. Ranch hands, most likely.

Across from Mrs. Alvord stood Louis Vance and his man set to run the new store at the mine. Morgan something. He was a big man, a freed Negro who'd worked his way west when the railroad came through. Bought land from Alvord outside Carbon but married and moved into town. Paula remembered since Alvord made a spectacle out of saying he didn't believe in discrimination, just honest work. Morgan's wife was there too, but Paula didn't know her name.

Owen P. Rudolph entered Paula's view from where he'd been sitting in an empty horse stall. He lived in Bob Jack's Boarding House across from the Professor, worked for the Union Pacific and oversaw their interests in the mines. He had no love for the way Alvord asserted himself on Carbon but was out here doing business with the rancher frequently enough. She could have sworn she'd seen him in town even as Crowe and his gang pulled in, but apparently he'd broken away before they locked things down.

Rudolph seemed to position himself between Mrs. Alvord and Vance, as if to lower some tension. A dispute was clearly in progress. When Paula heard more voices, she silently repositioned herself in the eastern end of the loft, crouching behind a wooden divide and a ladder to the ground level.

Mrs. Dunlap, whom Michael had married out here on the ranch only a few months ago, if town gossip was accurate, walked from another man propped on a stool. Looked pretty torn up. His left arm was in a sling, his jacket on the ground crusted with blood. A blue jacket, epaulets and all.

Paula's eyes went wide as they peered around the corner. Sure enough, there was one more person in the barn.

He was younger than Paula might have guessed. Probably not much older than her, in fact. A year or two, maybe. For all she'd heard of savages on the plains, she'd never seen one before. As ragged as the soldier looked, the Indian was far worse off. Most of his upper body was dirtied and bruised. Bandages wrapped his back, though they looked in dire need of a change. His face was swollen, one eye completely shut. He wore no shoes or shirt, only stitched pants, such as they were. He seemed awake, though she wouldn't have gone so far as to claim him conscious.

Savage or not, she just saw a boy, pretty normal other than the hair and clothes. He was fit, though most boys his age were probably taller.

"Mr. Vance!" The voice was Mrs. Alvord's, raised and aghast, drawing Paula's attention. "I will not entertain a notion of spilling blood on this property. We are all of us Christians here."

"And what about all the Christians in Carbon?" Vance returned, his volume escalating as well. "You heard what Owen reported—they're in Carbon with our friends right now. If I hadn't brought my family along, they'd be there under the gun right now."

Mr. Dunlap saw his employer's wife upset and stepped in. "They wouldn't dare hurt women or child—"

Vance seemed beside himself, pointing toward the barn door as if to Carbon. "This is the Sibling Gang we're talking about, Dunlap!" he said, practically shaking. "We don't have time for this, they could be firing the town right now! Everything we've built!"

"We've been over this, the Union Pacific men will have driven them away by now," Rudolph said.

"These people kill by the scores," Vance insisted. "I've seen them gun down a train full of armed guards. They destroyed the posse out of Evanston and they've killed Marshal Boyle. The railroad can't save Carbon."

"The sooner we resolve this the sooner we can go check on the town," Mrs. Alvord said.

"Vance is right about the Siblings," the solider said from the bench, his voice irritated. "No railroad men can fight them off. They picked apart my regiment last night. But Crowe can't take on an entire garrison at the Fort, especially without his sister."

"That's not the point, Delsman!" Vance shouted. "That Indian boy. If we let him live, let him leave, they'll find him. They'll trade him. General Crook couldn't care less about Virginia Crowe measured against Red Cloud and the Sioux. If Crowe gets free, she'll come back here to destroy whatever her brother hasn't already."

"Is Virginia Crowe really so intent on destroying Carbon?" Mrs. Dunlap asked. "What did we ever do to her?"

"Morgan and I were there on the train with her," Vance told them. "We gave her up to the marshal, I was there for her arrest after Boyle dragged me in for a statement, and Boyle pointed me out, the idiot. She knows I'm from Carbon, she threatened me from the jail cart."

"My husband's men can protect us from the Sibling Gang, Mr. Vance, but they can only hold off so many Indians," Mrs. Alvord reminded him. "What if this savage has information that could finally end the threat of Indian raids?"

"Every moment we waste sitting here arguing is another Roderick Crowe could pick up our trail," Delsman reminded them. "The Indian is a federal prisoner. If you want to make sure he doesn't end up with this gang, help me ride him in."

"You want us to go up against the Sibling Gang?" Morgan asked, as skeptical as Vance. "You just said nothing short of a garrison stands a chance. There's three of us. Vance is a trader, Dunlap's a cook, Rudolph is... I don't know what. I'm the only one who's even fired a gun, and you're shot half to hell. Don't make for great odds against eight killers on the warpath."

"We don't fight, we run. And what about you men?" Private Delsman asked, pointing at the ranch hands. "You two know the plains, you can help me get to this Alvord and his men on the trail, they can —"

"None of us know the trail well enough to lead you, certainly not in the dark with killers breathing down our necks," Dunlap maintained. "These two are ranch hands, they're no cowboys. And I'm new here, I've only ridden the full trail once to Nebraska. Mr. Alvord left all of us here to watch the ranch and look after Mrs. Alvord and her son. You're crazy if you think we're gonna abandon them to help you deliver some Injun who's already half dead."

"Then I'll go alone," Delsman insisted, rising from his chair past Mrs. Dunlap. "I have a duty to—"

"They'll find you," Vance said again. "They're probably already on their way here, rifling through all the nearby ranches. It's bad enough we'll have to lie about seeing you, but if they find you, they'll know. They shot Blanchfield in the head for lying, no questions asked."

"You've already brought hell on us just by comin' here," Morgan's wife lashed, nearly to tears. "Everyone in town could be dead right now because of you!"

Mrs. Alvord stepped forward to calm the room. "It isn't this man's fault that the Sibling Gang is bearing down on us," she said calmly. "Mr. Rudolph, can you not summon more men from the mine to help us?"

"I already told you, I sent word for Union Pacific security to drive Roderick Crowe out of town. But even if they succeed, Crowe's gang will still be out there looking for the Indian. Mr. Vance is right. We have to get rid of that boy before they track him to us."

"So you'll kill him? Bury him on in the prairie?" Mrs. Alvord pressed, disgusted. "He may be a savage but—"

"He's the end of Carbon, of your ranch, Mrs. Alvord," Vance said, his voice strained. "There's nowhere to hide him and this soldier. Roderick Crowe has eluded capture for years, he's cunning. He'll find the boy, make the trade for his sister, and come back here with her for revenge."

"Your cowardice is disgusting," Delsman said.

"I'm trying to keep my family and our town alive!" he shouted back. "None of us asked for this! We're running out of time, let's just get this over with—"

"Crook will offer a reward for this Sioux," Delsman said, growing desperate. "I can see to it you're all paid the maximum."

"You're on Curtis Alvord's land," Dunlap said. "We have money aplenty so long as we stay out of trouble."

"Well you've got trouble headed your way now. You can either help me do the right thing or see me off to it, but if you threaten my prisoner or my duty one more time," Delsman said, reaching for his rifle, "then you'll find trouble has already found you."

Quiet fell over the barn. Vance and Morgan exchanged glances, but Delsman ordered Morgan to throw his gun to the ground and kick it toward him. He did, Mrs. Alvord still calling for everyone to just leave guns out of this.

"Whatever happens next will be on your head, then," Vance said, signaling for Morgan and his wife to follow him out.

"You'll stay where I can see you," Delsman said, his gun still extended as he reached for his coat. "You don't have to help me saddle my horse but I won't have you disappearing to shoot me in the back."

"You're the killer here," Vance snapped. "Your delusions are going to cost us all our lives."

"I won't have my wife held at gunpoint," Morgan growled. "She's leaving so long as you're holding that rifle. You say otherwise you'd best get to shooting, soldier boy."

Delsman glared at Morgan but gestured for Mrs. Morgan to leave. She did. Vance and Morgan stood by the door, seething as they watched Dunlap and one of the ranch hands prepare Delsman's saddle.

"You've got plenty of water and rations, but you'd better ride quick," Dunlap said, clearly unhappy but following his mistress' order to get them on their way. "As fast as you can go carrying the boy, at least. Vance is right, they'll run you down."

"Too bad I won't have any help," Delsman returned, still eyeing Vance. The private lifted the boy up from his corner in the barn and onto the refreshed horse, practically hogtied.

Paula froze when she heard movement in the loft. Looking to the opening, she saw Morgan's wife creeping in from the ladder with a pistol. Paula's heart beat so loud she feared it would betray her position. The woman made her way to the opposite side of the loft and a better vantage to the boy and the soldier.

Paula didn't know who the woman intended to shoot. She considered shouting for Mrs. Alvord or the soldier. She wasn't sure which side was right or wrong. Maybe the boy did have to die.

Morgan's wife cocked her weapon just loud enough to draw Delsman's gaze. He spotted her immediately and raised his gun, firing first. The shot missed. Morgan charged the soldier with all his strength. Delsman fired into the burly man, dropping him.

Paula wasn't sure if Morgan's wife meant to hit Mrs. Alvord or not. When her husband fell, she screamed and fired indiscriminately, probably catching the mistress of the ranch by mistake. Either way both of the armed ranch hands drew and unloaded into the western side of the loft. Vance shot one of the ranch hands but fled when their fire shifted his way. He called for Morgan's wife on the way out but Paula couldn't hear her moving. Only her pistol was visible in the hay, spattered with blood. Rudolph sprinted after Vance.

Paula found the courage to look down after the shooting stopped. Vance's horse could be heard galloping away, probably to collect Margaret and his wife somewhere nearby. Mr. Dunlap had been shot as well. He looked alive but his hysterical wife had to drag him out of the barn, sobbing, left with no one else. The surviving ranch hand was already out the door with Mrs. Alvord's body, shouting for help. Paula didn't know if she was alive. Delsman lay bloodied beside Morgan.

Suddenly the only living people in the barn were Paula and the Sioux.

He'd fallen off the horse during the chaos and frantically looked around, maybe listening since he was still blindfolded. Paula felt her heart beating like a drum, listening for activity outside as if to make up her mind. Swallowing hard, she rose and made her way down the indoor ladder for the surface level. Stepping over Delsman's body, she rushed to calm his horse. Grabbing the prisoner, she pulled him up and led him to the animal. He didn't look to have been shot or hurt any worse than he already was.

With all her strength and then some, Paula pulled him onto the kneeling horse then jumped on behind him. Riding through the open barn door, she started east away from the Alvord ranch at a hard gallop. No one followed.

8. Hell Followed With Him.

MICHAEL DUNLAP WOKE TO THE SMELL of smoke and blood filling his nostrils. The blood was his own. He felt it oozing through bandages hastily wrapped around his gut where a slug remained lodged. He could barely lift a hand to graze his middle, his fingers dampening with the warm liquid.

"Lost a lot of blood, Mr. Dunlap," a man said above him, withdrawing the hand that had lightly slapped him awake. The evening dark didn't help Dunlap's blurred vision, but he focused on the face aglow with warm colors from a fire somewhere nearby. The man stood over him, hands on his belt. "Your wife did a fine job patching you up, but I expect you'll need that Irishman back in town if you want to make it through the night. Your missus is fixing a wagon to ferry you there as we speak."

Dunlap experimented with squinting and widening his eyes until the man came into focus. He wore dark colors but his face looked friendly enough. Dunlap tilted his head to the source of the light.

One of the barracks was on fire. He saw a handful of men walking from it, laughing. Two of them made their way into the Alvord house. He heard a gunshot from inside.

The man above him let out a sharp sigh but kept his gaze on Dunlap. "Thing is, I need your help in exchange for safe passage back to town," he continued. "Your fellow ranch hands weren't feeling too cooperative.

Considering your situation, I'm hoping you'll be more reasonable."

"…What?" Dunlap managed, struggling to keep his eyes open.

"Just need to know what in the hell happened to your lovely ranch, is all," the man said with his smile almost mocking. "Heard tell of commotion out yonder. We arrived just behind it from the looks. When this cattle baron gets back, he'll be stacking bodies—a boy in blue among them. Lucky for you, I don't see a dead Sioux prisoner. Where did that boy get to, I wonder?"

Dunlap swallowed hard. He turned to look for the wagon. "My wife," he said.

The man turned and pointed into the darkness toward the south side of the ranch. "Just over yonder, safe. She'll stay that way. So long as you're honest. I can't abide liars."

Dunlap dipped his hand against his middle again, feeling the blood continue to empty even as he lost feeling in his hand. "I've seen gunshots on the trail, Mr. Crowe. Gonna die."

Crowe nodded and leaned over to pat Dunlap's shoulder. "Well, I respect your courage, Mr. Dunlap. Now you just need to be brave for your wife. Where's the Indian?"

"I… I don't know," Dunlap said.

"Start with what happened."

"There… there were men who wanted the boy killed. Men who didn't. Somebody drew. Mrs. Alvord…" Dunlap seized up, sure his failure to keep her safe would haunt him well after his death.

Crowe let out a huff, his smile weakening. "Is dead. Sorry. Who made it out alive?"

"Just… Louis Vance and… a man named Rudolph. Works for the railroad.

"Where did they head?"

"I don't know. Carbon, I expect. Maybe out on the trail to Mr. Alvord."

"Burnside!" Crowe yelled toward the house.

A man previously relieving himself on Alvord's porch approached. Crowe directed his voice back at Dunlap. "How many men does Alvord have?"

"More than yours."

"No need to be testy in your final moments, Mr. Dunlap, I ain't the one who shot you. How far out on the trail is Alvord? And how many men strong is he?"

"I already failed his wife. I won't help you kill Mr.—"

"I ain't looking to gun down cattle barons, I just want that Indian. And it's worth 250 cash dollars to me." He snapped, and another man on horseback rode up. He tossed a stack of bills from the saddle bag. Crowe set it on Dunlap's bloody chest. "This ought to take care of your wife for a good while. More than even Alvord pays, I reckon. Just be honest with me."

Even dying, Dunlap could see the desperation behind this man's eyes. Crowe would offer and threaten anything to get what he wanted. It was only a matter of time before things got nasty. Dunlap nodded. "Fifteen men on guard, twenty-one with the cowboys. Probably at the border to Nebraska by now, Alvord will catch up with them soon, but word will get to him 'bout Mrs. Alvord. He'll be bringing hellfire for you."

"How many times do I have to tell this boot-licker I wasn't the one who shot this place up?" Crowe shouted to his men, rising full length over him. "Burnside, get to work on tracks, I need to know where this Vance and Rudolph went with our prisoner."

"They don't have him," Dunlap said. "Leave them be."

"What makes you say that?" Crowe pressed.

"They were the ones who wanted him dead, to keep him from you. They would have shot and left him here."

"Or taken the body," Crowe countered.

"They left the Indian boy in the barn before they rode off. They ain't got him."

"Then it looks like your count of who made it out of this scrape is incorrect, Mr. Dunlap. Indian sure as hell didn't limp away, not in the state he's in."

"There was no one else."

"'Cept you and your wife," Crowe said, having one of the men fetch her. "She was too hysterical to talk much but maybe I need to ask more poignantly. While I'm doing that, my boys are going to rip this house down board by board looking for hiding places and burn it with the Alvord boy inside when they've finished. Is that what you want?"

"Boss."

Crowe turned at the sound of Esteban's voice approaching from the south. He rode up with another horse behind him, reins in hand. "Found this mount tied to brush behind the main gate, off the road."

"The miner's girl rode from Carbon on that mount," Reece said with edged voice.

Crowe turned to him with intolerant eyes.

Reece looked down.

"You didn't see little Paula, did you?" Crowe asked Dunlap, his feigned empathy vanished.

"The Maddox girl? N-No."

"You didn't see her either?" Crowe asked, wheeling around to Mrs. Dunlap.

She said nothing, so Crowe held the gun to her forehead. "Did she have the boy with her?" he asked.

Mrs. Dunlap broke down with tears, so Crowe rested an arm around her back, cooing her down. "Alright now, enough of that. I just need a yes or no. But I need it right now."

She tensed again when Crowe put the pistol on her husband.

"Yes," she said, sniffling. "I saw her ride off. She had the boy."

"Which way?"

"I don't remember."

Crowe cocked the gun.

"I don't know, I was tending to Michael," she pleaded, falling to her knees.

Crowe sighed then holstered his revolver, leaving Dunlap to die and his wife wailing over him. Crowe whistled and the men gathered around their horses. "Bold little shit, isn't she?" he mused, rummaging through his saddlebags for the bottle he'd relieved from Carbon's saloon. "Couldn't shoot this Alvord to avenge her Pa so she'll settle for sticking it to me for holding her up. Won't ride back for Carbon or the mines, she'll figure we're still there. She's smart enough to ride for law."

"Little Holstein is half a day southeast, that's closest," Reece offered. "Not much law, though."

"But it's all she's got," Crowe said, taking a swig. "Look for tracks, we'll start after her. Probably only has an hour on us. Little girl riding in the dark carrying a half dead Indian won't get far." He allowed another chuckle from deep in his throat. It was rare circumstances surprised him anymore. "Bold little shit," he repeated.

There was a long pause before Burnside said, "Probably shouldn't have let her go back in town, though."

Crowe turned to him, bottle still in hand. "Virginia wouldn't have," he said casually. "That what you're thinkin', Burnside?"

Burnside glanced at Reece. "Just loose ends, boss. The woman over there too. I know how you and Virginia feel about women and kids but—"

Reece and the gang, even Burnside, weren't really surprised when Crowe pulled his pistol again. The shot dropped Burnside at once, piercing his chest. It missed his heart by at least a few good inches. The man squirmed and mouthed something for a few seconds.

Crowe kept hold of the pistol. "I don't think Virginia much cared for Burnside anyway. She likes you boys, though. You just take orders and your pay. Don't you." He looked to Reece, still sitting idly on his horse with as neutral an expression as a face could muster.

Reece nodded once, then turned his horse. "Let's get lookin' for tracks," he said, setting off at a gallop for the east.

The other men mounted and followed with Crowe bringing up the rear. He left the 250 dollars on Dunlap's chest.

9. Bold Little Shit.

For all the fears and doubts jostling for control of Paula's mind, she suddenly wondered if Jessamine would make it home okay. The old mustang had often been the closest thing Paula had to a friend on the ranch.

The soldier's horse was uncooperative as Paula directed it blindly through the night. Neither she nor her borrowed steed were confident of their path. Paula had only made the ride to the miniature cattle town of Little Holstein once before. On that trip she'd started out from Carbon on an actual road. Riding a wagon. With her father driving. In the daylight. Not saddled with a prisoner.

The boy occasionally strained and struggled, but he was so bruised and beaten he obviously lacked strength to fight his way free. Paula glanced at him in the dark. Perhaps he was only biding his time, preparing to leap clear and run when her guard lowered.

A threat surpassed only by the one riding after them, possibly that very moment. Crowe's sunset deadline for information at Carbon had long passed. She had to assume he'd already picked up her trail.

Roderick Crowe. A warm-blooded rattlesnake. He might have been fit for the stage with his affability, but Paula had seen his eyes up close.

"Men can lie with their words, their smiles, even their deeds, but never their eyes," Ma told her after Paula's first encounter with Alvord. The next time Paula saw the burly rancher she noted the fiery ambition. She noted Vance's avaricious desire, Red's buoyant spirit. Her father's waning hope.

But for all she'd seen in men's eyes, she'd never seen gleeful sin before. It frightened her. Past all of Crowe's charm, she believed he'd kill her to claim the boy.

Paula strained her neck looking back, expecting a row of shadows and torches over a ridge any moment. The soldier's horse neighed in rebellion, focusing her attention forward. Paula glanced at the stars, confirming her eastbound heading. Clouds veiled some of the sky, but she could make out the Little Dipper. The moon was over half full, just bright enough for Paula to spot vital landmarks on the trail. If she kept just right of the bowling ridge to the south, she should cut into a grassy valley with Little Holstein straight in the middle.

The railroad ran through town there. She didn't have any money, but maybe if she told a conductor what was happening, or if she found some law straight away…

Paula had considered taking the boy to the Cullen Mine where there'd be more armed men, but it would have meant doubling back toward Carbon and Crowe. Plus, that was where Louis Vance had probably ridden for backup. The boy wouldn't be any safer around him. At least this way there'd be a chance of…

What?

What exactly did she think she was doing? Did she really believe herself capable of ferrying a prisoner all the way up to Fort Laramie in hopes Private Delsman's tale of reward was true? Even if she found enough law in Little Holstein to neutralize the Sibling Gang, which she certainly would not, who would believe her story with no soldiers left to corroborate the boy's identity? If she got there, what if the boy's information was worthless? Maybe they wouldn't offer any reward at all.

Paula tensed when the boy shifted. Maybe he was dying. She hoped not—she needed him alive, yes, but she wasn't sure if she could cope with another person dying today.

Pa…

He'd be furious if he knew what she was doing. Even with the wildest reward Paula could fathom, no sum could protect a family of four women on a ranch in increasingly contested territory. Maybe Pa had been right.

Maybe his dream died with him.

And yet here she was riding to save it.

Paula gritted her teeth as tears slid down her cheeks. As much as she wanted to retreat home and fling herself into Ma's arms, to pack what little they had left, to sell the sickly cows and infertile land for train tickets to Chicago, she couldn't.

For all the things Pa wasn't, he was a loving father. He'd held onto the ranch because it was his only chance to earn what his daughters deserved— fine clothes, abundant meals, something worthwhile to inherit. Some part of him, the deepest, truest part of him, she believed, had held on through drought, assault and indignity just for her.

Pa's death laid a path away from all this, toward something safer, but she couldn't accept it this way. Not with Pa's murderer riding free. Pa had given too much of himself, as Paula had given too much of herself, to just walk away destitute and defeated. She had watched Pa lie down for Alvord, for Vance, for Blanchfield, for the Union Pacific, one too many times. Someone had to stand up.

She was taking this boy to the Fort.

✦ ✦ ✦

Paula rode until the first hues of light appeared in the sullen eastern sky, then brought the soldier's horse to a halt on what looked like the road. She was exhausted in a way no hard day's work could rival. The constant adrenaline made her entire body ache. The memory of Pa sapped and fueled her strength at the same time.

She'd have kept riding, but the horse needed rest. As did its riders. The boy hadn't moved much for several hours, and Paula felt warm blood on his back. For a moment she worried he hadn't survived the night, but when she pulled him down to the grass he coughed and tensed. His bruises were clear even in the pale light, along with a poorly bandaged cut down his back. It gave off no alarming aroma but had to be redressed.

Rummaging through the soldier's saddle bag, Paula found a can of water and a roll of bandages, along with a tin of tobacco, beef jerky, a hunting knife and rounds for a revolver she didn't possess.

She had cleaned enough of her father's scrapes to know what she was doing and washed out the boy's wound before freshly bandaging it. He grunted in pain but she didn't ease up. "Don't have time to waste," she said, then paused when she saw the boy's head tilt toward her. "Do you understand me?"

Silence. He remained tense.

Paula stood over him when she finished, stretching. "Course you don't." Glancing at the brightening horizon, she risked another moment to catch her breath. "I'm sorry about this. Might be no more than you deserve if you been attacking folks but… I'm sorry this is happening to you." Paula took the water and gingerly knelt beside him. Nervous to bring the canteen to his lips, she opted to lower his blindfold first.

He flinched and blinked. His eyes weren't what she was expecting. Where she'd anticipated an animal's blank or hostile stare, there was only fear and surprise.

He accepted the water, lapping as much as she offered. She wondered if he'd consumed anything at all in the last few days. Guessing he was equally hungry, she turned for the saddlebag and the beef jerky. "We really need to get going after this," she said. "I'll see about finding us a meal when we…" She dropped the food when she turned back. The boy was gone. Vanished.

Eyes wide, she reached for the hunting knife and scanned the grass in a panic. He couldn't have gotten far. Could he have broken free of his ropes? No, he—

The grass shifted ahead of her. Paula leapt into it. She toppled when a foot connected with the back of her knee. Somehow he'd slipped the bonds on his feet. He was up and running north by the time she realized what happened. Even with his limp, he was faster than she might have guessed.

But not fast enough. Paula gave chase and tackled him. Even with her smaller weight, the force was enough to bring him down. He dropped with a painful yip onto a root or rock but froze when he felt the blade on his back.

"I said I was sorry," Paula managed, panting, "but that don't mean you have a choice in this."

The boy turned his head, resentment burning in his eyes. Paula didn't like it and pulled his blindfold back in place. She led him to the horse then bound his feet in a sailor's knot. He struggled when she pushed him back up the horse, but with the knife against his bare skin, he didn't have much choice. She thanked the Lord she could get the beast to kneel or she'd never have managed.

Paula set off at a quick gallop, again scanning the darkened horizon for any movement.

10. Father Waite.

THE TOWN OF LITTLE HOLSTEIN had gotten ahead of itself. In fact "town" was probably a misnomer. A main street ran from one side to the other, but tents and makeshift shacks left by the railroad crews decorated the majority of its length. The only proper buildings were a diminutive general store, a half-finished hotel-saloon and the mismatched rail station at the far side of town.

The Union Pacific had extended a line there expecting Little Holstein to be a prime hub on the Laramie Plains for the booming cattle industry. Cowboys from Arizona wound herds through the area bound for Nebraska or further east, and with decent soil, the area was an easy sell for homesteaders.

Or so the railroad assumed. Even as the line was being laid, most cowboys started charting routes further south, finding safer paths around the plains altogether. Homesteaders exercised equal caution, as if the valley was a spoiled Garden of Eden. Rumors of the increasing Sioux savagery had spread far. Though the plains were barely halfway to the edge of the continent, they'd taken on a reputation as the edge of civilization.

And so Little Holstein had remained just that—little.

There wasn't much in the way of opportunity at the outpost. Or law, for that matter. A wonderful combination for degenerates. Paula had heard the stories. Unsavory characters—army deserters, laid-off railroaders, professional gamblers, an unscrupulous criminal element—had more or less claimed Little Holstein for their own. She heard tell men played hands of poker for fingers in a whore house where women never wore clothes at all.

It didn't look all that vile when Paula rode into town that morning. No riotous shootouts erupting in the street, no public deviance leaning out windows, no ragtime piano from the saloon. Only two horses stood hitched along the entire length of main street. The only sounds in the air were the distant clanging of a blacksmith hammering horseshoes and the hiss of steam from the train idling at the station.

Maybe everyone was still passed out drunk from the previous night, Paula mused. Or maybe fear of the Sioux had emptied the camp.

Either way, Paula offered a silent prayer of thanks to the Almighty that no one was about, seeing as she carried one of the aforementioned Sioux. Before they'd ridden into town Paula had stopped to wrap the boy in a blanket from the saddle, cloaking his face and chest as best she could. She knew a lone girl riding in with a hidden figure would draw enough stares, but surely someone would stop her if they saw her riding with a heathen boy coated in crusted blood and bruises.

Paula kicked the horse's flanks and sped straight through town. Still no sign of the Sibling Gang behind her, but when they did catch up, even they couldn't run down a train. Paula gulped. She wasn't sure if she believed that—they were train robbers, after all—but surely she'd be able to put more distance between the Indian boy and Roderick Crowe with a steam engine's help.

Paula ran the soldier's horse straight to the rail house before pulling it to a stop on the boarding platform. A greasy operator with a thin mustache and balding head exposed through a visor emerged from the rail house waving his arms in protest. "What do you think you're doing?" he called, dabbing his head with a kerchief.

"I need to board," Paula said.

"The next train should be here this evening," the operator replied, obviously taken aback.

"I need to board *this* train!"

"This train is leaving," the operator said, pointing to the engine already creeping ahead as it belched a sharp breath of steam.

"Can't you hold it a moment?" she begged. "There are men chasing me—they'll kill me if they find me."

"What? Who are you, young lady?"

"Please, I don't have time to explain! Can't you fit us on?"

"Do you even have money for a boarding pass? And who is this?"

Paula grabbed the reins of the horse and presented them to the man. "You can have everything I have, the horse included. I just need to get on the train."

The operator released a huff that rivaled the train's. "We take money on this line, young miss, not horses. This train is leaving, I suggest you come back this evening to catch the 5:20 to Cheyenne."

"I told you, I have to leave now or they're going to catch up to me!"

"Where are these men supposedly after you? And where are your parents? I have half a mind to fetch the marshal. He'll get to the truth soon enough."

"Marshal?" Paula exclaimed. "There's a marshal here?"

"Father Waite. He rode in this morning."

Paula's brow furrowed. "The marshal is a priest?"

"So they say. Now you best run along before I—"

"Where is this marshal? Where's the church?"

The operator summoned a single piercing laugh as if for effect. "Even if Little Holstein had a church, which it certainly does not, you wouldn't find Waite there. The saloon's about the only place you'll find him unless he's riding the territory hunting outlaws."

"Is he a good gunman, this marshal?" she pressed. "Does he have a posse with him?"

This time the operator's laugh was long and riotous, though swept away with the train whistle picking up speed out of Little Holstein.

"It's just him, then?"

"Waite is the posse 'round these parts. He's a pitbull. Why do you think it's so peaceful this morning? That's how I know he's here."

Paula climbed her way back onto the horse while the operator watched in bewilderment. She raced for the saloon she'd passed.

"Where do you think you're going?" the operator shouted.

Paula rode on. A few townsfolk had made their way to the street, lethargically trudging to or from their tents as if woken by the train's whistle.

Paula kept her head down and a tense hand on the boy. One or two of the townsfolk eyed her peculiarly, but most ignored her even as she bolted to the saloon and hitched the horse.

Paula helped the boy down. Leading him to the window, she casually glanced in. She'd never set foot in a saloon before. The building was incomplete, under construction. A staircase with no railing led to a second-floor hallway. One room looked like it lacked roofing based on the light beaming in.

Only four people occupied the bar, one surely the barkeep. He stood on a footstool mending a gunshot in the ceiling he looked none too happy about. Another man sat at a round table pouring himself a drink into a glass smaller than one of Ma's teacups, though the beverage was certainly not tea. Across the room a man lay passed out on a cheap poker table, moistening green fabric with his drool. A woman sat beside him staring out the window. Even from so far away Paula could read her sadness, as if longing for a distant home she would not likely see again.

None looked particularly threatening, but none resembled a marshal. Much less a priest.

Paula mustered the courage to push past the swinging doors with the boy in tow, deciding to ask the barkeep for the marshal's whereabouts. The barkeep turned when he heard the creaking doors. Paula watched his expression shift from shock to annoyance. "This is an adult establishment, miss."

"I just need help finding someone. Do you—" Paula paused when the boy stumbled over a loose floorboard. His blanket remained fixed to his person but when the barkeep peered closer into the makeshift hood his frustration escalated to horror.

"The hell are you doin' with an Injun!" he shouted, reaching to the bar for a pistol the size of Paula's forearm. "Damn thing looks feral, get away from him!"

Paula put her hands up but stepped in front of the boy, trying not to shake. "He won't hurt anyone. I need to find Father Waite. I heard he was here."

The barkeep refused to angle his weapon at the girl but maintained his heated tone. "I won't have a damned Injun in here raisin'—"

"Only hell bein' raised in here is yours, Wauldruff," the man pouring alcohol at the table said.

"If you want part in this take it outside, I won't—"

"What you won't do is tell me where I will and will not go, barman. They're my business now, both of 'em, so shut the hell up and mind your own."

The barkeep vented an overly loud huff but returned to the bar, hand still around his weapon even as he turned for a rag to wipe the counter.

Paula watched the man at the table throw back the contents of his glass. Pa always allowed a momentary wince when she'd seen him down his drink. This man didn't.

The way he sat made him look younger than his graying hair or leathered skin suggested, lazily slouched in a chair as he balanced on its back legs. The top of his head was mostly bald, but the gray hair around his dome fell long and flat past his ears and neck. The man's upper lip was home to a bushy mustache, long enough to overtake his bottom lip.

His gaze swept between Paula and the boy. Paula studied his eyes. Pale blue. Not those of a priest, surely. He wore no white collar either, only a gray duster that stretched nearly his full length.

She felt her mouth dry when she opened it. "You're Father Waite?"

"Marshal Waite," he returned. "So what brings a pipsqueak girl and a…" He paused to lean his chair forward and peer past the hood of the cloaked figure. "…Sioux boy to the Little Holstein Saloon?"

She paused longer than she expected. She hadn't really decided how much she'd tell anyone. What if he tried to stop her? To kill the boy or deliver him to the Fort without her to collect the reward? "May I see your badge?" she asked.

The man raised the lapel of his duster to show a star pinned to a waistcoat.

A door opened behind the bar. Paula tensed, her hand flying to the knife she'd fixed to her belt. It was only a woman carrying a plate of food.

"Jumpy little thing, aren't you?" the marshal observed, pouring himself another drink. The woman set the food in front of Waite. He attacked it without offering thanks. "What's got you so spooked, then?" he asked with a full mouth of eggs.

Paula chose her words carefully but swallowed her doubts, reminding herself time was short. "The Sibling Gang is on its way here," she said.

The marshal paused mid-bite. "Bullshit," he said, shoveling the previously suspended bite of toast through his hairy maw.

Paula blinked as if it was the last thing she'd expected. It was, now that she thought about it. "I'm not lying. They just rode through Carbon. Said they'd burn it to the ground."

"Did they?" he asked nonchalantly.

"I… They said they would. They killed Sheriff Blanchfield. In front of everyone. Said they'd kill more. They almost killed me."

"Why?" He kept chewing, taking a long gulp of water from a mug.

Paula wasn't sure if the man was probing to get at the whole truth or just completely tactless, but whatever the case she found herself increasingly irritated. He'd backed her into a corner with as single word.

"They said they were looking for someone."

"Let's see if we can't speed this up some. Who were they looking for, why were they looking for this unfortunate soul, and what happened in Carbon that would lead the notorious Siblings here? And bear in mind that if I have to ask 'why' one more time I'm going to go about my breakfast and let Wauldruff there throw you out."

Paula stiffened, her fists balling. "They're looking for an army prisoner they wanted to take to Fort Laramie to trade for another prisoner, one of their gang. They're coming here because the prisoner got away.

"You got him away, you mean," Waite said, pointing to the boy.

Paula nodded.

"How'd a pipsqueak from Carbon get roped into all this?"

She steeled herself. "I'm riding this prisoner to Fort Laramie for the army reward on him. He's my prisoner and I need help making sure the Sibling Gang can't take him from me."

Waite slowed his chewing, his mustache arcing up in a smile as his eyes passed over Paula's small frame. "What's your name, pipsqueak?"

"Maddox," she said.

Again Waite's smile spread, though it did little to ease the tension.

"Well, Maddox, it seems I misjudged you. And you'll be happy to know that your problem with the Sibling Gang is already solved, because the Sibling Gang is disbanded and scattered to the winds. Another marshal brought in their leader a few weeks back, likely the one in question at the Fort. I'm sure you've seen her artwork on the Carbon sheriff's office—Virginia Crowe. Her brother got tagged in Denver a few days later and the rest of them boys either rode off for Deadwood or shot each other to hell over who'd wear the outfit's pants. Hopefully the latter. Either way, the Sibling are no more."

"That's not true! I'm not lying!"

"You may well not be, Maddox, but whoever held you up back in Carbon wasn't them. Trust me, I know these boys, and without a leader—"

"I saw Roderick Crowe with my own eyes!" she shouted, marching closer to the marshal. "He kept our doc from getting to my Pa when he was bleedin' out from a gunshot. His man Reece held a gun to my head after he kicked me to the dirt in front of our whole town. The only reason I'm alive is because Crowe let me go to kill the man who killed my Pa, but instead I found this boy. I ran with him here hopin' I'd find someone to take me to Fort Laramie or keep him safe, but it looks like I only found a geezer lawman more worried about gettin' fat and drunk than killin' outlaws."

Paula felt her face flushing red and her breath short but couldn't stop. "You think you know the men after me and what happened to them but I clearly know 'em better than you, so whether you believe me or not, I'm tellin' you that Crowe and seven others are probably on that ridge right now, and there ain't nothin' gonna stop them from gettin' what they want. 'Cept maybe you. So are you gonna keep sittin' there stuffin' your face or are you gonna get up and get a posse together?"

Waite stopped eating about halfway through Paula's tirade, his tickled smile vanished. "You got a good look at all eight, then?" he asked softly.

"Crowe wears a black gambler's hat, Reece a poncho. He's got a scraggly beard and a stupid accent. There's a Mexican with them, a Negro and a short one with big teeth. The rest look normal enough 'cept for all the steel loadin' down those horses. One had a gun longer than me, a spy glass on it and everything." She paused, watching Waite soak in the descriptions. "You gonna let Wauldruff throw me out?"

Waite stared at her before pushing his plate away in an annoyed huff. "Tell me exactly how you picked up the boy and where you last saw Crowe."

She did, recounting how Crowe let her go after Pa died and the shootout at the Alvord ranch.

"And how long was your ride here?" Waite pressed, urgency finding its way into his voice. "Exact, no guessing."

Paula's eyes darted back and forth as she quickly calculated the figure for him. "Near... ten hours, including the stop to rest and water."

"Maybe a nine-hour ride here at full bore," he said, mostly to himself. Waite rose slowly, telling Wauldruff to keep an eye on both Paula and the boy.

"Where are you going?" Paula asked as he strode outside to his horse. He ignored her, digging through a saddlebag for his spyglass. Finding it mixed amid fresh biscuits, he brushed off the lens and hurried through the saloon to the stairs.

Again Paula asked what he was doing and again he ignored her. Climbing up a ladder from an unfinished room, he stood full length on the saloon's roof and raised the spyglass to the west. He could see for several miles up the valley ridge. Waite searched for a few minutes. Nothing.

He lowered the spyglass and spit on the roof, tapping the side of his leg. He started back for the ladder when he saw it with his naked eye. A dust cloud. Waite raised the spyglass again. One, then two riders appeared from behind a ridge. The two riders turned into seven.

He couldn't make out any faces but lowered the spyglass. "Well, shit," he murmured before racing back into the saloon.

11. Tip Your Server.

"ALRIGHT, PIPSQUEAK, TELL ME EVERYONE who saw you ride in," he asked, racing downstairs. "I mean anyone and everyone who saw you, don't skimp."

Paula flinched. "I... I don't know, not like I know anyone—"

Waite grabbed her hard around her shoulders, pulling her uncomfortably close. "Kid, I have maybe two minutes two save your life and this entire flea-bitten town thanks you ridin' in here. Now obey me and describe *everyone* who saw you ride in."

Paula swallowed hard and tried to focus. "I... the railman, I talked to him. Half the town was still asleep, weren't nobody else on the road. Saw two drunks waking between those tents when I rode up but—"

"What did they look like?" he grilled, then wheeled her around to a window. "You see 'em out there?"

Paula looked around the street at the few townsfolk milling between the livery and a campfire beside the row of tents. "Don't see em."

"Anyone else? Life or death, kid."

Paula's heart beat like it had when Reece held the gun on her. "I... no, I don't think so. Bunch'a drunks were still asleep."

Waite wheeled around and led her to the woman sitting at the window.

Where she'd once looked listless staring at the horizon, her attention was now rapt on Waite and the girl. "Pipsqueak, Clementine. Clementine, pipsqueak. And prisoner. Clem, hide them both upstairs. No sound. No nothin'."

When he ran for the door, Paula's brow furrowed. "What are you doin'?" She watched Waite mount his horse, then take the reins of Delman's horse and lead it away from the saloon. "Hey!"

Waite tore away down the street eastbound, away from Crowe.

She prepared to run out after him and curse him out, but Clementine held her close. "If Waite says hide, I think you best hide, sweetheart," she said.

Paula looked between Wauldruff at the bar and the other women, as if for guidance, but none came. Swallowing hard, she followed Clementine up the stairs with the boy behind her.

They settled into one of two completed rooms. Maybe Clementine's, given all the clothes scattered about. When Clementine opened a closet, Paula shook her head. "I want to see what happens," she said, pointing to the window.

"You want my help or not, kid?" she pressed. "We're not alone. Now hide."

Paula huffed and pulled her prisoner into the closet. When Clementine shut them in, Paula gazed through the closet cracks. Only now, looking at the purple corset hanging from the metal bedframe, did she realize Clementine was probably a whore. She glanced at the boy, wondering if he'd shout for help, give them away. Either way he'd end up at the Fort. Not much sense in that, she supposed.

The room was quiet for an agonizingly long few minutes, then the thunder echoed into town. Paula felt herself sweat as she heard them stop just beyond the hotel.

"Listen up! Listen *up!*" shouted Reece.

The next voice was softer but it frightened Paula far more. "Good morning," Crowe said.

She could hear his smile and visualize the tip of his hat to whoever had roused and sauntered to the street.

"Name's Roderick Crowe. These are my friends. Lookin' for another friend of mine, girl by the name of Paula Maddox. Cute little thing—brown hair, probably five feet from the ground. She would have just ridden in this morning with an Indian boy. Hard sight to miss, really. Who's seen 'em?"

Silence hung for a moment.

Crowe laughed. "Come on now, it's hardly that early. Where is she?"

Silence.

No laugh this time. "Thing is, I'm going to find her one way or the other. Whether that means tracking down whatever law she took off with or upturning every one of those tents to make sure she isn't hidden away." He paused. "Come on out, Paula. You're in there somewhere, aren't you?"

The cold swept from her fingers and stabbed into her heart. For a moment she wondered if someone had whispered her location to him and men were creeping up the hotel's stairs even now. When Paula glanced at Clementine through the cracks, the woman's stare was a mix of pity and betrayal, likely from having all this thrust into her bedroom. Paula could relate to the betrayal—where had Waite gone? Probably halfway to Cheyenne by now.

"Clemy, you seen my… what the hell are you doin', woman?" a man's voice said from the door.

Paula froze. A half-naked man still wet from a bath sauntered into the room, puzzling at why Clementine was hunched near the window. "What's all this commotion?" he asked, gazing down at the horsemen in the street.

"I won't hurt you, Paula," Crowe continued. "I know you're scared, but I'm not even bent about all this." He chuckled. "The boys are a bit put off you made them ride through the night, true enough, but hell, I take my hat off. Takes sand to steal from a thief, and you knew just where to hit me, didn't you?

"But we'll let bygones be bygones, alright? All you have to do is turn the Sioux loose, and I'll forget this ever happened. I'll even pay your way back home to momma, give you something for your trouble. How does a hundred dollars sound, Paula? Hell, let's make it two. Could probably use that money with your Pa gone, couldn't you? It's nothing to me, Paula, I only care about making sure you get home safe. The same way I want my sister safe. You have a family, you can understand that."

He gave her a moment, but Paula stayed firmly in place, watching Clementine and the man watch Crowe.

"Holy shit…" the man beside Clementine said. "That's Roderick goddman Crowe. What's he doin' offering money to a woman?"

"I don't know, Jeb," Clementine said.

Jeb looked at her, puzzled. "The hell's got you so spooked, woman?" he asked.

"Nothin'," she said. "You best find your gun and get downstairs, Wauldruff will want help if things get—"

The boy repositioned his leg. Made just enough of a sound to catch Clementine's attention.

And Jeb's. "The hell?"

"Jeb, come here," Clementine said, pulling off his towel. "Don't all this commotion get you fired up?" she said, pulling him onto the bed. Paula closed her eyes tight, but they opened quick enough when Jeb pushed passed Clementine to throw open the closet door.

"I'll be damned," he said out loud.

Paula wasn't sure what to do but found herself too petrified to react.

"Jeb, I can explain," Clementine said.

"How the hell did you get mixed in this?" Jeb said in a harsh whisper. Clementine didn't have time to respond before Crowe continued, harsher.

"I'm not going to hurt you, Paula, but I need that boy you got. That's why I'll also give those two hundred dollars to whoever brings you out to me. They'll be gentle of course, if they want a dime, but they'll bring you and the Indian to me right quick. And if anybody gets in the way, well, the boys here are still pretty sore about all this riding."

Something of a commotion arose outside, a few shouts to see the money, a few more asking if the girl had anyone else with her.

Clementine stepped in front of the closet. "She's just a girl," Clementine said. "He's a killer."

"And who do you think he'll kill when he finds her here?" Jeb whispered, rifling on his trousers. "You heard him, Clem—two hundred dollars."

"Jeb, no."

"Said he ain't gonna hurt her."

"Waite left her with me. You want to cross him?"

Jeb ignored her, pulling on his boots.

Paula thought about charging him, taking his gun, holding it on him before it was too late.

Clementine beat her to the punch.

Jeb held her gaze, silent fury building behind his eyes. "Clemy. Give me that gun."

"Leave her be," Clementine said, her voice shaking. "She's just a girl. She's innocent."

"Look who else she's got in there. Look who's after her. Clem, this is two hundred dollars. We could get gone with that. Make a decent woman out of you."

Clementine held fast. Until she turned for Paula, eyes teary. "I… I have to get out of here. I'm sorry, sweetheart."

Jeb rolled his eyes. He stood and yanked his gun from her, then put it on Paula. "Get up, kid."

Paula braced for a struggle but realized it would only cause a commotion. She'd have to think of something else. Maybe Wauldruff would help. She stood, then Jeb pulled the boy up beside her. He started walking them out the door.

"Mister, there's more reward money than that on my prisoner. I'll split it with—"

"Shut your yap, kid. Not passin' up on—"

The waitress was waiting near the stairs, staring up as if in anticipation. Then Paula heard the gun cock. She assumed it was Jeb, then she heard a quiet voice from behind the door. "Don't get jumpy now, Jeb."

Paula turned to find Waite positioned behind the door, gun extended at the back of Jeb's head. Clementine froze behind him, hand over her mouth.

Jeb managed a dry, nervous chuckle. "Gonna shoot me, Waite? Give us away?"

"Only reason I didn't just snap your neck was to keep ol' Clementine here from screaming," Waite said back. "But you keep quite 'til this blows over and you get to walk out of here alive."

"Shouldn't you be out there dealin' with this?" Jeb asked.

"Already did."

Paula glanced at the graying lawman, but he kept his steel eyes between

Jeb and door.

So, same as Jeb and Clementine, and the waitress downstairs gazing up with apprehension, she waited. Waited for Jimmy Reece to burst through the swinging doors with pistols blazing. Waited for Crowe to announce they were burning the town.

Sure enough, it was Crowe's voice that raised next, after a muffle from a familiar voice. The railman? "I know his esteemed holiness the marshal," Crowe said. "What was he doing in Little Holstein?"

When no one else replied, the railman continued. "Putting his boots up at the saloon, I'd guess."

"That where the girl found him?" Crowe pressed.

"I suppose, I wasn't there."

"Who *was* at the saloon, then?"

Another familiar voice sounded. Wauldruff. "I own the saloon," he said from somewhere outside. "The girl came stumbling in looking for help. Ran out with Waite."

"What help did he offer exactly?"

"I wasn't listening all that closely."

"You weren't interested that a twig of a girl burst into a saloon with a bound and bloodied Indian?"

"Just said she needed help, and Waite said he'd get them out of here. Didn't say nothin' about the Sibling Gang, I'll tell you that much."

Another pause. "Where are their horses, then?" Crowe asked.

"Loaded them onto the storage car. Against procedure but he flashed his badge."

"Esteban?" Crowe asked.

"Tracks end at the station, boss," the Mexican said.

Paula didn't know what was happening but dared to hope it would work.

"Want to turn the place upside down to make sure?" Reece asked.

"Waste of time, train'll have to stop at the mailpost and the foundry. We can catch it there."

With that, Paula heard only the sound of hoofbeats thundering away. No one in the hotel moved or spoke for a long moment, then, without warning, Waite cracked Jeb on the back of the head. He collapsed in a pile to the ground, to which Clementine gasped with horror.

"Spare me, woman," said Waite. "This ain't the sort to entangle with. Even in your profession." Waite proceeded to hogtie Jeb, then tossed him against the bed in the next room. "Keep him there for a full day, don't want him doin' nothin' foolish until we're well clear. If he wakes with an appetite for vengeance, remind him I let him clear of that barfight in Evanston last winter. Or shoot him if it's easier, I won't mind."

Waite pushed pass the boy and Paula, holstering his pistol. "Get a move on, pipsqueak, they're only gonna be a day behind us by the time they catch that train," he said, heading down the stairs. "Long ride ahead."

Mouth agape, Paula glanced at Clementine in the doorway to her room, whose eyes watered with sadness and shame. She slowly pulled the door shut.

"Maddox! Now!" Waite called from downstairs.

With the boy in tow, Paula followed Waite to the back of the hotel. They waited for the crowd to dissipate, then made a dash behind the buildings for the rail station. The Marshal pushed his way into the back, where both his and Paula's horses stood uncomfortably.

The railman greeted Waite with crossed arms. "Can't believe you talked me into that," he muttered in a hushed voice. "When they come back—"

"You won't be here," Waite said. "Get to Cheyanne southways, steer clear of the railroad. You'll miss 'em and I'll get you your share."

"50 percent," the railman said. "If either of those beasts had made a scene, I'd already be dead. You owe me—"

"Well let's be careful when it comes to what's owed, George," Waite said, tightening his saddle straps and shoving the Indian boy back up Paula's horse. "'Cause if I recall I've turned a blind eye to your fair share of contraband pullin' in here from Lincoln City. Be a shame for one of those shipments to come spillin' out before a marshal." Perhaps sensing further protest from the railman, Waite turned to him full length with his cold eyes. "Or I could just kill ya."

The railman took a step back, unfolding his arms.

Paula said nothing.

After the coast was clear, she and Waite made out on their horses past the edge of town northeast. Paula was sure they'd been spotted by someone, but even so, the lawman didn't seem to worry. With Little Holstein far behind, Paula's shock finally gave way to her curiosity. "How many men did you pay off?" she asked.

Waite turned to her in the saddle. "Just ol' George," he said. "Threatened a few more. Gangs come and go. I don't. That lot knows who to fear, push comes to shove. Still, got lucky, mostly. If those horses made a scene, next marshal to come along would be burying that entire shithole town."

"What about the barkeep? Wauldruff."

"Got especially lucky, there. He doesn't care for me much but 'spect he remembers how well I tip. He'll want a cut of that reward money when we turn over our prisoner."

When he offered nothing further, Paula asked the next question. "How much do you want?"

"Seventy thirty," he said, hands on his belt. "The big piece of that pie coming to me."

Paula looked like he'd punched her. "He's my prisoner! You're a marshal, isn't it your duty to—"

"My duty is to patrol and capture dangerous outlaws, of which Roderick Crowe is and your hogtied Sioux is not. I should be mountin' a posse to get the jump on the Sibling Gang. Instead I just saved your life, and I'm offering you direction and protection through some of the meanest land in the territory. There's plenty worse than Crowe and his thugs in the Laramie Mountains between here and the Fort. You want to get there in one piece, it'll cost you seventy percent."

"Fifty fifty," Paula recoiled before she knew what she was saying.

"Seventy thirty are the terms. Some of mine will end up with George and Wauldruff too, you paid up front when I saved your pipsqueak skin."

"My family needs this money or we're going to get driven off our land! My Pa is dead, you heard it from Crowe himself. It's just me, my widowed Ma and my two sisters. We have nothing left. Why do you think I'm out here doing this?"

Waite released another aggravated sigh, but Paula halted her horse and cut short his next statement. "I thought you were in the business of jailing thieves, didn't know you was one," she scolded.

Waite glanced back with an arched brow. "Now that you mention it, suppose I could just take that boy. Leave you here."

Paula stared at him, her heart sinking.

Waite looked forward again, raising a hand. "Fifty fifty, then. Got yourself a partner, Maddox."

12. The Ruthless Sort.

INTERESTED THOUGH PAULA WAS IN the fables of Odysseus and conquests of Alexander, Plato and Aristotle's competing arguments of the one versus the many often left her dozing during visits with the Professor. More than once she'd woken not to the Professor's admonitions but the sensation of falling just before drifting to sleep.

She'd never imagined the same weightless sensation striking while on horseback, but two hours north of Little Holstein, she ended up on the dirt.

"When was the last time you slept?" Waite asked. He peered back from his horse, reaching out to collect Paula's as it walked along without her. Her prisoner had nearly fallen as well, but she could tell he was awake at least.

Paula's face flushed red as she scrambled to her feet, ignoring the ache on her elbow and side where she'd landed. She picked up the army hat from Delsman's horse which she'd taken to wearing and dusted herself off. "I'm fine," she answered.

"It's two days to Rigby's and another day and half through the mountains to the Fort. We ride until dark and wake at dawn, and you'll be on watch half of each night. The other half you sleep. Not now."

Paula tried not to stomp as she made her way back to her horse.

"Haven't seen bags under eyes like that since my grandmother's open casket."

"I'm fine," she repeated.

"Don't got time to brew coffee or catnap."

"I didn't ask for either."

"Gonna ask me to heft your prisoner for a spell?"

"No."

"Gonna complain we didn't get food back in town?"

"Aren't we in a rush?" Paula asked as she slid back into the saddle.

Waite turned back and kicked his horse forward, nearing a trot.

The silence resumed.

Even the hoofbeats seemed lost amid the endless, empty plains. Paula silently sang a song to keep awake, rubbing an eye with the butt of her hand. She'd have given anything for an hour's rest. For a horse all to herself. For fresh water and food in her own saddlebags. She still wasn't sure if Waite was goading her to scare her off or merely out of resentment he'd partnered with a teenage girl. Either way he was content to withhold assistance.

Apparently Rigby's store lay in the foothills of the Laramie Mountains. A remote homestead more than an actual store, Waite told Paula the owner would barter for food and essential supplies. A welcome reprieve for the few riders who traversed the mountain.

They might even commission a deputy there, Waite hoped. The Sibling Gang would only be a day behind them once they uncovered the deception, and the marshal was eager to amass additional firepower. He hadn't bothered recruiting in town—none were reliable in a fight or trustworthy to bed down with, he'd assured her.

The only thing that had kept Paula from dozing off as the day pressed on was concern that she'd enlisted the wrong sort of man to help. "I've never heard of you," she said after nearly an hour of silence.

"Imagine my disappointment," he returned.

"But all those men in Little Holstein knew you. Everybody in Carbon knows... knew, Marshal Boyle, and he worked land farther off than Little Holstein."

"You're fixin' to ask a question, ain't ya."

"Why were they all so scared of you?"

"Who's more scared of a lawman than the Sibling Gang?" he rephrased, rhetorically. "Them that know what's best for 'em," he said.

When the girl said nothing further, he glanced her way, stretching on his saddle. "You never spent much time outside that ranch of yours. Have ya."

"I've been all over Wyoming," she answered.

He nodded. "Well I don't usually ride so far west or south as Little Holstein. I patrol the Dakotas mostly, the wild Lakota nation. Only made it back to Wyoming hunting an outlaw named Hamilton on the run from subpoena. He owed testimony against a mine owner outside Rapid City."

Waite spat on the trail, annoyance twisting his mustache. "Gave chase all the way from Rapid City only to find Hamilton shot dead in Little Holstein yesterday afternoon by some drunk cowpoke named Sinclair. Because Sinclair didn't like the way Hamilton dealt cards. Weren't Sinclair's first killin', neither. Mean bastard. Strangled the girl taken up in that hotel before Clementine, I heard tell. And supposedly he drew fast when he wasn't drunk. Maybe faster than me, at my age.

"So, I waited on him to bed down last night then knifed his two outlaw friends, quiet. Quiet but messy. Roped Sinclair by the neck, pulled him out into town. Knifed him too. Let 'em all watch. Told 'em what happens when they obstruct justice."

Waite glanced at the girl, staring back pale. "What do you think keeps a town like that in line, Maddox? Full of men like that? Full of depravity and sin."

She waited for him to answer his own question until she realized it was a test. "Justice?"

"Fear!" he said impatiently. "You payin' any kind of attention? Fear. Bein' a marshal is bein' one man out here amid hundreds. I'm old and getting older. They have to know I'm meaner. Colder. That if they break a law, I break a bone. That if they raise a fist, I raise a gun. That when I ride in—rare as it may be—I ain't there to sniff flowers. It's the only thing keeps me alive out here."

When he looked Paula's way, she had broken eye contact, staring blankly ahead of her. "Wishin' it was Marshal Boyle you'd found in that hotel this mornin', mmh? Well, Boyle is dead. Didn't know him well but well enough to know he never stood a chance against Crowe."

"You ran from him," Paula observed.

"You can scare a town, but you can't scare the devil. Most certainly can't outgun him. But the devil deals in theatre too. Sometimes while he's preening, if you're lucky, you can outthink him. That's what saved your life, pipsqueak—luck, brains and fear. Fast and strong ain't got nothin' to do with it."

Paula swallowed her doubts as she watched the gray lawman ride ahead of her. Whatever he lacked in compassion and integrity, maybe he was the sort she needed. Ruthless. Unafraid. The railman described him as a pitbull. He hardly frothed at the mouth, but apparently he could maul.

They stopped by a creek to rest and water the horses a little past midday. Paula walked to the other side of her horse to shield herself from Waite while he relieved himself into a bush. She found her sleepiness abated despite her exhaustion, as if her body had written off and absorbed the last 24 hours in the face of another 72 promising more of the same. Paula stared aimlessly at the horizon toward Carbon and their ranch now and again, wondering if her mother had made it to town yet to discover Pa dead and her oldest daughter vanished.

A sudden sob soared up and out. She gritted her teeth to keep it from Waite, shutting her eyes and setting a hand over her mouth. She quickly wiped tears from her eyes.

When she turned she found a pair of eyes on her. The boy hung only a foot away, still sprawled over the horse in his bonds. His bruises were still bright and heavy on his skin. Waite had dressed his cuts fresh on the trail to ensure nothing got infected. The boy's blindfold must have slipped off at some point. He stared at her with eyes as calm as they were intense. She couldn't help but return his gaze, momentarily prisoner to his silent resentment and curiosity.

Paula jumped when the boy flew off the horse, pulled from the other side onto the dirt. Waite sent a boot to the boy's stomach.

"Ain't no call for that," she yelled.

Waite leaned over to refasten the boy's restraints and tie the blindfold back in place. "Ever seen a Sioux raid, Maddox?" he asked.

"I know what they do."

"I asked if you've seen one."

She didn't say anything.

"I have. Seen boys as young as this, younger than this, cut down girls your age and take their scalps. You think this one would do any different if he wasn't beat half to death and roped?"

"Beating him the rest of the way dead won't get us our reward," Paula managed.

"When you hold a man against his will, hell, even a boy, the thing that keeps him held ain't the bonds on his hands or feet, not the gag in his mouth. It's keeping his spirit broken."

"I thought priests were supposed to nurture spirit."

He glanced at her impatiently. "I'm good at breaking spirits because my daddy was a slavemaster in Arkansas. Wasn't never a priest. Now get back on your horse." Waite lifted the boy up and over his shoulder, then tossed him atop his own horse.

"He's my prisoner," she said.

"We got ground to cover and you're nearly as beat as this boy," Waite said, mounting up. "He's stronger than he looks, this one. Don't want him gettin' ideas as we tire. Keep focused on yourself, stay watered. I need you and those young eyes sharp out here."

"I thought you said Crowe would be at least a day behind us."

"I thought I told you there's worse than Crowe out here. Think this boy is the only Sioux on these plains? Might be he's a magnet for more."

"What does that mean?" Paula asked as she rode up to Waite's side.

He snorted and wiped his nose, keeping his steely eyes ahead. "I rode down this same way we're headed. Rigby, he heard talk from trappers of a Sioux party on the hunt for an army patrol. Sounded specific."

"How could they know the army had this boy?"

"What *we* know is the important part, Maddox. Might just be they're out for retaliation, but you don't want to get caught with a Sioux prisoner out here. Roderick Crowe will seem like granny handin' out cookies then. Best keep an eye out."

Waite glanced at the boy as he squirmed for a better position over the saddle. "You hear the private call him anything? A name?"

"Why would it matter?" Paula asked.

"There are a few important Sioux, I reckon. He must be some kind of important for the army to want him so bad. Makes him worth more."

"No," Paula said, deciding Waite was more interested in the pay than justice. Either served her purpose, she supposed. "No name that I heard."

Waite nodded, cocking his head. "Well, everybody ought to have a name, boy," he said. "With the state of your face maybe yours will be Pulp." He glanced back to Paula as if checking to see if he'd made her smile. He shrugged when he found only a grimace. "Don't make eye contact again. It'll only embolden him."

"I just wanted to see what kind of man he was," she said, to which Waite raised an eyebrow.

Paula reddened again but decided to continue if only to show her partner she was more mature than he assumed. "Men's eyes show you who they are." Her heart dropped in her chest when he laughed.

"Did a woman tell you that?" he asked.

Her hands gripped the reins tighter. She regretted saying anything.

He smiled and shook his head, taking a moment to gather his thoughts. "Men show you who they are, Maddox, who they really are, starin' down what scares 'em. Weak men, anyway. Strong men show you who they are starin' down opportunity. Remember that."

She would.

13. A Wider Aim.

HUDDLED BY THEIR TINY FIRE that night, Paula spoke for the first time since the afternoon. "Why do they call you Father Waite, then?"

Waite was already bedded down, his hat tipped over his face to his mustache. He left it there. "My abundance of faith, I suppose."

Paula's expression remained the same. "So you weren't a preacher or anything?" she pressed.

"What's your guess, Maddox?" he asked, raising the brim enough to flash belabored eyes.

Paula let the moniker go, accepting that for whatever reason he saw fit to hide its origin. "So have you always been a marshal?"

"Have you always been so full of questions?"

Paula's huff was loud and deliberate. She turned to gaze out at the horizon.

They'd made camp under a small depression of rock in the plain to hide the fire. Paula didn't even know why they'd bothered to spark such a small blaze. She held her legs tight to her chest in the cold. Waite had given her his blanket while he slept under his coat.

The lawman laughed under his breath.

"Is something funny?" Paula snapped.

"Just that women are women from a very young age, it appears. And here I am partnered with a miniature one on the trail. Jesus."

"Do you hate women or something?"

"No one hates women. I just prefer them indoors."

"You hate young people then?"

"No one likes young people except their mothers. But you're not a child. You struck a deal with a federal marshal to ride an enemy combatant into an army garrison under pursuit of a criminal outfit through hostile Sioux territory. I reckon you're more a man than most of my deputies through the years."

Paula wasn't sure if he was mocking her or not. "Is that what you're doing?" she asked. "Treating me like a man?"

"Like it or not you're in a man's world now, Maddox. I don't hate you, I respect you. That's why I won't powder your bottom and tuck you into your blanket out here."

"Friendly conversation is powdering my bottom and tucking me in?" she asked.

"You need sleep a lot more than you need to know about my nicknames."

"I slept while you kept first watch."

"Then now it's my turn to sleep, isn't it?" he asked. "Can't do that with you yammerin'."

Again Paula huffed and stared off into the darkness.

Waite shook his head and let his hat dip back over his face, folding his arms. "Been a marshal for eleven years, mostly in the Dakotas and Nebraska. Fought for the Confederacy before that. Was a policeman before that. Guess I just like firearms."

Paula let the silence hang a moment after he finished. "That's it?"

"What the hell else is there? You fixin' to become a biographer?"

"Do you have a family?"

"Some husband and father I'd be out here killin' outlaws if I was."

Paula gave up, accepting obstinance as a condition of her journey to the Fort. She skipped ahead to the question she hoped to ask a paragon, but settled for Waite. "Would you help me bring in my Pa's killer? After this is over, I mean."

Waite pushed up his hat again, his eyes finding hers. Even in the dim light he could see them red and puffy.

"Best focus on the task at hand for now, Maddox," he advised. "Tell me more about your murdering rancher once Pulp is giving up Red Cloud and Roderick Crowe is strung up next to his sister."

Paula looked to her feet. She sat in silence for a few minutes until forced to choke back another sob.

"None of that now, Maddox," Waite said. "Teary eyes won't be able to make out Roderick Crowe or a Sioux scout creeping up on us in the dark."

"You think Crowe could catch up to us that fast?" she asked, shifting the subject.

"They will have caught up with that train before sundown. Crowe probably split his boys. His man Reece will be on the way back to Little Holstein to interrogate at gunpoint, probably ridin' with Ross Burnside and Piano Bill. Crowe will be on this way to the mountains with Red Esteban, Mic Buchanan and Sonny Greaves. He'll know we have to cross near Rigby's to make the best time. He'll be riding hard, probably already killed his horses and stole new ones. He knows there's only a day or two left for his sister."

"You've tracked the Sibling Gang before," Paula observed.

"Every lawman from here to Salt Lake has been after the Crowes at one point or another. I nearly had Reece and Esteban in Painted Bluffs a year ago but Virginia rode in with the rest. Had the bitch dead to rights but her brother jumped in, gave her a window to flee. I chased 'em over a month but they split. The trail I picked ended with a Chinaman who Virginia paid to lead me the opposite direction." He paused to pick his teeth.

Paula could see the resentment in his eyes.

"Was tracking Reece again after their last split a month ago. Then Boyle tagged Virginia in Evanston. I chased her halfway across the west and Boyle practically bumps elbows with her at some damn bar after an anonymous tip. The sack of shit..."

Waite pulled a bottle from under a coat pocket and took a sip, earning a frown from Paula.

"Suppose I should be grateful though. Half the challenge with the Siblings is knowing where they'll strike next. Nothing else would have brought the gang back together like this, and now I have them barreling right toward me. Fixin' a collar on Roderick Crowe… Well, that's retirement right there."

Paula blinked, her mouth slipping open.

"Tell me your intention," she said, far louder than she meant.

"Keep it down, Maddox," he countered, gesturing to the dark night.

She stood. "What kind of lawman are you?" she nearly shouted. "You're only using me and this boy to lure Crowe and his men into a trap! You never meant to honor our agreement to deliver him to Fort Laramie or collect his reward, which is probably more substantial than the entire Sibling Gang, by the way, and… and you lied to me!"

Waite offered the same taxed look as before. "Are you finished?" he asked.

Paula remained on her feet.

"Jesus Humboldt Christ, Maddox. Perhaps I acknowledged your uncommon maturity a bit prematurely."

"Then, you don't aim to—"

"I'm riding that boy in with you." He said it emphatically, as if insulted. He shook his head and leaned back into his restful position. "Your prisoner is the task at hand. If Crowe forces us to take him in advance of our arrival to Fort Laramie than we'll respond accordingly. But while I'm sure you're a seasoned marksman, I'd prefer to have a few additional guns at my side before riding at seven killers. Point is, I'll get backup at the Fort. Then I'll have him, tired and desperate."

Waite yawned and rolled over, taking a sideways swig from his bottle. Liquor dripped down his mustache. "If my shot had hit its mark that day in Painted Bluffs, I'd have bagged both Crowes. Almost $11,000 in reward between them."

Paula sat back down, wrapping the blanket over her legs. "Why do you talk so much about money?" she asked, foregoing an apology for her accusation of betrayal.

Waite's mustache rose with his smile. "Clementine don't come cheap." When he saw her distaste his smile only widened. He leaned up on one elbow. "I'd wager I'm not the first man to acknowledge that you are brighter than I gave you credit for, am I?"

"Why is money so important?" she repeated.

"Are you not riding to collect the reward for this prisoner?"

"I told you how desperately I need it."

"So because I have no mother and sisters awaiting foreclosure on a ranch, I couldn't possibly have need of such compensation?"

"How would I know? I tried asking about you earlier."

He nodded, holding his smile. "You did," he acknowledged. His gaze fell into what remained of the fire. "Just need something to retire on, is all."

"Most people don't retire with $11,000."

"Most people aren't as good a shot as me. And it's about time I got what's due after all these years."

"Marshals don't make fair wages?" she asked.

His laugh was harsh, grating his throat as it escaped. "Maddox, I spent six years training and commanding men to fight and die for a country that didn't come to pass. A bankrupt business and destroyed estate were my only remuneration. Eleven years after I started over out here it feels like I've killed just as many men keeping what passes for peace. I've been shot up, cut up, blown up and spit up by judges who tell me my methods are excessive and by people who don't give a shit about the law until it's broken against them. None a'them have a clue what it takes to keep monsters at bay. They've never slept in hostile territory, staked a hideout from a muddy riverbank, had to shoot a hostage to save another five."

He kicked the last burning log in the fire, simmering it to coals. "And I barely make more than a Chinaman hammerin' rails together. I want out, Maddox. I've had enough law to last a lifetime. There is no justice, no fairness, out here. Not for me. Not for your Pa. Not for the trail of dead the Crowes leave in their wake. Not even for that boy lyin' yonder."

When the fire all but failed, Waite seemed to wake from the darkness he'd let settle around him. He wordlessly blew the fire back to life with another few twigs and log over the coal bed. "I'll keep an eye out 'til first light. Get another few hours' sleep, Maddox.

"But I already—"

"You already managed through one full night, riding the whole way. Two in a row ain't healthy at your age. Get to sleep, we can't afford any more dead time from you fallin' off your horse."

Paula felt something soften as she watched him rise into a sitting position, looking out into the darkened plain. She rolled to her side with the blanket wrapped around her and shut her eyes. "Thank you," she offered.

Waite nodded.

14. Two Kinds of Soldier.

"Why?" Paula whispered.

Waite didn't budge, extending the butt of his carbine rifle to the girl. The old lawman awkwardly contorted his upper body from where he lay on the rocky knoll. He couldn't rise for fear of giving up their position, but Paula found it more likely Waite was simply too lazy to lift himself upright. He tended to expend the least amount of energy needed to accomplish any task, even if it meant risking ridicule.

"You're hungry, aren't you?" he answered, equally hushed.

"We have biscuits and jerky."

"Stale corndodgers and dry beef are hardly adequate for a growin' young lady."

"I'm a young lady now?"

"You're a young lady on the prairie. Which means you'd better know how to shoot."

"I know how. I told you."

"Then let's see it."

"Why does it matter?" she repeated.

Waite grunted. "I can think of seven reasons furiously catching up to us with each second you sit here stalling," he said. "Not to mention reasons with fangs, reasons with tomahawks, and other reasons you'd best just trust me on."

"You honestly expect me to help you fight off the Sibling Gang if they catch us? I'm only..." She caught herself from finishing but Waite's face was already contorting along with his upper body. He swung the butt of the rifle along the horizon as if to present the whole of creation. "You see any other deputies out here with us, Maddox? You think Roderick Crowe or Jimmy Reece are gonna let you ride away back to your momma because of tender age and freckles? We're partners straight down the middle, remember? Unless you want to hand your prisoner over to me and skedaddle back to Carbon, that is."

Paula glared at him before easing down the rocks to his position. Flattening herself out beside him, she gingerly accepted the weapon from his grasp. It was heavier than Pa's. A different action, too—lever rather than bolt.

"It's already chambered, all you gotta do is line it up."

"I know," she whispered harshly.

He flashed the inkling of a smile that told Paula he knew she was lying.

The gun felt slippery in her grasp. She closed one eye as it gazed down the barrel to the deer lapping water at the base of the knoll. Pa had let her shoot cans off the fence and spokes on a busted wagon wheel. She'd even gone with him hunting pheasant last year, collecting the birds he downed and ensuring their end with a quick twist to the neck.

Somehow this was different, though. She'd eaten plenty of venison but the creature in her sights felt so... alive. The lean muscle was artful, certainly more than the bulky cows at the ranch.

Paula thought of the calves she'd nursed back home. Her father had reminded her they were only livestock when he caught her cradling one, talking to it as she might with the dog. She tried applying his words to the deer, imagining it was Pa flat beside her whispering gentle encouragement rather than the crass marshal goading her.

The deer tensed as a shot resounded over the knoll. Their prey skipped up and away from the creek bed. Paula flinched—it wasn't her shot.

Waite seized the barrel of the weapon. "Easy, Maddox," he cooed, seeing her finger still strained on the trigger. She gradually released the weapon but frantically scanned the horizon. "Don't worry, that was off a good spell. Best not divulge our location with a nervous trigger finger, though."

"What if it's them?" Paula tensed again when another round of shots echoed over the prairie. There had to be at least two or three guns out there.

"It ain't," Waite said, pushing himself up with the rifle and a groan. "That's war shootin'. Frantic. Desperate."

Paula rose beside him. "What do we do?"

Waite stayed quiet a moment, likely judging distance and location. "Best see what the commotion is about," he said. "Whatever it is lies on our trail."

The two mounted their horses behind the knoll and rode north another few minutes. The gunfire stopped as they came to a ridge. Smoke trails drifted along with the breeze to the west. Paula froze when Waite halted and raised the rifle, pointed at approaching hoofbeats in the grass. They waited until a lone cow strode around the ridge, ambling past them without offering so much as a glance.

Paula caught sight of a dotted diamond on the creature's backside. "That's the Babcock's brand," she said.

"They from Carbon?" Waite asked.

"They go past us sometimes. They drive herds up from New Mexico. Alvord hates them for being free grazers. They're bringing people up with them to resettle at some ranch east, in Nebraska I think."

Waite listened more than he looked. "Huh." He kept the rifle close but urged Paula east until they maneuvered around the ridge. They dismounted and scuttled to a position behind rocks. The marshal pulled the spyglass from his saddlebag and took in the view, squinting but failing to react in any discernible way.

From the distance Paula could only make out a wagon and a few horsemen. Cows walked or ran away, splintered in all directions. "What happened?" she asked.

He didn't respond, still analyzing whatever scene had played out. Then he brought the spyglass down, resting it on his thigh. The faint sound of screaming made its way to the ridge.

"Let me see," Paula said.

The look Waite gave her told her she didn't want to see, but knowing her stubbornness he said as much.

"I'm old enough to help you kill the people after us but too young to see?"

"Yes."

"That's horseshit." She felt momentarily big to give him what for, but saw he wouldn't budge. "You're not being fair."

"Fair?" Waite repeated. He shook his head as the screaming continued, hardening as if throwing away whatever empathy he'd held before. He handed the spyglass over. "Look out yonder and tell me if you see anything fair."

Paula hesitated as if she'd walked into a trap. Her curiosity won out. The view remained poor but a shiver raced up her spine at the sight of dead men scattered about the wagon. There were smaller bodies too.

Two men ambled about, throwing supplies from the wagon into a pile. Another four were grouped together, struggling with something. At first Paula thought they'd taken a hostage or prisoner. Then she realized where the screams were coming from. She pulled the spyglass away after witnessing one of the men ripping a woman's dress over her head. "You have to do something," she said, her voice shaking.

"What would you like me to do, exactly? Charge down there on open ground one against six?"

"They're… She's…"

"She's as dead as the others," Waite said. "This Babcock outfit brought this on themselves."

"How can you even say that?" Paula whispered harshly. "Those bandits killed children! They're… attacking her! It's your job to—"

"My job is getting you and your prisoner to the army," he spat. "This is no country for women and children, they were dead the moment those cowboys decided to ride out here in the open without ample firepower.

"So you're just going to leave her."

Waite took his hat off to run a hand over his balding dome, staring out at the blurred attackers as the screaming persisted. His voice was calm and measured despite his frustration, weighed down by what Paula assumed was practiced apathy.

"Go ahead, Maddox. Tell me I'm a coward who only keep the law when it's convenient. But being a lawman ain't about law. Not out here. An army of marshals, hell, the actual army, couldn't right all the wrongs out here. First rule of this country, lil' partner—don't bite off more than you can chew. Else a bigger, meaner set of teeth sets upon you while you eat. You want fair, get back east of Nebraska."

Paula's rage bubbled under her flush cheeks but she didn't have the words to express it. She thought about lashing out at him as he'd instructed, but then the screaming stopped.

After a final gunshot.

It felt like the gunshot that tore into her father, and Paula saw him fall, saw him slip away in her hands, all over again. She was as powerless to stop one as she was the other. Another unspeakable crime, another life taken, another murderer who would walk away laughing.

The tears on her cheeks simmered from the heat beneath. She cried atop her horse, looking down and away from the open plain. Waite grabbed hold of Paula's reins, lightly pulling her horse after his.

✦ ✦ ✦

Waite allowed a larger fire that night, sheltered under the bows of a vale in the northern plains. Trees were more common now, on the edge of the Laramie Mountains. "I'm sorry you had to see that," he said.

Paula lay wrapped in her blanket with her back to the fire. She hadn't spoken since pulling away from the massacre late in the afternoon. Neither had he. "You were right," she managed after a moment. "I didn't want to see."

"But you had to," he affirmed. "*You* were right."

"You don't think I belong out here. Do you." She didn't turn from where she lay but she could hear him shift, feel his eyes on her.

"You're a decent sort, lil' partner. You care. About fairness."

"You don't?" Paula waited but only heard him pull the cork from his bottle.

"There ain't none either way," he offered at last. "What you or I care about doesn't mean spit out here."

"Why do you even bother then? How'd you get to be a marshal?"

"I was only ever police or a soldier. Not much call for a man with those skills."

"You could have thrown in with Crowe."

"I live amid injustice. Don't mean I have to be party to it."

"But you are. You killed Sinclair and his friends in Little Holstein. Even if they had it comin'…"

Waite didn't say anything. Only took another drink. "I was like you once, you know," he offered a few minutes and a few swigs later. "Young, full of right and wrong and nothin' else." Another swig. "That was why we seceded. It was about some Yankee a thousand miles away telling Franklin County what to be. I killed men, sent men to die, for what I thought was right. For a place of our own."

Another swig.

"Probably for the best we didn't get it. Not much of a home for the Negroes." He dug around through his saddle bag.

Paula turned when she heard a fresh cork pop.

"When you don't get what your heart's set on, suddenly fairness goes out the window. Had to clear out after the war, lost everything. If this business with Pulp doesn't work out, you'll see that a man…" He paused, glancing Paula's way. "…A pipsqueak, can't stay in a house with dreams scattered about the floor like shattered glass. Every time you step on them you bleed a little deeper.

"But out here, they said… A new world where a man can be whatever he wants to be." He laughed, then took another swig. "No, but a man can take whatever he wants to take, even if it belongs to someone else. I tried to stop it, to take out all my disappointment and rot from the war and fight another war out here.

"That's the worst kind of soldier to have, of course. The one who cares. When he wins, he's the moral absolutist vindicated, the hell with the loser. But when he loses… well…"

Waite spread his arms wide, his smile twisted as if presenting himself for display at a zoo or a freak show. "He keeps on fightin' even after the war's over. Always has to fight. Everything and everyone—every injustice that's out there. 'Til one day, he fights so hard, he cares so much, he turns around and sees the line of the law and the line of decency are drawn so far behind him that he can't find 'em anymore. He realizes the only place to actually get at what's right is to go beyond. Where the law does not reach and decency does not abide."

A long drink. Half of the second bottle was gone.

"You fight and you kill and you deny mercy. You wreck God's terrible vengeance on the guilty. To avenge the innocent and your innocence. To keep your soul from fallin' apart. Then, when the blood is spilled and the innocent avenged, you open your book and tally the cost. That good soldier, the one just following orders, he sees debt on his soul he can never pay back."

Waite smiled again, his glazed eyes falling over Paula. "But the bad soldier, the one who cares, well… the books all add up to him. It all balances out."

His smile faded as he finished the bottle. He didn't look sad or empty, just… blank.

"He can't find that line of decency because it's covered in blood. And he doesn't care. He's angry all the blood didn't mean anything. That he never got his due for all the justice dispensed, all the vengeance taken. It gets to be such a bloody mess he gives up trying to clean it." A chuckle escaped more from this nose than his mouth. "That part of him leads to the Bloody Baptism of Father Waite."

Paula blinked, almost taking advantage of his drunken state to ask about the nickname. "What about the other part of him?" she asked instead. Her voice was as vulnerable as it had been since meeting him, as if her belief in this man, her only possible champion, hinged on his answer.

He glanced at her and shrugged. The bottle fell from his grip, sliding between his legs. "That part of him will always hear that woman screaming today," he said, barely audible.

Most of what he said was lost on Paula, but before she had the chance to ask further, his eyes slipped closed and his head tilted over his shoulder. She might have checked his pulse had she not heard him snoring. Paula stared at him for a few minutes, then the fire.

Then she heard Waite get up. But when she turned to him, she saw it wasn't Waite who'd stirred.

Paula sprung toward Pa's rifle, thankful she'd left it close. The boy had risen to his knees across the fire from her, his blindfold removed as he stared her down. His bonds remained tight, but Paula leveled the gun at him, her mouth open but no words coming out. She almost shouted for Waite, but the boy unhurriedly took a seat near where he'd been laying. He stretched his back over a rock, shuffling his feet as if to get comfortable. He closed his eyes and rested his head against the stone.

Paula wasn't sure what to do with the rifle. She fell asleep torn between fear and guilt.

15. Escape.

PAULA WOKE TO THE SOUND of hoofbeats. She assumed it was a dream at first, opting to remain under the comforting warmth of her blanket. Then she felt the warmth of sun on her skin. Her eyes shot open and she threw the blanket free. It was well after dawn from the yellows and blues in the sky. Light stabbed through the tree line like infinite daggers, gleaming from the empty bottle in Waite's lap, unmoved since it fell empty. The marshal hadn't budged either.

Surprise escalated to panic when she found the boy missing.

The only trace of him was the rope that once restrained his wrists and ankles, cast idly in the grass beside the rock he'd moved to in the night. Pa's rifle had vanished as well. "Waite!" she yelled, running to kick his boots.

He jolted and swung forward, reaching as if to seize something he meant to kill.

"He's getting away!" Paula was shocked at how fast the man scrambled to his feet, snatching the carbine from under his arm. He slept with all his weapons. "Where is he?" he spoke so fast the words slurred. Paula wasn't sure if he was panicked or still just drunk, but she pointed to where they'd tied the horses and shouted for him to hurry. They took off. "He got your rifle?"

"I think so," she returned. They spotted the boy on Paula's horse at the bottom of the slope, veering sharply to the south. Waite's horse trailed, its reins in the boy's hands.

Waite stopped Paula from running after him, instead pulling her toward a stubby cliff atop the incline.

"What are you doing?" she shouted.

He didn't answer, nearly tripping over roots and rocks as he slid to a halt at the cliff. The boy was galloping full speed below them, already pulling away through the thin trees.

Paula's deflated heart flared again when the marshal raised his rifle, taking aim. "He's too far," she protested.

Waite closed one eye, steadying his right over his left forearm.

"What if you kill him? We need him alive!"

Still Waite kept silent. Then the shot.

It was the longest delay Paula had ever witnessed, but through the trees she saw her horse buck and fall, toppling the boy as it dropped. Waite's horse jerked away and continued running south. The marshal tried a strident whistle but the animal kept going. Unlike Paula's horse, the boy pushed himself back to his feet, dashing along the same path. He didn't look back.

Waite raised his rifle again but lost line of sight, marked by a loud obscenity. Pulling his hat lower he dashed past Paula for the decline. "What are you waiting for?" he yelled.

Paula started after him uncertainly. "Shouldn't we get our supplies at the camp? Our food—"

"Your prisoner is getting away, Maddox!" he bellowed. "The little sonofabitch is a goddamn chameleon. If we don't keep a warm trail he'll vanish like a puff of smoke out here."

"But he's injured, he can't—"

"He look injured to you?" Waite was irate. "Bastard has probably been mobile for days, just biding his time. What in the hell happened?!"

Paula matched his ire as she slid down the incline after him. "You passed out drunk is what happened! He was moving last night so I kept my gun on him but..."

"You fell asleep," Waite finished.

"It was your watch! You left me holding a gun on him."

"And you didn't think to wake me up?"

"I'm sure you don't remember but you nearly drank yourself to death last night. I didn't much feel like dealing with you anymore."

Waite might have said something more but groaned and paused by a tree to take a breath, already straining.

"Can you even do this?" she asked.

He glared and tossed her his rifle. "Welcome to the glamour of law enforcement," he snapped. "Keep up. And if I hear so much as one whine outta you..." He took in a large breath until he was practically shaking. Then he pushed off from the tree and started south at a hobbled jog.

✦ ✦ ✦

Waite looked close to death when they emerged from the thin trees onto the plain. The morning sun cast thick shadows over his face. She recognized the pale skin and bloodshot eyes adorned with dark bags beneath. Her father had stumbled out of the barn more times than she cared to remember in that state, but a pot of coffee and a few hours in bed usually brought him back to life.

Waite had no such luxury. Within an hour his wheeze was comparable to one of the Maddoxs' sick hogs. Paula wished she'd gone back to camp for their canteens since he refused to take detours to search out water. His insistence that every second counted would kill him at this rate.

Watching him claw up inclines and race through straightaways, his wheeze seeming louder with each step, Paula found Waite a captivating distraction from her guilt of letting the boy escape. She'd never seen him like this. Determined. Outthinking Roderick Crowe in Little Holstein with little more than minutes to orchestrate a town-wide conspiracy had shown his wit and focus, but this was something else.

Unfulfilled dreams and bloody injustices left him sour, but surely somewhere under the seasoned apathy a flame still burned for more than whiskey and a fistful of dollars.

Relief, and possibly Waite's salvation, came when Paula spotted his horse lapping stale rainwater from a depression in the plains. She worried that Waite, plodding eight or nine paces ahead of her with his gaze fixed forward, might have missed the animal altogether had she not shouted his way. Waite's whistle brought the horse over at an unhurried pace, as if it had been waiting for them all along. The marshal drained half the water from the satchel on the horse in a single voracious gulp, then handed the rest to the girl.

"Let's go," he said, pulling her into the saddle behind him. Paula's arms locked around his torso as he started forward at a gallop. Except he pointed the horse back north toward the mountains.

"You're going the wrong way!" Paula shouted, convinced the marshal's exhaustion had turned to delirium.

"You think he's running aimlessly into open ground?" Waite returned. "He's still wounded. No chance to outrun us. We passed him somewhere in the rocks or trees. He's doubling back into the mountains to disappear."

"How long have you known that? And what have we been doing running this way then?!"

Waite patted the horse's neck. "I'm too old and fat to walk him to Fort Laramie once we catch him."

"What are the odds we'll be able to find a lone boy in that?" Paula gestured toward the rising mountains on the horizon. "He's had hours to burrow in somewhere."

"A marshal wouldn't be worth much in Sioux territory if he couldn't track."

His words might have instilled more confidence had he not ran past his own horse in the field a few minutes prior.

Waite slowed pace once back in the rocky terrain, sometimes pausing altogether to hop off the horse and kneel in inconspicuous brush. He plucked a berry off a shrub and threw it up to Paula on the horse. "He's headed west toward Beaker's Plateau. Probably for the river in the gorge."

"You can tell that from this?" Paula asked, rubbing the berry between her thumb and index finger.

"From the lack of 'em. This branch was picked clean."

"What if it was someone else?"

Waite's chuckle was mean. "You see an abundance of other travelers out here, lil' partner?"

"Animals eat berries all the time."

"They don't pick a single branch, and they sure as hell don't walk their little hooves into this rocky basin. If our steed could talk he'd be cussin' us out plenty about now." He mounted and rode them further into the basin toward the gorge.

"Do they teach you how to track when you become a marshal?" Paula asked a few minutes later.

"They teach you how to track in Franklin County Arkansas. 'They' being any father with a son."

"Did you have any brothers or anything?" she asked.

He sighed, as if suddenly accepting that young girls were more inquisitive than his usual stock of deputy. "Only child," he answered. "Lived far enough out that the kids I saw most regular were Negroes. Spent plenty of time with one for a few years, my age. Francis. Tended to horses. Not sure how he died, but he didn't make it to adolescence."

"Do you think slavery was right?" she asked, remembering his confederate background.

"Do you?" he countered.

"Pa said it was cruel to keep any man in chains for being born apart from other men. That's why he fought for the Union Army."

"Didn't ask what your Pa thought."

Paula paused. "The Professor said God made colored folk different," she mused. "That their brains or hearts or both aren't the same someways. I've never seen one up close 'cept for Morgan and that fella in the Sibling Gang so I don't know."

"They ain't no different," Waite offered. "'Cept for the skin, far as I could ever tell. Met plenty smarter than me. I couldn't read for shit until I made it to lieutenant."

"Then why did you think slavery was right?"

"I didn't. Not the way most folk considered it, leastways. But one man can't change a country."

"You could have let your slaves go," Paula offered.

"Never owned any. Had three or four that worked to keep up the house, mainly while I was gone at war. Didn't offer pay, but I kept a roof over their heads. Kept 'em fed."

"While you were at war fighting to protect slavery."

"What do you want from me, Maddox?"

"Just say it was wrong."

"To you? A springy little white girl who's seen two Negros and spoken to neither?"

"Who else you gonna say it to?"

He looked back, incredulous. "You like to get under people's skin, don't you?"

This time she said nothing.

Waite sighed. "Expect you're right. For all the good that does the Negros of the world." They rode a moment before he chuckled, surprising her. "Can't remember the last time I admitted wrong. To a pipsqueak, no less. Nothin' more dangerous than a woman's mind."

Paula might have smiled under other circumstances.

16. The Element of Surprise.

FORTY MINUTES LATER THE RIVER was still several miles off, but Waite stopped the horse in a bowled ravine heavy with vegetation. When he dismounted, taking care to do it quietly, Paula whispered to him. "You see something?"

"There's a party on the other side of this bowl up by the river," he said. "If Pulp's still on this track for the gorge he'll be boxed in until they move on."

"How do you know there's a party ahead?" she asked. "I didn't see anything."

"Observed a heavy set of fresh tracks back in the plains. Headed northwest. Only one easy way into the mountains for a group that big, straight through to the gorge. They'll have stopped at the river to rest up before turning west for Casper or east to the Fort. Either way, chances are they're roadblocking the boy's escape."

"And you think he's hiding somewhere down there?"

"We're about to find out."

"It would take hours to search all that."

Waite nodded, sweeping his gaze over the brush to the open air above.

Paula watched a pheasant swoop down while he waited, disappearing into the greens and browns.

"Stay on the horse," he ordered at last. "Ride back behind those trees, keep hidden and ready to ride, we might have to skedaddle right quick."

"Why? What are you doing?"

"Saving us a few hours," he said. Waite loosed a single shot into the air, the rifle jerking against his arm. A flock of pheasants kicked up from the grass and shrubs, lifting off in unison for the north. Waite only glanced at them, his gaze trained on the vegetation they'd left. "At the expense of our position. Stay hidden." In a low crouch, the marshal waded into the bowl through the grass.

Paula lost sight of him quickly.

She scanned the grass for any sign of movement for long, agonizing minutes. The pheasants landed back on the other side of the bowl. At first Paula wondered if the shot had been meant to scare up the boy, but watching the birds drop to safety away from the marshal she guessed his true aim. The pheasants had taken flight from everywhere but a small pocket by the trees—the direction Waite disappeared.

After twelve minutes, Paula's confidence in his plan waned. Maybe the boy wasn't there after all.

Paula's heart leapt high in her chest when she heard hoofbeats across the ravine, veering around a wall of rock. She peered from behind the trees and saw three men on horseback uprooting the pheasants once more. It couldn't have been the Sibling Gang. Could it? She risked more of a look with Waite's spyglass, still tucked in the saddlebag. Thankfully she saw no gambler's hat. No poncho.

What she saw was nearly worse.

The bandits from the plains started on the path around the bowl to Paula's side. She frantically searched the vegetation for Waite. Did he even know they'd been found? Was he waiting with his rifle, taking aim as they approached his horse? Paula wished she still had Pa's rifle but clutched the hilt of the skinning knife Waite kept in the saddle.

She could leave. Try running back the way she'd come. Waite would be safe if he remained hidden, but there was no way for her to hide the horse. She could come back for him later. No, it was already too late. If she took off now they'd spot her and give chase. She remembered what they'd done to the last woman they came across.

Paula shook violently, feeling sick. She couldn't summon breath fast enough. They were already halfway around the bowl. Another thirty seconds and they'd spot her.

Still no sign of Waite.

"Lookie here," the voice called from the rise of the bowl.

Paula was frozen. Every instinct told her to run the horse, to leap into the vegetation for Waite. But she couldn't, still just clutching the knife.

"Not often you find anyone in these hills, much less a child." The man was gaunt, his dusty beard the only thing filling out his face. The other two looked at Paula with equal parts fascination and glee. They stopped in front of her, one on the other side to block her escape back onto the trail.

"What are you doing out here, miss?" another asked, leaning forward to rest on his saddle.

"I'm bound for Fort Laramie with Marshal Waite and his posse of deputies," she said, her voice cracking.

The men exchanged a volley of concerned glances then set skeptical eyes back on her. "Posse?" one man pressed. "How many?"

"Twenty," Paula said entirely too fast. She immediately felt the number was too high but couldn't take it back.

The man's expression didn't shift. "What's a posse after in the mountains?"

"They're hunting a prisoner. He's wanted by the army."

The one doing the talking seemed to ease back, nodding. "A posse of twenty hunting one," he repeated. "Strange that there'd be any marshals after an army prisoner as opposed to actual army."

"The army private escorting him was killed. Marshal Waite and his men—"

"Strange that they have a little girl with them, too." The man slid down from his saddle, his smile wide. Wicked. "Why'd they leave you all alone?"

"Marshal Waite is riding here right now," she sputtered.

Another man, a heavy-set Mexican, dismounted.

"I'm telling ya, he's riding from..." Paula paused when she saw him. Waite was crouched, choosing his footing carefully as he inched out of the bowl. His duster was removed along with his hat. He'd left the carbine behind as well, instead clutching his revolver and a rock the size of his fist.

His eyes were alive with something ethereal, commanding Paula to remain where she was.

"He's comin' from Rigby's. I just rode out to look around while the posse rested. I'm looking for water," she said.

"Well it just so happens we're camped out by the river a piece west of here," the gaunt man said. "Best you ride back with us. Can't rightly leave a cute little thing like you on your own."

Waite shifted his icy gaze to the man closest to him, increasing his pace.

"I don't know you," Paula said. "I—"

"You'll get to know us," the man said. "Real well. Get down off that horse."

Paula worried her heartbeat would somehow give Waite away. "You're scaring me." She said it because she thought it would sound real and prolong the discussion, though it happened to be true.

"Ah, no reason to fret," the heavy man said. "We're real friendly. We'll show—" He turned when he heard the thud from behind him.

Paula flinched but couldn't shut her eyes at the sight of Waite caving in the gaunt man's head with the rock. The marshal dropped his bludgeon, reaching for the knife in the fallen man's saddle. The man on the horse turned to draw his weapon but froze when he saw Waite's gun pointed his way. Waite didn't fire, instead using his perfectly good melee weapon as a projectile. He threw the knife, lodging it into the horseman's neck. The animal bucked and retreated from the bloody scene.

By then the remaining man, the heavy one, had his pistol drawn. He fired and pierced Waite's shoulder. The marshal stumbled and shouted something feral. Then, to Paula's shock, threw his revolver at the foe rather than fire it. Waite charged. His punch dropped the man, even forty pounds heavier.

Paula watched the marshal pummel his fists into the Mexican. Before long it looked like Waite had used a rock on him too. Hearing the horseman squirming from where he'd fallen, Waite picked himself up and raised his boot to the man's head. This time Paula forced herself to close her eyes. She might has well have seen the act from the horrible cracking sound upon the stomp.

Her face as white as Waite's hands were red, Paula remained where she was. Waite stood silent a moment, content to breathe and revert from whatever primal state had engulfed him. Without looking at Paula, he leaned over to pick up his revolver and holster it. He left the knife firmly lodged in the corpse.

Waite disappeared back into the bowl, reappearing over a minute later with his hat, duster, carbine, and the boy. He walked the boy with a belt around his hands. Fresh bruises decorated the young man's middle and arms. Blood ran from his lips.

"What… why did you do that?" was the question Paula arrived at as the marshal draped Pulp over one of the bandit's remaining horses.

"It's the same group we spotted yesterday. More will be at the river. Have to hurry, they might send a few more to check things out."

"Why didn't you just shoot them?" Paula asked.

He grunted as he mounted the horse with the boy. "One or two shots, they might assume the boys were huntin' or dickin' around. Storm a'shots and they know trouble's afoot. Don't want a group chasing me on horseback while I'm saddled with a girl. Now let's go. Rigby's ain't far and these boys'll be comin' for blood when they eventually find their pals."

"Should we hide the bodies?" Paula asked.

Waite rolled his eyes and prepared to say something unkind, but saw the girl's expression and seemed to contain himself. "Best we just get to the road." He kicked his horse forward to a gallop after she mounted the other. "Oh. I found Pulp, too."

17. Rigby's.

WAITE WAS MORE GRAZED THAN PIERCED by the gunshot to his shoulder. Crimson stains ruined his gray duster, but only a dime-sized layer of flesh was missing underneath. He didn't bother to wrap it, insisting Rigby would take care of it once they arrived at his place.

"Barely an hour north of here," Waite said once they made it back to his intended route through the mountains. He drained the remainder of the canteen he'd picked off one of the dead bandits, easing the horses to a walk. "Rigbys are good people. Their shop sits on a butte—we'll have view back near ten miles in case them marauder cowboys decide on holdin' a grudge."

Paula didn't ask more about the Rigbys or their apparent outpost, too shocked to speak. The shootout in Alvord's barn had been one thing, but Waite's assault on the bandits... She'd never even heard of something like that.

One could argue a gun battle was more explosive, it's capacity for destruction heightening the threat. The sheer volume of the clash in the barn had reverberated through Paula's ears during her ride to Little Holstein.

A gunfight, though, was something Paula could understand. In the dime novels, there was a cleanliness, poise, even civility to a duel. The eruption at Alvord's ranch had been anything but, of course, but she recognized the emotions on display between Louis Vance and Private

Delsman as they frantically blasted at each other. Fury. Terror. Desperation. More than once since that night she'd imagined herself standing in the heat of the fight, wondering what she'd have done.

Past the moral implications, Paula supposed the act of shooting someone was fairly simple. A bullet was so instant and absolute in its lethality, she mused, that one could only point and pray, really. Depending on one's aim, the gun did all the work. It took bravery to stand and fire, but she supposed anyone could do it if desperate enough.

She couldn't imagine anyone doing what Waite had just done.

Where a gun held the mess of killing at bay and inserted a comfortable distance between the killer and the dead, Waite still wore the dead on his clothes, hands, even his face. His own blood was lost amid all the rest.

Paula recognized nothing on Waite's face as he stomped, stabbed and smashed. Something animal had gripped him, driving out any semblance of compassion, any vestige of humanity. The truly alien part of it was that while Vance and Delsman had been completely enveloped in their desperation, Waite's barbarism had been summoned at will. Cleaving the skull of the first man with a rock, the second with fists and the last with his boot—none of it had been blind rage. From the moment he crept from the ravine to the moment the three bandits lay dead, his eyes burned with cold fire. Calculating. Plotting every move as the situation progressed.

That the marshal could toggle his compassion so absolutely with his reason intact was far more frightening than the sadism of the bandits or Crowe. That's why what he said next startled her so much.

"You don't have to worry, you know. Nobody's going to hurt you so long as you're with me."

It was the way he said it that most affected her. Paula had heard the promise throughout her life, but it rang hollow from her father. He hadn't even been strong enough to protect himself, much less Paula or her sisters. His heart was up to the task, but that hadn't been enough.

Past all Waite's inner tumult, past all his selfish motives and his damaged worldview, his word carried no doubt. No ambiguity. No question. Whether for her brightness or bravery, maybe just for her willingness to keep up with him, he'd taken a liking to her. He'd been rough on her, flippant, but he'd offered her a place at his campfire and the respect of his honesty whenever they spoke. She'd seen the guilt on his face after allowing her a view through his spyglass the day before, as if caught between teaching her the truth of his world and guarding her from it.

Whatever responsibility or even fondness he felt for her would never translate to paternal devotion but, unlike Pa, she believed this man when he promised to keep her safe.

Waite noticed his partner ride closer in the final stretch to Rigby's.

The store was little more than a cottage on a grass trail branching from the main road cutting through the mountains. It sat in a depression of sorts, lodged between two granite monadnocks rising from the earth as colossal cylinders, resembling ancient stone towers of a bygone civilization. A ridge rose from the back of the house toward a miniature peninsula jutting from one of the monadnocks.

The marshal dropped from his horse without hitching it and stomped up the few stairs to the house porch, grunting from the sting of his wound. A woman emerged from the door before he got to it. She was younger than Paula expected, having pictured a hardened woman living in such a remote place. She had fair skin and light blonde hair under a thin bonnet. She seemed to be smiling until she laid eyes on the marshal. "Marshal Waite," she said, less in greeting and more in shock. "I didn't expect to see you again so soon. What happened to your shoulder?"

"Need a stitch or two, likely, maybe just a patch. Where's Rigby?"

"Tending to livestock, I'm sure he saw you come in…" She trailed off at the sound of a horse winding its way down a thin trail up the ridge.

Paula tensed at the rider—his skin and hair were nearly identical to the boy's. He was Indian, possibly Sioux himself, yet his clothes were that of a farmer. His expression mirrored the woman's when he came to a halt by the house.

"Supplies," Waite said when he saw the man. "For myself and the girl." He threw his coat onto the porch railing and showed his gunshot to the woman. "Let's start with whisky."

The woman glanced to the Indian man then mustered a thin smile. "Of course," she said, pushing the door open for him. "Why don't you have a seat in the back, I'll fetch the medicine tray."

"Come on, lil' partner," Waite said, ambling inside.

Paula wasn't sure she cared to be around the marshal as he numbed pain with restocked whiskey but decided she'd rather stay close. She didn't care to be left alone with any strange men, Indian or otherwise.

It turned out the man was Ben Rigby. Waite introduced the Rigbys to Paula while Mrs. Rigby set to cleaning his wound and another few cuts on his chest. Waite explained the purpose of his return while he drank. The couple seemed unaffected by his latest mission to deliver Pulp to the army, as if they'd known him to undertake far stranger jobs.

Rigby spoke English well enough it sounded like he'd done it his entire life. Perhaps he'd been rescued as a child or born to mixed parentage, Paula thought.

Rigby rose at the completion of Waite's story. "I have to finish tending my livestock."

Waite instructed Paula to follow him. "Make sure ol' Ben doesn't turn our prisoner loose before he heads back to his goats," he said with a laugh that let everyone know how funny he found the idea. He was already a fourth into a bottle, after all. "Then see if you can give him a hand with anything. She's a farmgirl, and we'll be short on payment for supplies until we collect the bounty for Pulp." Waite turned to Mrs. Rigby with a gaping grin. "My I-owe-you still valid, dear Mrs. Rigby?"

She forced the same smile she summoned at the front door. "Your credit is running thin but you know we always do our part for the law."

Waite's laugh filled the room. "Got a real Georgia peach here, Rigby," he said, smile wide as Mrs. Rigby leaned closer to begin her minor stitching.

Paula looked to Rigby, calm and collected. "These men that shot you up," Rigby said, shifting the topic and tone. "There were more in the lower gorge?"

"Could be," Waite said, earning a frown from Paula. He knew there were. "I'd be more concerned about the Sibling Gang, though. Odds are they'll blow through here sometime tonight. I'd batten down the hatches if I was you."

"They're hunting you?"

Rigby's question didn't carry accusation but Waite inferred such anyway.

"They're bound north for Gentry, so they'd be on this road one way or the other shortly. You can count yourself lucky I got here first to warn you off. Occupational hazards of owning a shop along a road, Rigby—undesirables tend to travel the same as the law."

Paula watched Rigby swallow something rising in his throat, then turned to his wife. "I'll move the livestock to the far field," he said. "Fire a shot if—"

"I'll be fine, dear," she said, not turning from her work. "We have the marshal here, after all."

"I'll drink to that," Waite said, all smiles again. He lightly beat his chest as if to emphasize vitality. The old lawman was flabby from his neck to his belly but still thick with enough muscle to conceal his age had his chest hairs not been gray. Paula could make out four scars on his chest alone, two likely from gunshots.

Rigby took his leave without another word. Paula followed, putting her hat back on as she stepped down the porch steps to their horses. She packed a fresh canteen of water into her saddle bag but stopped when she heard Rigby speaking something she didn't understand. She turned to find him talking to the boy still strung over the horse. He lay a wet cloth over the boy's back and the fresh wound there.

"What are you doing?" Paula asked.

"Your prisoner won't make it out of the mountains, much less to Fort Laramie, if his wounds aren't treated," Rigby said.

Paula hesitated but eventually gave him the nod to continue.

Rigby helped Pulp down from the saddle and sat him on the porch steps. He left the boy's blindfold on but washed the cuts and scrapes down his arms, neck and torso. When Rigby spoke in the strange language again Paula asked what he was saying.

"I'm asking him if he's sore in any strange places around his chest or his middle. Most of these are light wounds but he could be injured inside."

The boy was quiet for a long moment but eventually spoke for the first time Paula had heard. His voice was dim and dry. The two continued conversing while Rigby cleaned the boy up, replaced his bandages and gave him water.

"What is he saying?" Paula asked at last. She took a seat on the far side of the same step as the boy.

"He aches," Rigby offered. "But he is strong. He will recover."

"That's all he said?" Paula pressed.

Rigby glanced at the girl as if searching for something in her expression. "He's frightened. He asked me to help him escape."

Paula nodded, not sure why it made her so sad. "What did you say?"

"I told him I was sorry for him but he should remain strong. There may yet be an opportunity for him to break free. The marshal has many enemies."

Paula blinked. "Would you help him if you could?"

"Would you?" he returned.

Paula looked down. "I... I can't."

Rigby nodded, tying the boy's restraints to the side of the porch.

When he rose to make his way for his horse, Paula stopped him. "Can you... ask him something for me?"

"What would you have me ask?"

Paula searched for the words. "I want to know why he didn't kill me this morning when he escaped."

Rigby looked taken aback but leaned toward the boy and spoke.

Paula tensed when the boy turned toward her. Even with the blindfold it felt like he could see her. He said something, then leaned against the porch railing, tired.

Rigby rose, collecting his thoughts.

"Well?" Paula asked.

"He won't say."

18. Dust.

LEAVING THE BOY TIED TO the porch, Paula followed Rigby up the trail to the outcropping from the mountain. A small shed and chicken coup lay tucked against the rock, along with a pen containing a cow and two goats.

Paula was entranced by the view. She could see for miles south and west, all the way back into the plains bald of pine. The late afternoon sun painted the granite rocks in gradients of deepening orange. "It's beautiful," Paula said more to herself than Rigby.

He dismounted, gathering the goats and herding them out of the pen. "It is," he agreed. "There's another open area around the rock where we sometimes take the animals. It should be safer there until this gang passes us by."

"I'm sorry we put you in harm's way," Paula said. "Can I help you?"

"No. We see our fair share of trouble living out here."

Paula noted the contempt in his voice. "Are you sure it's okay leaving Marshal Waite down there…"

"The marshal is crude and cruel but he wouldn't hurt Samantha," Rigby maintained.

"I don't care for him when he's drinking," Paula offered.

Rigby set to moving the cow from the pen, pushing her into a waiting area while he went to the chicken coup. It looked as if the animals knew what to do.

"How long have you lived up here with your wife?" Paula asked, as much out of curiosity as courtesy.

"Four years. My parents were killed by cavalry and I was delivered to the railroad to work. She was the daughter of a preacher who took me in during my adolescence. When Samantha and I fell in love her father disavowed her. As did most others. So we ended up out here. No one else will brave the Sioux so we have the land to ourselves."

"The Sioux know you're here?"

"These are their mountains, or were until they were driven further north. I'm one of the few who remain. I know these mountains well. We make a fair profit selling goods to trappers, miners and law like Waite. Well... not Waite, of course."

"It seems you know each other fairly well," she said.

"He seems to think so," Rigby said with a grunt. "He isn't here often but he's always like that when he is. We hear talk of him from other marshals, mostly."

"What kind of talk?"

Rigby paused locking the coup after bringing his few supplies inside. "How well do you know him?" he asked.

"I'm not sure. But he's all I have."

Rigby nodded slowly. "I'm sorry for that," he said. He mounted his horse, ready to lead the livestock around the side of the rocks.

"Do you know why they call him Father Waite?" she asked before he could get started.

Rigby frowned, as if battling what he should say.

"Please tell me."

"I don't think he likes people to know."

"But I need to know. He's my partner."

"Then he should tell you."

"You know he won't. Please. I need to know what kind of man he is."

She watched Rigby cave in, searching for where to begin. "Marshal Reilly told me the story," Rigby began. "Waite was younger, still based in Arizona. There was a gang of Mexicans terrorizing towns along the border. Los Lobos. Supposedly it was easy enough to scoop up their thugs but their leader was well protected. Waite was after him for over year but couldn't get close.

"The story goes Waite heard the leader was going to baptize a godson in Mexico. Waite posed as a priest from the mission to get into the church, then he opened fire on everyone inside during the ceremony. No one was armed. He killed everyone, the leader's whole family. They called it the Bloody Baptism."

Paula swallowed hard, remembering the name from the previous evening.

"Afterward, Los Lobos ran wild in retaliation, completely destroyed a few towns looking for this Father Waite. When the government heard they tried to reprimand him or take his badge but there was no proof and it was on foreign soil anyway. Either way they had to reassign him north to get him away from the assassins. With the leader gone, Los Lobos splintered into other groups, but the Bloody Baptism remains a dark legend." He stopped to judge the girl's reaction.

She started blankly toward the cliff. "Do you think he's an evil man?" she asked at last.

"I think he cares as little for manners as he does about justice," Rigby returned. "I don't know if he's someone you want to ride with a moment longer than you have to, but I'm sure he'll get your prisoner delivered."

Again Paula noted his contempt. "I'm sorry that…"

She stopped. Something moved on the horizon. Dust rising from the hills. She squinted, heart pounding as she made out riders.

Rigby spotted them as well. "Is that the gang?" he asked urgently.

They were still far off, but Paula had seen enough folks ride into Carbon to know the dust cloud behind this group was too large to be a few remaining marauders. "It could be," she admitted.

Rigby didn't bother moving his livestock any farther. Instead he left them to make his way back down the trail for the house. Paula followed.

"Samantha!" Rigby shouted as he leapt off his horse by the porch. "Get your things, we're leaving!"

Waite burst out of the door by the time Paula caught up, rifle in hand though his shirt remained off. "What did you see?" he barked.

"There are men riding this way in a hurry," Paula answered. "Big dust cloud from the edge of the plains."

"How far out?" Waite grilled.

"Six miles, maybe," Rigby said, moving into the house to get his wife.

Waite cursed. "Get Pulp situated," he ordered Paula, "I'll gather supplies."

Paula obeyed and helped the boy back onto Waite's horse. When the marshal emerged he was fully clothed, draped in a new brown overcoat and loaded with a full saddlebag of supplies. His argument with Rigby from inside spilled onto the front steps.

"Out of the question, why should I risk my life for you?" Rigby nearly shouted. "We have shelter behind the rock columns."

"Then send your pretty wife there and you can ride northwest," Waite insisted. "You know these hills, you'll be fine. Just lay some false sign to mislead them to that broken bridge, is all I ask."

"You're asking me to leave my wife," Rigby maintained, as he saddled up on his horse.

Mrs. Rigby looked more frustrated than frightened. She only had a small bag in hand.

"What if they go looking up there?"

"Some logic, Rigby—you're trying to herd her up there either way," Waite blasted.

"I'd be with her."

"Won't make no difference who's with her if Roderick Crowe finds her. If you're worried about your hiding spot take her with you, disappear into the trees then double back."

"They'll double back too when they get to a blown-out bridge," Mrs. Rigby said. "You brought this on us and now you want us to get involved? I've known you to be selfish, Marshal Waite, but—"

"Selfish?!" he repeated, aghast. He pointed up to Paula with the butt of his rifle. "I'm asking for a little help keeping another lady safe. Give Paula here the same chance."

Mrs. Rigby readied another outburst but her husband cut her off. "Fine," he said. "There isn't time to waste arguing. We'll lead them to the west bridge. Just be sure you cover your tracks."

"Much obliged," he said, almost sarcastic. "I'll send some of that reward your way. Get goin'." Waite turned to march back into the house after depositing the refreshed saddlebag onto Paula's horse. "One last load, lil' partner, then we're gone."

Paula turned to the Rigbys as Ben mounted up behind his wife. He rode to her, glancing at the door of their house, then leaned in close. "You should know," he began. "Your prisoner isn't just some boy. He claims he's the son of a tribal chieftain. I believe him, and that means this gang in the distance aren't the only ones looking for him. A party of Sioux warriors passed through the mountains east of here yesterday. They might be after this boy. Either way, they'll be watching these roads. Is all this worth it?"

Paula's heart skipped a beat. She didn't have an answer. "Why are you telling me this and not Waite?"

Again Rigby glanced to the door, then whispered back to her. Something like guilt pulled his head low. "You're only a girl. You deserve to know what you're riding into." He paused. "The water is rough, but you can survive if you have to."

Before she could ask what he was talking about, Rigby kicked the horse forward and he disappeared with his wife around the path ahead. Paula waited in silence for Waite to emerge, staring at the boy draped over his saddle.

A few miles north of Rigby's, the mountain trail (if one chose to call it that—Paula certainly didn't) split east and west to paths even less resembling trails. Both routes would have ended at the gorge carved out by the Laramie River if not for the bridges constructed at either site. The western bridge was the widest and safest (which wasn't saying much, built by trappers and expeditionaries years prior). It had recently been torn apart by a rockslide. The remaining eastern bridge was little more than planks on lines of rope. Waite had taken a horse across on two occasions, he assured his partner, though they'd certainly want to take it one at a time.

Paula was less concerned with the structural integrity of the bridges and more with which Crowe and his gang would select. If he took Rigby's bait it would grant Paula and Waite another few hours to speed ahead. If not, well, maybe the eastern bridge could hold two horses.

So, Waite led them east at the break. Paula's heart raced, mainly because their pace didn't. The marshal maintained a gradual trot up the rocky slopes, careful to guide them around patches of soil that would leave obvious tracks, occasionally dismounting to brush away what sign they left.

"If they take Rigby's bait they wouldn't see any of this anyway," Paula pointed out. "If they don't, we need to get to that bridge faster. This is a waste of time!"

Waite ignored her, continuing to brush over a series of hoofprints in the dirt. "Suppose they split up, lil' partner," he said, hiding his brush within a tree so as not to be found. "Four men this way, four that, with orders to fire a shot at the first recent sign. That's what I'd do if I was Crowe, no matter how obvious the sign Rigby leaves. Manhunts and gunfights are just hands of poker. You can be dealt shit and still take the hand if you know how to play the man across from you."

"This isn't a game, Waite," she nearly shouted.

"Because games are supposed to be fun, is that it?" His mustache arched up as his grin spread. He slapped her on the back as he rode by. "You aren't having fun right now?"

Paula bit her tongue rather than lash him with accusations of drunken recklessness. Not because he was right about the tactics, but because somewhere deep down in the place where she'd felt trapped on the ranch, confined by inaction, she felt unexpected release. A foreign exuberance. Despite her terror from the violence, her moral apprehension to deliver the boy, the looming threat of death every step of the way, being out here—forcing things to work out rather than praying for them—ignited an excitement that made the world a little more surmountable.

Waite stopped at the top of a ridge. He pulled out his spyglass and gazed past the treetops to the split in the trail. "We'll wait to see which way they break then take off for the bridge," he said, as if sensing the girl's sweat bead.

"Will we have time to cross if they follow us?" she asked.

"Yes. It'll just mean no sleep until we make it to the Fort."

Paula sighed. She hadn't offered much to the Almighty since collecting the boy, but guardedly folded her hands.

The sun was nearly down by the time the dust arrived in the distance. Paula could make out what looked like seven or eight horsemen pausing at the split. She knew something was wrong when Waite's head tilted. "Is it them?" she asked.

"Not unless Crowe found himself a new roster of killers," he said. "Which upon closer inspection, these men are not. It's a posse of townsfolk with a pitchfork up their ass about somethin'." He handed her the spyglass.

Paula blinked when she made out the figures dismounting to investigate the trail, talking and pointing either way.

Waite narrowed his eyes when he saw hers flash with recognition. "Who is it?"

"His name's Louis Vance. He's got folks from Carbon with him, other men who more or less work for Alvord. He's the man who started the firefight in Alvord's barn. One of the few who made it out alive. He must have went back to town for reinforcements."

"Reinforcements for what?" Waite asked. "He wants to collect on the boy himself?"

"Vance wants to kill the boy to keep Crowe from finding him and trading him for his sister at Fort Laramie," she summarized. "Vance thinks if Virginia Crowe escapes she'll remember him as the man who helped make her arrest and burn Carbon to the ground. He must have found out I was riding the boy to the army."

"That shopkeep road his fat ass into the wild to save his skin from the Siblings with the Siblings right on our tail?"

"Didn't say he was smart," Paula returned. "Reckon he has a lot to lose, though."

Waite grunted and swiped his spyglass from her hands.

"Any other vengeful townsfolk I should know about?" he snapped.

"I didn't think he had the sand to follow us."

Waite released a soft sigh and patted her back. "At least it ain't Crowe," he said, peering through his spyglass again. "Think any of those boys know how to shoot?"

Paula shrugged. "I think two of them were soldiers, they work out at the Cullen Mine as security."

"Shit," Waite said casually, watching through his spyglass. A moment passed and he gritted his teeth, tightening his grip. "Shit." This time it was passionate.

"Are some of them splitting off this way?"

"No. All of them are headed this way. Goddamn Rigby, you'd think a born Sioux would know how to lay sign."

Paula tensed. "What do we do?"

"Ride," he said, headed back to the trail at a gallop. He didn't bother hiding his tracks in the dirt. She followed after him, at least relieved to be moving full speed. So much for sleep the next few nights.

19. A Rock and a Cold Place.

"Sonofa bitch!" Waite's shout echoed from across the gorge, defiant of the roaring rapids below.

Paula heard it before she emerged from the trees, having fallen behind in their race to the bridge. She braced for the worst as her horse skidded to a halt in the gravel beside Waite's, half expecting Crowe to be waiting for them on the opposite side of the bridge. Her heart dropped like a stone into the churning water below.

"Did Rigby mix up the bridges?" Paula asked, staring at the planks dangling against the far side of the gorge wall. It looked like the support ropes had been smashed or cut. Boards protruded from the river, wedged between the rocks like food caught between teeth.

"Our good friend Mr. Rigby sabotaged us, lil' partner," Waite said, every word stabbing as if for Rigby himself. "That's why this party from Carbon set after us so quick. He probably doubled back another way to leave sign on our trail."

Paula thought about asking why but she could make a guess. It sounded like the good marshal made a habit of imposing on the Rigbys. This probably wasn't the first time he'd put them in harm's way for his errands. Or maybe Rigby wanted to help the boy escape once the marshal had been shot down by the approaching party.

Whatever Rigby's reasons, the question of why didn't matter much at the moment. "What are we going to do?" Paula asked.

Waite was silent, teeth clenched as he scanned the area. "We're gonna play the man across from us," he asserted, pulling his rifle out from the saddle.

The powerful confidence Paula longed to hear wasn't present in his voice, but she could already see his eyes going cold with focus. It would have to do.

"Heyah!" Waite drove his horse away from the bridge toward a slope leading down to the riverbank. The slope was rock and gravel. Hardly inviting to hooves, as the animals let them know all the way down. Paula followed regardless, already hearing the thunder of horses behind them.

She thought back to Rigby's cryptic final words. *The water is rough, but you can survive if you have to.* Did he mean for her to cross alone?

It looked as though Waite had the same idea, but even with horses, the white rapids were no less threatening. Preparing for the assault of cold in the rushing current, Paula was surprised to see Waite stop short and turn about.

"Come here," he shouted. When she brought her horse beside his he heaved the boy off his saddle and onto hers. "Hide him and the horse as best you can behind them rocks." He pointed his carbine to the larger formation along the bank about thirty feet downriver, then handed the weapon to her. "Once I fire, I want you to start shooting with this. Try to make the first shot count."

"You mean to fight them?" she asked, shocked. "There's eight of them!"

"Eight gentle townsfolk. Most of them will fold if bullets start flyin' their way."

"And the ones that don't?"

"We'll kill 'em," Waite said.

Ice hung from his words, and Paula felt cold. "Can't we just try walking the river until we find a crossing point?" she countered.

"There ain't none. The rocks have us boxed in further up where you can't see. Only way out of this gorge is back the way we came or across."

"Rigby told me the water was safe, that we could—"

"Rigby told us the bridge was here!" Waite blasted. "Does that look forgeable to you?"

Paula glanced to the roaring rapids, then the heavy rifle in her grip. "I... I've never shot someone," she said, barely audible over the river. Her hands were shaking even with the weight of the weapon.

Waite saw it, saw her eyes, and his seemed to thaw some. "Hopefully you won't have to, lil' partner," he said. "But if you do, remember why you're out here. This is for your mother and those sisters. Now get down there, we only have a few minutes."

Her nods were small but vigorous. She didn't say anything, concentrating on keeping tears at bay.

Turning the horse around, she trotted toward the largest of the rocks and dismounted. She helped the boy down after leaning the rifle against the boulder she intended as cover. The horse wasn't easily led so close to the crashing water but she hid the animal as best she could. She propped the rifle on the rock as Pa taught her with the fence post.

Her heart raced at pace with the rapids. The boy was tense beside her, as if aware what was about to happen. Waite sat firm in a comfortable but purposeful stance atop the horse, revolver drawn and ready.

Vance's party arrived barely two minutes later. The shopkeep spotted Waite and stopped, studying him for a moment. He led the eight men down the slope.

Waite didn't flinch other than to spit to his right when they assembled before him. "There are better ideas than linin' up in front of a Federal Marshal," Waite called.

Vance flashed what he must have thought was a disarming smile. "You must be, Marshal Waite, then."

Paula was surprised he knew the name.

"I'm—"

"I know who you are, Louis Vance," Waite yelled, challenging the river for dominance of the air. "Bearing in mind I already know the answer, why don't you explain to me why the hell a shopkeeper is driving a posse of Carbon townsfolk sixty miles across the plains and mountains in three days?"

The hopeful expression on Vance's face became dour. "I have a responsibility to my town, to my friends, marshal," Vance declared. "I take it you have the boy we're looking for."

"My party of deputies has the boy," Waite shouted back. "They just forged the river. Was about to do the same when we spotted a rabble bearing down on us."

Vance and his men looked across the river for activity. He seemed to let the assertion pass without debate. "It's imperative we keep that Indian out of Roderick Crowe's hands," Vance said.

"You're in luck then, because I don't give up prisoners."

"I'm afraid that's not good enough, marshal. I'm not sure where the Sibling Gang is but they're going to find you no matter how many deputies you have. They could be waiting for you on the other side of the mountains, or riding to cut you off at Gentry."

"I'll say it again," Waite returned, unyielding. "The boy is in my custody bound for Fort Laramie. I intend to collect on his reward and no Sibling Gang, nor a ragtag posse of townsfolk, is going to relieve me of my prisoner. If anyone tries, they will find themselves impeding federal law and either arrested or shot dead. Depending on how sporty they feel."

Vance's men exchanged nervous glances but their leader held firm. "If it's the reward you're concerned with, Curtis Alvord and the citizens of Carbon have put together a—"

"It is not the reward I'm concerned with, it is the completion of my duty to return a federal suspect to the 7th Cavalry for questioning on native enemy strongholds."

Paula knew better but he sounded so convincing she almost wondered if an inkling of principal had taken root somewhere within him.

"Heard Paula Maddox got mixed up in this at Little Holstein," Vance said, shouting louder as if in hopeless attempt to carry his voice over the river. "Hard to imagine a girl that young surviving those rapids. Where is she and this posse of deputies?"

Waite grit his teeth but kept his weapon aimed upward. "Let me tell you what's about to happen, Louis Vance. You're going to walk back up that slope with these men and head home. Because if you hold me up one more goddamn second, I will be back to Carbon with another three marshals bringing a whole different kind of hell with us. Arresting you in front of your wife on federal charges of hindering a marshal on duty will be the least of your problems. And if any a'you sonsabitches pulls on me, you'll be dead. That simple."

Vance hesitated this time, looking to his men to gauge their faces.

"Go on home, Vance. If you care about your family and your town then don't kill these men here today because of your paranoia. Go on home."

Paula saw the indecision on their faces, the conflict. Vance may have rallied them to fight the Sibling Gang, but who among them would gun down a Federal Marshal in cold blood? She dared to hope she could lower Waite's rifle as one of them turned his horse to start back up the slope.

That's when she heard the splash behind her. At first she figured it for a rock tumbling down the slope, then she turned to find the boy gone. Vance began shouting frantically. The first shot sailed past her toward the boy, missing both. The second was Waite, unloading his revolver as he reared the horse up, charging into their ranks.

The gunshots quickly faded from Paula's concern as she leapt into the freezing water after the boy. He was slow, his hands and feet still bound. Even in the shallows up to his knees, the current fought to claim him with each step. Paula clutched Waite's rifle if only to help secure her footing. As the boy paused to saw at the bonds between his feet, she leapt for him. She dropped the rifle when he slammed his head back into hers. She lost her balance and they both fell into the rapids.

The water's roar shifted between deafening and muted as the current pulled her under and bobbed her back up. Already stunned from the boy's headbutt, she slammed into the first rock. She bounced off like a ball, violently twisted down by a surge in the current that grazed her along the bottom. Paula surfaced spitting water, frantically clutching for anything to keep her head in the air. She managed to grab the edge of a log torn up from somewhere upstream but only cut her hand along the ragged edge of the wood.

The current finally pushed her against a flat rock, the pressure bruising her back even as she gave in, allowing herself a moment to rest. She turned to the shore to look for help. There was only a cliffside. The gravelly slope had vanished along with any sign of Waite or Vance.

Paula shrieked when something sharp cut into her back. She nearly slipped off the boulder but clung with nails digging at the granite, fingertips red and raw. With one eye open she saw Waite's rifle dart past her as if bidding her a painful farewell in retaliation for losing it to the wild.

She wasn't sure how much time passed on the rock. Hopelessness drew out all the terror and self-pity she'd held at bay these last few days like a poison. An overwhelming loneliness pounded into her as hard as the river itself.

Paula only knew she was crying when she tasted the salt. It didn't feel real. None of it did. Pa's death, escaping Crowe, her ride north with Waite... all of it was like something out of a dream. She'd woken to find reality had caught up with her. She asked the questions sure to be posed by whoever would find her body down river. What business did a scrawny fifteen-year-old have out here all alone? Did she really think she'd be able to survive this country?

Blood added to the unpleasant taste in her mouth. She glanced downriver. The rapids heaved upward in a swell then broke against another wall of rock. A calmer section lay to the left, but she couldn't tell what lay beyond. The sun was nearly gone. She couldn't hold on through the night.

Whatever strength remained in her little body drained away with her courage. Maybe Waite's promise that morning, that he'd keep her safe, had given her a false sense of invincibility when she ran into the water after...

The boy.

He was nearly submerged but she could still see part of his head in the water of the calmer side. It looked like he was caught on something. His hands looked unbound, but she couldn't tell about his feet. Paula felt instinct take hold again. Studying the current to gauge where she'd end up if she slid off the boulder, she decided to push herself left in the hope she'd miss a violent swell on the right. It was a long shot but she had little to lose.

It took everything she had to fight the current and slide off the boulder, but soon the river had her again. It plunged her under the surface, twisting her around. When she emerged she saw the lethal swell. She swam at its edge but missed it. She fought to paddle herself to the calm spot, reaching for the rocks around the boy.

Most of her left side felt numb where she'd ricocheted against the first boulder, but pain reignited when she caught hold of the boy's arm, pulling hers taut. She screamed. Something was wrong. Dislocated, maybe. Thankfully the current wasn't as savage here, allowing her to kick her way alongside the boy. He stared in shock when she swam into view, his eyes pure panic as he struggled to keep his head above water. He looked pinned in place by more than the current.

He frantically grasped for her. She took his hand, trying with no avail to pull him up. Aware he was running out of strength and breath, Paula summoned hers. She pushed underwater with open eyes. The water was clear but with the sun all but set there wasn't much to see. Feeling down the boy's legs, she found the ropes at this ankles caught on a branch.

"Hold on!" she yelled, down again. This time she set to yanking the branch. Her hand bled as she pulled so she set to kicking. She didn't feel it snap but she felt the boy rise, maybe finding a ledge to pull himself higher. Paula kicked herself up on the rock.

In her desperation for air, she swam too far away from the boy. She screamed as the current violently caught her, throwing her back into the mainstream. She only caught a glimpse of the cliff before smashing into it, then she blacked out.

20. Hunters in the Night.

PAULA WAS WALKING BEFORE SHE REALIZED she was awake, staggering from tree to tree as if the raw instinct that took hold in the river still clung for control. Darkness lay thick around her. "Pa," she heard herself say.

She had forgotten he was dead. She told herself to call for Waite instead. No, one was as unlikely to hear her as the other.

She collapsed beside the thick tree trunk on which she'd been leaning. Paula didn't thank the Lord for safeguarding her through the rapids. She didn't check herself over for injury, despite the pain in her arm, on her head. She didn't scan the darkness for a sign of where she'd ended up. None of that mattered.

The boy was gone, probably at the bottom of the river. Waite too, though riddled with bullet holes. What remained of her family would never see her again. Wherever she was, Paula couldn't find her way back. She had no supplies. No energy. No help.

She knelt for a time. Maybe a few minutes, maybe an hour. Tears came and went. She wondered how she would die. She wondered if it would hurt. Holding Pa's hand in his last minute, she couldn't tell if he'd been in pain or not. He hadn't cringed or winced, just lay there. His expression hadn't been of agony. Just sadness. Failure.

Paula wondered if her mother would look for her, follow her to Little Holstein or beyond. Elizabeth wouldn't understand all this. She'd cry and hide herself in her room, throwing tantrums until they found her sister. Then one day the tantrums would stop. Paula wondered if her sister would remember her decades from now when she was married and had children of her own. Hannah would never even know her face.

Paula started walking again if only to take her mind off her sorrows. Her entire body ached. The cold penetrated her the same as the darkness. She fought to keep from shivering. Her clothes and hair were still damp and her core was cold in a way she'd never felt on the iciest winter nights. Breath rushed from her lungs when she walked her right shoulder into a tree. She realized she couldn't move her arm. The slightest twitch of her finger stabbed.

A sound came from somewhere ahead. A twig breaking, the ruffle of foliage. The forest had been quiet otherwise, shielded from wind and muffling the roar of the river. Paula held her breath, suddenly terrified. She didn't move. Didn't breathe a sound.

She backed up slowly, feeling her way for a tree with low branches. Perhaps she could climb up, hide.

Then she saw the eyes. Twin pearlescent jewels glittering in a shaft of moonlight. They only flashed once, but they were too low to the ground, too big to be anything but threatening. The adrenaline immediately dispelled the cold from her core as if to brace her for the inevitable pounce of the creature.

Taking grip on a low branch of the tree beside her, Paula found the courage to climb. It came too late. She heard the creature's cry before she saw it move, but another sleek animal flashed through the darkness. The second creature didn't lunge at her, but rather at the first. Roars echoed through the trees. Paula climbed.

From the minimal safety of the lowest branch, she watched the first creature tear away as if in retreat, then lunge back with claws extended toward the second creature waiting low on the forest floor.

As soon as it began, it was over. When the attacking creature landed on the other, a pitiable cry replaced its feral roar, followed by a pained, wet gurgle sputtering into silence.

Paula held her breath, waiting for whatever had killed the beast to turn its deathly claws on her. Foliage rustled, and the weight of the dead creature landed heavy on the earth. When it fell into a beam of moonlight Paula saw its face—a mountain lion, she guessed, half as big as a horse.

The shuffle of the second creature came Paula's way. Not sure if she should lunge, scurry farther up the tree or wait for the inevitable blow, Paula's mouth fell open when the creature stepped into a moonbeam. And spoke.

"Paula," the voice said. She tilted her head as if she'd been dreaming all along.

It was the boy.

✦ ✦ ✦

She screamed when he popped her arm back in place at the shoulder. Even her beating in the river didn't equal the pain, but as terrible as it felt, it quickly abated. Pushing herself up from the tree trunk the boy made her lean against, she rotated the limb as if to inspect its functionality. Everything still worked, despite the lingering tingle of numbness. "Thank you," she managed after a long moment, wiping the spit from her face with her dirtied sleeves.

Her clothes were still damp but the fire he built had saved her from the cold. The boy tended to the fire under a rocky overhang close to the river, setting another dried branch over the coal bed. He rested his back against a rock, groaning as he tried to relax his muscles. Despite what he'd done to the mountain lion, he remained the most heavily injured between them.

"Thank you." She repeated it, directing her inflection to communicate the most genuine gratitude. "For saving me. In the river. And in the woods."

The boy nodded but kept his eyes on the fire and the spit of meat roasting over it.

Paula didn't think the big cat smelled particularly appetizing but let her hunger rule. The boy hefted his kill back to their camp after carrying Paula there. He left his weapon with her—a spear or sorts, fashioned from a tree along the river. Paula didn't know how he'd sharpened the ends so quickly but it had proved effective enough.

"Why did you save me?" she pressed in his silence.

Still he kept his attention on the fire and spit.

"Why didn't you kill me yesterday morning before you left?"

"You should rest," he said. "Eat and sleep. It will be a long day tomorrow. A long way to go."

"Where are we going?"

"A safe place."

Paula could scarcely believe he'd spoken English all along. That he'd been privy to all their plans. To her worrisome monologues and Waite's drunken self-reflection. His command of the mother tongue wasn't formidable but it was certainly serviceable.

"Where did you learn English?" she asked.

He didn't answer.

"How did you get us out of the river?"

Again, he refused to answer. Paula was ready to give up, but after a long moment he spoke. "I found you. The river was strong but then weak. I pulled you on land."

Paula was stunned.

He continued. "I found wood and food. I found Igmutalca. Her marks. I came for you, but you were not there. I made this and looked for you." He held up the spear. "Igmutalca was strong. I surprised her." He seemed to search for a word. "Lucky."

The remains of the creature—including its hide—was close as he cut meat to cook. "Why did you help me?" she asked at last.

"She would have killed you." He handed her a smoldering chunk of meat on a stick.

It tasted about as good as it smelled, but it was food and Paula forced it down quicker than she imagined. "What's your name?" she asked while he ate.

He glanced at her as if hesitant. "It is not a name like yours."

"Am I not allowed to say it or something?"

He rotated the meat higher on the spit. "Misun," he said.

Paula tilted her head. She didn't know a thing about Sioux names but it didn't sound very boyish to her.

"Does it mean something?"

"Does your name mean something?" he countered.

Paula wasn't sure if she'd offended him but answered anyway. "I don't think our names—Welsh, or something, maybe—I don't think they mean anything at all."

He nodded once, keeping his gaze on the fire.

Paula leaned back. She wasn't sure if he just didn't like to talk or if he didn't like her. Either way, he was there, listening. After her state of mind stumbling through the forest, it felt good to be in anyone's company. In a way, it meant more to be with Misun than anyone else. After all she'd put him through, all they'd been through together.

She realized she cared what he thought about her. She wanted him to know she wasn't a bad person. That she hadn't lightly planned to hand him to the army like a coin for barter. Even though that was exactly what she intended.

Paula suddenly felt as low as she had since that last morning with Pa.

"Sometimes I hate my name," she said after a moment. "I feel like it's not even really mine. I only got it by accident. It's the girl version of the name meant for the son my parents never got. If I had a brother, I probably wouldn't be out here. Everything would be different. Pa would still be alive."

Misun seemed to consider saying something for a long moment. "But I would be dead," he offered at last.

Paula's brow furrowed. "What?"

"You saved me. In the barn. From the man named Louis Vance."

"I was trying to take you to the army," she reminded him. "They probably wouldn't have let you live if I had."

"Then in the river. You saved me."

The way he looked at her reminded her of Waite seeing her as a person, not a hapless child. "Why didn't you talk before?" was all she could think to ask.

"I did not trust you. Or the marshal."

"You trust me now?"

"I know you. You will not hurt me."

At first Paula bristled, assuming he was calling her weak or inept. His eyes told another story. Of compassion. Maybe of pity. "I'd… still turn you in if I could, Misun," she said, lowering her eyes from his. "Even after you saved me. I have to."

"You do not want to."

Paula wasn't exactly sure what he meant. "It's actions that matter. What I want doesn't make what I was doing to you right."

Misun said nothing.

Paula raised her legs to her chest and folded her arms around them. "It's okay to hate me, Misun. I hate. I hate that Pa died for no reason. That people see a difference between men like Alvord and Crowe. That good gets twisted into men like Waite." She found his eyes. "I hate what I was doing to you. Everything is so complicated…"

The crackle of a splitting branch in the fire echoed into the forest. Misun's eyes betrayed the same mixture of curiosity and resentment from the trail, but she could see something more. As if, despite everything, he'd found something to identify with. He lifted away the last of the meat from the fire to cool, then kicked in the sticks he'd used to cook their meal.

"Small brother," Misun said, lying back against his rock. Paula tilted her head. "That is what my name means. My brother died by men from the railroad. He took men into that battle. He was a warrior. He led. I was a boy. Now my father looks to me. To give courage in our people. My brother had courage. I have fear. I fear death. I fear the future. I am not a warrior like my brother. I do not lead. I am not the son my father needs."

Paula saw his head dip heavy. "But you're going back to him." She said it more than she asked.

"Of course. He is my father. They are my people."

"Of course," she repeated, absently staring into the fire.

A few minutes passed before Paula's eyelids grew heavy.

"You should sleep," Misun repeated.

Paula suddenly felt nervous. "Are you… going to leave?"

He seemed confused by the question. "Leave the fire?" he asked, already getting up.

"No, I mean, if you want, but… Will you be there when I wake up?"

"Yes."

Paula nodded, her right leg starting to ache. She tried a smile. "I guess I'm your prisoner now."

"You can go if you wish. Now or when you wake. But you should not. You need a guide to leave the mountains. I know the path."

"Where are you going to take me?" she asked.

"Down the river. There is a camp of your people. If they are safe you can stay. I will go to a place of my people." By then the resentment had dissipated from his eyes, as if he'd been straining to hold it there in the first place. "I cannot go to the Fort with you."

They stared at each other a long moment, no words exchanged. "I still don't understand why you'd help me like this after everything I did to you," she said.

He didn't blink. "I do not hate. If I did, maybe I would be stronger."

21. Peaceful River, Tempestuous Creek.

"You told Rigby you were the son of someone important. Are you?" she asked Misun in the morning as they walked.

He glanced back as if agreeing with Waite's earlier assertion that the girl asked too many questions. "You would not know my father," he returned.

"But he's someone important," she pressed.

"He is respected by our people."

"Is he a chief or something?"

"Why ask?"

"Why don't you answer?"

Again he glanced back, seeming to study her expression to glean if she was serious or not.

"Perhaps I do not want my people known by white men you would tell. If you took me to your Fort, your army would force me to tell about my family. That would lead to death."

"Well neither of us are going to the Fort now, are we?"

When he stayed silent, marching along the graveled riverbed, she let a groan fly that made him cringe. "Who would I tell?" she pressed.

"You behave like a child," he said.

Paula blushed. She supposed her current aggravation stemmed not from Misun's reluctance but rather from the fact that he still didn't seem to trust her as much as she trusted him.

Whether from seeing the disappointment on her face or tiring of the banter, Misun finally spoke. "He is like a general of your army," he offered.

"Why do you keep saying that?" she asked, surprising him with a flash of anger. "*Your* marshal. *Your* army. *Your* general. You act like I'm the one responsible for all your problems. They're not mine. I don't own them, I'm not a part of them and I don't really care about any of them."

Misun's brow furrowed as he paused to study a track Paula didn't recognize in the dirt. "But you are here in this land with them."

"I have as much right to be here as anyone."

"No."

They walked in silence for the rest of the morning. She was more hurt than she let on as they wound their way north along the river. They covered impressive ground despite their fatigued and battered bodies.

Misun seemed used to such grueling excursions but was still worse for wear, his many bruises dark against his skin. He walked with a minor limp in his left leg and shivered randomly.

Misun paused to rest around what felt like early afternoon, sipping water and foraging a few plants Paula had never seen. He offered her something green with wide leaves, wordlessly, and she took it. Then they started again.

Paula felt guilty as the day drew on, though she wasn't sure why. She wouldn't apologize for being there, for Pa's dream of owning a ranch in the territory. Perhaps because whatever connection she and Misun had, whatever common ground they'd fostered, would be lost once they went their separate ways. They'd be two people from two different worlds at odds once again.

Paula helped lift him up a series of rocks north of the river. He strained on his bad leg but she kept a firm hold until he regained solid footing. Paula felt warm at his touch. His hands were rough, calloused for someone his age, but even in his condition he felt strong. Familiar. Somehow it felt like she'd known him far longer than the few days they'd been together.

She decided she'd rather continue talking while he was around. "I have two sisters," she blurted, not sure what else to talk about. "I'm the oldest. 15. Beth is 11. Hannah's just a baby, two years old. Beth doesn't know as much about animals or farmin' as me, she mainly just helps Ma with the garden and throws feed for chickens. Ma says she has more traditional sensibilities. That just means Beth acts girly to get out of doing most work. She's annoying but smart like that. Hannah will probably take more after her than me."

Misun looked back while they walked as if he'd missed something.

"Do you have sisters too or just brothers?"

"Only brothers," he responded. "Three. All warriors. I am youngest."

"Did you spend much time with them?"

"When I was a boy. We would laugh. But they became men after their Hembleciya. Rite of passage, you would say. I did not see them often after. They left to fight."

"Did you do a Hembl... a rite of passage?" she asked.

"Yes."

"Did you have to fight or something?"

"No. It is crying for a dream. Going to a high place like these mountains and waiting. A spirit comes in the dream and shows a path. Then men are ready to walk it."

"You saw a spirit?" she asked, hoping her voice leaned more toward rapture than skepticism.

"I... do not know," was all he offered. "My brothers came back confident of their path. A holy person tried to help understand my dream. I am not sure of my path. I am not a man like my brothers. I am less sure without them."

"Did all of them die?"

He nodded. "They died fighting. I did not."

Paula bristled. "That makes you less of a man?"

"They were stronger. My father knows. He saw me unsure after my Hembleciya. I shame him."

What he said upset her but she wasn't sure what comfort she could offer. "My sister isn't like me. Don't mean my Pa loved her less. You said yourself he still needs you."

"He has no other sons to help him."

Paula's frustration gave way as a familiar sensation set upon her. "I know what it's like for your father to need something you can't give him."

Misun slowed his pace beside the river. They didn't talk for a stretch but Paula began walking beside him.

✦ ✦ ✦

Misun counted eighteen in the camp. Eleven men, seven women. Panhandlers, from what Paula could see. She hadn't heard of any gold in the Laramie Mountains—in any of Wyoming, actually. All the activity was northeast in Dakota. Waite told her most of his time was spent around Rapid City keeping order as men gunned each other down in the creeks and mountains over specs that turned out to be sand.

This bunch didn't look so extreme. Women were outside churning butter. Surely there were one or two children at play somewhere in the tents or further downstream. Paula saw three men wading with pans. One sported a white beard long enough it dipped into the stream. Another man slept in the open. The only particularly dangerous looking one chopped wood by a tent, though Paula suspected he wouldn't look as formidable without the axe in hand.

Still, she had little desire to join their party. "They look like they've been out here a long time," Paula mused, watching Misun for his reaction. "They're dirty. Unkempt."

"These people are foolish," he said after studying them a few seconds more.

"Because there's no gold here?"

"Because they do not belong here. When my people come, blood will spill."

"Looks like they're pretty settled in," Paula said, pointing to the fenced in livestock. "Wouldn't they have already been caught if they were going to be?"

"My people will return to the mountains soon."

"Why?"

"They are angry. And they are searching for me."

Paula blinked. Perhaps the boy's father was more important than he had let on. Waite had surmised as much. She wished the marshal was here. "Do you think it's safe with them?" she asked.

"You prefer we keep going?"

She worked to formulate her response but found words caught in her throat. "No," she said at last. "I mean… don't you need to get back to your people?"

"I told you I would take you somewhere safe. I do not know if these people are safe."

"I doubt I'd be safe even if you took me back to Carbon," she said. "There are women here, it must be safe enough. You've done plenty, Misun." The trickle of the creek and the chopping of wood filled the silence as the two stared at each other. "You think the warriors will leave the mountains if you're found?"

"I do not know. It will still be dangerous for you."

"It was dangerous coming out here." She paused, shifting her gaze to the strangers in the creek. "Maybe they'll take me home. Or I'll find my own way."

"It is not safe alone. Not for you."

"I wouldn't know where to go," she admitted. This wasn't the Laramie River anymore, but rather a tributary branching off a few miles back. She'd never been this far north. She knew Gentry lay ahead on the road to Fort Laramie but she had no idea how to get there. No idea how to find the road back to the plains. With the Sibling Gang, the bandits from the gorge, the Sioux and Lord knows who else in the mountains, Paula had no intention of walking days in any direction alone. Especially unarmed.

Misun nodded, his eyes flickering. "I will go. Be careful when you appear. Do not surprise them. I will watch to make sure you are safe."

Paula allowed herself the smile she'd considered most of the morning. "Alright," she said. They sat another few moments before Paula noticed Misun shifting his weight from his bruised right leg. His cuts were mostly healed, though it was a miracle he hadn't suffered an infection. Her own cuts were sore but probably not that threatening. She asked him to take a final look at her nonetheless.

"Are you in pain?" he asked.

"No, not really. It's just… you're the closest thing I have to a doc. Might not have one down there in the camp. Maybe you should check me over."

Misun said nothing, glancing to the creek and men, then back to Paula.

He inched closer over the dirt and ran his hand along her forehead. Paula closed her eyes as he rubbed away some of the crusted paste he'd laid along her cuts. Paula tried to keep her breathing at a steady pace, to soak in the last few moments before their connection would be severed forever.

The boy ran his fingers over the skin around her forehead. His eyes were closed and he mumbled something, perhaps offering some kind of prayer or blessing with his treatment complete. Paula's smile held while he spoke low and mysterious sounds, batting away the notions of traveling further with him, of selfishly asking to be led to a town or larger group somewhere further north. No, she'd caused him enough trouble already. They both—

She knew something was wrong when he tensed and turned. By then it was already too late. Paula followed his gaze to the double barrels of a scattergun extended through the trees behind them. A man with two dead squirrels tied to his belt held the gun. He was probably fifteen paces back, but he had a clear shot.

"Get away from her!" the man shouted. He marched forward with the weapon shaking. He hesitated when Paula rose between them, arms outstretched.

"This is my friend, he's not going to hurt anyone," Paula shouted back.

The gunman continued his approach but his eyebrow arched skeptically. "The hell are you doin' out here with an Injun?"

"We're lost," Paula lied, at least on Misun's behalf. "We were with Marshal Waite but he was attacked upriver and we were washed down here. We need help."

"Don't worry, girl, he twitches wrong and I'll take his head clean off. Get out of the way, now." It was as if the man hadn't heard her.

Paula remained between them. "Just put the gun down," she pleaded.

The man seemed equally frustrated that she wouldn't listen. "Mitch!" he yelled. "Get over here with your gun! Injuns!"

Paula heard shouting behind her. "There are no Indians, it's just me and my guide and we're just passing through. Just let us get on our way."

Footsteps rushed across the creek behind them. His weapon still pointed at Misun, the gunman reached forward to grab Paula and jerk her away. The instant he laid a hand on her, Misun bolted. It happened so fast. She screamed when the gun went off, not realizing Misun had pushed it skyward until he and the gunman were on the ground. The boy drove an elbow into the man's temple. Then Misun had Paula by the hand, hurriedly leading her away from the body of the gunman, motionless on the earth. A knife was wedged in his neck, likely plucked from his own belt.

"What did you do?" Paula whispered.

It turned out the man named Mitch hadn't been at the creek, but rather behind the first man in the woods. His gunshot missed Misun, tearing through the bark of a tree instead.

"Stop!" Paula shouted, waving her arms wildly. Misun tried to push her behind him but another two men from the creek arrived with revolvers in hand, shouting.

When one of them grabbed Paula, Misun reacted again. This time he was overwhelmed, struck with the butt of a gun as Paula fought to stay in the line of fire. She guarded his body on the ground.

"Holy hell, he killed Jackson," the man named Mitch called as he stood over his companion's body.

"It was an accident," Paula insisted. "My friend was only protecting me. You can't hurt him."

"Get away from him right now," one of them said.

"Promise me you won't shoot him," she insisted, arms still around Misun. The two men with revolvers exchanged glances, keeping guns on the boy as they pulled Paula up. Guilt tore through her as she watched them bind Misun's hands with a belt.

"I'm sorry," she said, locked on his eyes. She couldn't tell if he shook his head but was smart enough not to speak as they hauled him to his feet.

Mitch met them as they walked back to the tree line near the creek. A large man in suspenders approached from the creek with rifle slung under his shoulder. "The hell's goin' on up there?" he shouted.

"Best take a look," Mitch returned.

The man glared at both Misun and Paula as he strode by, but his pace shifted to a dash when he caught sight of the body in the trees. Paula heard the thud when the big man slid beside the fallen gunman.

"We won't kill your Injun," Mitch said to Paula as they walked to the creek, "but I can't speak for Jackson's brother. Big Jack loved that boy."

Paula's blood curdled when she heard the big man release a pained howl that echoed through the trees.

22. Murderer.

PAULA KNEW THINGS WOULDN'T END WELL when she saw Big Jack's eyes, his cheeks tear stained as he carried his brother's body through the creek. Clamor had enveloped the camp when Mitch and the others marched the young girl and savage in, but a stunned silence befell the crowd as Big Jack covered his brother under a blanket beside their tent. He stood over the body in silence while a few of the women asked what happened in hushed whispers. Then Big Jack turned.

Paula's surprise came from the lack of rage in the man's movements. No veins bulged from his thick arms, no muscles tensed across his face. He almost looked at peace. When he disappeared inside his tent she hoped it was only to grieve in silence. Instead he emerged coiling a rope. Big Jack seized Misun by his neck and led him away from the tents to the tree behind them.

"Wait!" Paula exclaimed, the first voice above a whisper since Big Jack crossed the water. "You can't kill him."

The man didn't pause, didn't look back.

"Hey! Do you hear me?"

"Who is this?" another voice asked beside her. It belonged to the man with the long gray beard she'd seen in the river, still hobbled over as if his legs were stuck that way. He directed the question to Mitch but Paula spoke.

"My name is Paula Maddox, and that boy is my prisoner." She shouted the answer to Big Jack, but he continued forward.

The older man tilted his head. "What's a girl in braids doing in the mountains alone with an Injun prisoner?"

"I was with a federal marshal taking this boy to Fort Laramie. He's wanted by the army and there's a big reward out for him. I captured him and I intend to collect. If you kill him you'll have Marshal Waite to answer to."

Hope charged through Paula as she saw the panic on the old man's eyes. He turned to a burly man in suspenders standing beside him, arms folded.

"Cap, don't let Jack do anything hasty, maybe—"

"Wait a minute," the burly man cut in. He rested a hand on his hip as he stared the girl down. She got the sense he was the leader from the way the old man and Mitch looked to him. "I'm Travis, you can call me Cap. Where is this marshal of yours?"

"We were attacked by bandits at the eastern bridge through the gorge. I was guarding the boy when he tried to escape into the river, we were washed upstream and I walked him here."

"Not even Big Jack could survive those rapids," one of the other men who'd kept a gun on Misun said. "Sure as hell not any little girl. That Injun was—"

"Shut the hell up and let me talk to her, O'Malley," Cap said with a frustrated sigh. His gaze fell back to Paula with a furrowed brow. "Your Injun may not be full grown and looks a might thrashed to boot, but you ain't no prison master, Paula Maddox. Barely look strong enough to put on your clothes. You're tellin' me you chased this boy downriver through white water and walked him here in no chains, and he just followed you along?"

"You don't understand," Paula said, watching the faces of those in camp shift from sympathetic to accusing. Her mind wheeled trying to muster a version of the truth they would believe. "There are other men out to capture him from the marshal. The Sibling Gang. That's why the marshal and I were riding him in without a posse, Roderick Crowe is after us even as we speak. The boy speaks English, he knows the Fort is the only safe place for him. He's comin' willingly."

"Of his own accord?" Cap pressed.

"You didn't see what we did, Cap," Mitch chimed. "She said the Injun was her friend, her guide. He must have fooled her. He was touching her."

"Tell me the truth, now," Cap said, taking to one knee in front of Paula.

She reeled back, ready to shout that Marshal Waite would bring all sorts of hell on them if they harmed Misun, but she caught Big Jack from the corner of her eye. He threw his rope over a tree branch. Misun lay on the ground under his boot while the man knotted a noose.

Paula tore from the crowd toward him, shouting for Big Jack to stop. Cap caught her, locking his arms around her. "Dammit girl, there ain't nothin' you can say or do to save that boy. Your reward went out the window the second you let him loose to kill Big Jack's brother."

"I'll split the reward with you!" Paula shouted, her eyes tearing. She kicked Cap but wasn't strong enough to break free. "You can have it all! Please, just—"

Cap spun her around and gave her a violent shake. "What the hell did that savage put in your head? You're tryin' to save an animal. If his kin came through here and found us right now we'd all be dead or worse."

The notion gave Paula another idea. "He's a chief's son! He's important. That's why he'll be so valuable to the army. The Sioux are looking for him too. They're in these mountains right now, if you kill him they'll—"

"They won't find him," Cap interrupted. He turned for help. "Take her out of here. No cause for little girls to see this."

A woman came forward to soothe her, to lead her away, but Paula kept struggling and kicking, her tears bubbling over into sobs. Mitch passed her to the two gunmen. They bound her hands. "It's just until you calm down, dear," one of the women said.

"Wait, I still think we should try talking to Big Jack," the old man cautioned. "We have enough trouble without a marshal coming to clear us out."

"There probably ain't none. And we'll hide the body," Cap said, folding his arms as he watched Big Jack fasten the rope around the boy's neck.

"Are we going to hide hers too?" the old man pressed. "What happens when she—"

"It's a damn Injun, Clyde!" Cap shouted. When he saw the same hesitance in more eyes throughout the camp he shouted. "Did you all forget Bill Shipman and his wife? Found their bodies tied to rocks covered in blood. You think a mountain lion or a bear did that? This Injun's lucky we don't peel the skin from him and flay him out over a rock!"

A quiet fell over the crowd. Only Paula's sobs and the trickle of the creek filled the afternoon air.

Paula wanted to call out to Misun, to beg for his forgiveness, but she couldn't muster the words. She didn't want to watch but couldn't take her eyes from him. Misun resisted as Big Jack tightened the noose, but the man stopped him with a quick fist to his middle. The rope kept Misun from buckling over but it looked like he'd be sick from the force of the blow.

"I'll give you the reward," Paula managed again through her tears, begging whoever would look at her. "I'll give you whatever you want..."

No one responded.

The moments before Big Jack began pulling were surreal, stretching for eternity. Paula had seen more death in the last few days than most might in a lifetime. She'd felt it quench the life from someone dear to her, but to wait for it at the hands of an executioner was a different kind of anguish.

Paula screamed when the moment came. Big Jack didn't need to exert much of his strength. There was no malice in his eyes, no vengeance. He looked natural, almost serene as if performing a daily task as simple as washing his hands or chopping firewood. The rope lifted Misun a foot off the ground. His face tightened and rolled. He sputtered, kicked his legs, but before long it was little more than a twitch.

Paula wrestled herself from the men holding her and ran with her hands tied behind her back. She slammed against Big Jack's body. She bounced off him, and still he didn't look at her, holding the rope with both hands while Misun's strength gave out. Cap seized her again.

A warm splatter of liquid sprayed across Paula's face. Next came the return of a distant gunshot. Misun landed in a pile beside her, gasping for air. Then Big Jack landed in a pile, his mass crashing like a bag of bricks. Paula knew what landed on her face when she saw Big Jack's head caved in from a bullet wound. He was dead.

"Nobody move!" a familiar voice shouted.

Paula couldn't place it, but her face went pale when she saw a rider approach, his weapon extended to Cap and the crowd gathered behind him. "Unless you want the same as your giant here you best get your hands and those ropes off that girl," said Cliff Ritter, his voice low and icy.

"You just shot down an innocent man," Cap shouted, slowly removing Paula's restraints.

Paula was almost too shocked to move but rushed to help Misun. She removed the rope from his burned neck. The boy coughed fiercely, snot and saliva dripping down his face.

"That innocent man was guilty of obstruction of justice," Ritter said. "Impeding a federal officer in the delivery of a prisoner to custody. Not to mention kidnapping a 15-year-old girl."

"You're Marshal Waite?" Cap asked.

"One of his deputies tearing these mountains apart looking for our escaped prisoner and this girl. Lucky for you I heard that gunshot a while back. If your goliath here had snapped this boy's neck you'd all be up on charges as accessories. You're welcome."

Paula couldn't help her furious stare at Ritter. The relief that came from the rescue was paralleled only by the resentment of owing Misun's life, and probably her own, to the man who'd killed her father.

"How do we know you are who you say you are, friend?" Cap asked in a low rumble.

"Well I guess we could ride out together and find Waite with is badge, but to be honest, I couldn't give less of shit what a pack of dirty fuckin' gold-diggers believe about my purpose. I am who I say I am." Ritter looked back to Mitch and the two men armed with revolvers of their own. "And I see you thinkin' back there. You ain't fast enough."

"There's near ten of us, mister deputy," Cap said. "And one of you."

"And if I need to kill ten worthless gold-diggers to collect on my bounty I won't lose a wink of sleep over it," Ritter said, his voice still ice. "This is what I do for liv—"

Paula shook as another two shots blasted through camp. Both from Ritter's gun. They found the chests of the two gunman behind Mitch, who'd decided to test him after all. They were dead before they could point their guns. One of the women screamed from the tents. She tried to rush forward but another woman held her.

Ritter's expression didn't change. "Anyone else want to make a widow today?" he asked.

Cap glared hatefully but took a step back from Paula and Misun, hands in the air.

"Fetch a horse for Miss Maddox. You should have three available now."

"We don't," Cap said.

"You better," Ritter returned, angling his barrel at Cap.

Paula watched as Mitch called over a few men with horses. Ritter made Cap saddle them. Paula worried he would push the camp too far, that he was inviting more blood, but perhaps that was his aim. She could see the same glimmer of a smile on the corner of his mouth that she'd seen when he gunned down Pa.

"You ain't no deputy," Cap said as he finished tying down the saddle. "You ain't no man. I'm gonna find you after this. Tell your marshal what you did here."

Ritter tilted his head, then gestured to Paula as she helped Misun mount the horse. "What were you plannin' to do with little Paula here after you'd killed her prisoner?" Ritter asked. "Gonna tell the marshal about that too?"

"You don't know shit," Cap countered.

"I know that I'd love to see you again," Ritter said. "I sincerely hope you come and find me."

Paula watched the panhandler swallow his enmity, returning to the camp. "Back away until we get to the trees," Ritter said to her, riding so close they nearly touched. "Then follow me close." He reached over to pull Misun from her horse onto his. The boy nearly fell but Ritter kept him secure.

Paula started to protest but the ice in Ritter's eyes stopped her. "Back away slow."

They did, Ritter holding his gun on the group until they disappeared from view.

23. New Terms for New Problems.

RITTER DIDN'T SAY ANYTHING WHEN PAULA brought Misun a sip of water from her canteen. The boy sat against a downed log along the trail, hogtied and blindfolded again. Paula had protested it wasn't necessary, that the boy would cooperate. Ritter ignored her, commanding her to keep a sharp eye on the trail behind them. The gunman resumed his watch atop his horse, insisting Paula do the same while they waited.

Paula felt the man's eyes on her but didn't give him the satisfaction of a glance. Waite's gaze had been equally frigid, but the marshal's cold came from focus rather than heartlessness. Paula couldn't think of another word for Ritter. He took a twisted pleasure from pain. From inflicting it. He'd saved her, yes, but she was half surprised he didn't gun down the entire camp for the sport of it.

She'd heard stories about him shooting Negroes and Chinamen as examples for laziness on the railroad when he'd served as a construction foreman. And Pa wasn't the first man he'd killed for Alvord, she knew that much.

"How much longer?" Paula asked without looking at Ritter.

"We'll wait another ten minutes or move on without them," he said. "Too many enemies about to dawdle for a geezer lawman."

Paula didn't respond, waiting for Misun to finish his sip and give him another. He'd only suffered two blows at the hands of Big Jack, but they'd done a number on him. Paula worried he had a concussion from the strike to his head.

"Aren't you gonna ask me what I'm doing here?" Ritter asked when she took a seat beside Misun.

"I'll ask the marshal," she said, gazing down the trail. "Then I'll tell him we don't need you."

Ritter's wicked smile emerged with a dry chuckle. "How exactly were you fixin' to stop them gold-diggers from stretchin' your pal, then?"

When she didn't acknowledge him he shuffled in the saddle and continued as if to annoy her. "Mr. Alvord sent me and two men to help you, little Paula. Didn't know it was you we'd be helpin', a'course, but here you are. Waite told us you rode the boy from Carbon all the way to Little Holstein by your lonesome. Takes sand."

"How did you even know to come?" Paula asked.

"A hand rode out to us on the trail to tell us what happened between Vance and the soldier, told us the boy disappeared. Mr. Alvord wants Virginia Crowe to stretch, sure, but if he wants anything it's the Sioux cleared outta here. If the boy can help give up Red Cloud and the rest of his savages, he'll make damn sure your prisoner gets to the Fort safely."

"And you'll see to that?" she asked, her tone mocking. "You think you can fight off Roderick Crowe?"

He didn't take the bait, content to pick at the 15-year-old's temper. "Don't worry, sweetie, I'll keep you safe."

Paula thought about telling him to shut the hell up but maintained her cool. She held her gaze on the road. At least Misun was still with her, though relief quickly gave way to guilt. An hour ago, Misun had been liberated. He could have—probably should have—left Paula to the panhandlers once they found the camp. He should have left her to the mountain lion. He should have left her in the river.

But he hadn't. Against his own interests he'd saved her, only to end up right where he'd started.

It raised the question of what she would do next—restore the freedom Misun had earned, or resume her mission. The guilt gnawed at her either way. Without that reward the ranch was lost. Pa's death would have been meaningless. It was a reality she'd already accepted as she walked downriver that morning. The failure for her family was painful, but she'd taken some measure of comfort in seeing Misun walk free. If nothing else his liberation granted her absolution from condemning the boy to death at Fort Laramie.

Maybe torture.

This second chance to save the ranch, to safeguard Pa's honor, brought more pain than the notion of letting him down. After all Misun had done for her, could she still trade him for cash and ride away? He hadn't spoken a word since Ritter's rescue. She couldn't tell what he would do once he recovered his strength.

I do not hate, he'd said at the fire. She took in the boy's sweating chest, imagined his thoughtful eyes staring at her behind the blindfold.

Paula wandered through fields of guilt and confusion until she heard the faint rapping of hoofbeats in the distance.

"Finally," Ritter said from atop his horse, picking his teeth.

Paula rose and dashed a few feet past Ritter when Waite emerged from the trees, his duster blowing behind him. Another two riders trailed. She didn't know their names but recognized their faces. More of Alvord's men. Probably gunmen from the ranch.

Waite's smile was one of relief. He laughed when he saw the girl in the road and the boy tied up behind her. "I'll be damned and branded by Lucifer," he said, jumping from his horse to grab her by the shoulders. "You alright, lil' partner?"

Paula couldn't help her smile as he checked her over for injury. "Yes. Barely. How did you escape from Vance?"

Ritter groaned when the marshal tapped the revolver in his holster.

Waite frowned. "Had a bit of help from the cavalry here, as well," he admitted brusquely. "Vance's posse of shopkeeps wouldn't have held up under fire but Pulp's sudden retreat gave 'em a target and a spine. My horse went down but these fellas rode up from behind and cut Vance down in crossfire. Say they're from Carbon. You know em'?"

Paula felt a pang of guilt for Margaret Vance. Spoiled as she was, no girl deserved to lose her father. "I know them."

Waite's jovial expression hardened when he saw the girl sour. She pointed up to Ritter. "That's the bastard who killed my Pa."

"That so?" Waite said. The two riders at the marshal's back tensed, exchanging glances with Ritter and then each other.

"This bastard just saved your life, and your reward, from hangin' or worse," Ritter said.

"We can't trust them," Paula said. "I don't know what they told you but they work for Alvord. They probably aim to shoot us in the back and collect the reward, the greedy sonsabitches."

"Nobody's doin' anything of the sort," Waite said, both assuring her and announcing the fact to the rest. "They might well have saved my life though. Sounds like they certainly saved yours. Told 'em that if they help us ride Pulp to the army in one piece we'd split off a third of the reward their way to divide 'mongst themselves or their boss."

"The hell we will!" Paula shouted. "The whole reason I'm out here facing down rivers and mountain lions and crazy diggers is because of them! You want me to give a share to them threatening to drive my family out? To the man who killed my Pa?"

"Ain't like that, Maddox," Waite said with a defensive gesture. "I—"

"What's it like then, Waite?!" she bellowed. "You made me a promise! It's not my fault you drink so damn much and are so ill- tempered that you drove Rigby to betray you and fixed us in this spot!"

Waite exhaled sharply. "Now hold on one minute, you want me to split my share down to—"

"No! I don't want us giving a *penny* to these bastards! We don't need them!"

Waite looked more taken aback than she'd seen, his expression halved between frustration and guilt. Instead of exploding back at her, though, instead of demeaning or mocking her as she expected, he gave her a moment to simmer then leaned forward to speak in a calm voice.

"Yes we do," he said. "Ran into a Sioux scout last night. Nearly took what hair I got left. Spotted the rest of his party from afar a few hours back. Near twenty that we could see. If they don't already have our trail they will soon. Between them and Crowe, who is God- knows-where by now amid all our distractions and detours, we're gonna be lucky to make it to Gentry, much less the Fort. We can use all the firepower we can get about now."

Whether it was the gravity of the words or simply hearing them come from the usually confident marshal, they carried the threat home. Paula glanced to Misun. He'd pricked up as expected.

Even after accepting help from the likes of Ritter, Paula trusted the marshal. She just didn't trust herself yet. Even then she hadn't decided what she was going to do with Misun.

"Come on, lil' partner," Waite said, as sympathetic as she imagined his voice could ever sound. "This is the hand we been dealt. Too late to fold now."

She sighed. "Do you think we have enough firepower to make it through if the Sioux find us?" she asked.

Waite glanced quickly to Ritter. "Best we just get ridin' and don't find out," he said, mounting up. "Why don't you grab Pulp there and help him to my—"

"Don't call him that," Paula said softly.

Waite raised an eyebrow while she helped the boy to his feet and mounted him on her horse. The marshal eyed Ritter for any clue but found none. With everyone mounted, Waite nodded and looked down the trail. "Still a solid day to Gentry with only a few stops to rest," he declared. His eyes remained fixed on Paula. "Then we'll collect that reward. And I will personally escort you home to see it delivered to your family. While I'm there maybe I'll check into this Alvord and the exact circumstances around Mr. Maddox's death."

Paula felt something warm inside her even as Waite's cold gaze collided with Ritter's.

"How does that sound, Maddox?"

"Which way is fastest?" she asked with a nod.

Waite grinned and slapped her on the back harder than he should have. "That's my partner," he exclaimed. "We'll head for the fields straight north where the mountains round out. Can ride fastest there."

"That's open ground," Ritter protested. "Better to keep east in the trees as long as we can with all the eyes out for us."

"Trees ain't gonna hide us from Sioux, Ritter. This is a chase, pure and simple. Need all the time we can muster. Heyah!" Waite blasted ahead at a gallop for the main trail.

Paula saw Ritter's annoyance. She sneered at him before taking off after the marshal.

24. A Sordid Reputation.

FAMILY WAS ALL A MAN HAD. Everything else faded in time. Friends. Money. Power. Dreams. History was apt to forget the size of a man's ranch, the cattle routes he drew over fields and mountains, the scope of his empire and fortune. Family was the only true form of legacy.

A business, even one that touched all of America, was ultimately soulless. It could be passed to the ownership of others, its scope and mission altered. It would only be money when it came time to close shop.

The love of a wife, though... Surely if anything transcended life and death it was that. Family gave a man something to love while he was alive. Something to fight for. A child, with all its potential, was the most precious thing a man could hold and nurture. A child was a man's greatest accomplishment. His greatest weapon. His greatest hope.

A man would do anything—anything—to protect and nurture his family.

Alvord had told all this to the politicians in Cheyenne. Now he told it to General Crook at Fort Laramie.

"A beautiful sentiment, Mr. Alvord," the general said, "but sentiment doesn't dictate troop movements."

"My wife's been shot, is barely breathin'. My son was there. He saw it. How many more families have to be shattered before you send us help?"

"I'm sorry about your wife, sir, but it wasn't the Sioux who shot her. Township matters and the Sibling Gang are for sheriffs and marshals respectively, I am neither. I have one garrison here. It's barely enough to keep the Northern Sioux and the Lakota in check. I don't have the men to go gallivanting through the plains rounding up bandits and Indian scouting parties."

"The gold in the Black Hills will dry up, General. The cattle industry is just getting started. Carbon and railroad towns are full of hardworking, honest folks. Deadwood is a cesspool. You're protecting the wrong sort."

General Crook had been minding a large map sprawled over a table for most of the conversation, making notes and handing them to a lieutenant. Alvord didn't appreciate having only half of the man's attention, and finally let him know it with his tone and volume.

The general finally gave him eye contact, sizing up the burly rancher for the first time. "How did you get this meeting, Mr. Alvord?" Crook asked. "I don't take civilian requests."

"Next to the railroad I'm the largest employer in the plains," he returned. "I speak for many."

"I see. I've dealt with men like you before, Alvord. Your fortune may buy influence with politicians but this is the Army. If you want me to send a division to the plains I suggest you continue east for Washington and throw your money at the president. I could use more soldiers."

"I'm only asking for—"

"You're asking me to save your business. I'm trying to smoke out Red Cloud, and my best shot is this prisoner Marshal Waite is riding in."

Alvord paused. "Waite?"

"Says word from Little Holstein. Are we done here, Mr. Alvord?"

Alvord glared the general down. "I sent three men to help find the boy and get him here. You're welcome."

"Good day, Mr. Alvord."

Alvord made his way out of the garrison command building, silently cursing Crook. The shortsighted, presumptuous, egotistical fool. Alvord paused his march across the training yard, feeling nauseous at the thought of his wife's life in the balance and his son alone. He felt like scum for not riding home the moment the ranch hand delivered the message of what happened. He sent nine men back to protect the ranch, but only he had any chance of getting real aid from Fort Laramie. It was closer than Carbon from where Alvord heard the news on the trail, so he rode through the night to get there.

But what Crook let slip… "Waite," Alvord murmured outside. Alvord had never dealt with the marshal in question but had heard the name before. From former Marshal Jacob Buckman, one of his longtime security men, with him and McDermitt waiting just outside the Fort.

"Tell me about Marshal Waite," Alvord said to Buckman, riding up to he and McDermitt on horses. "You warned me off about him the last time I was here recruiting men. Told me he would probably take the job for the right price but he was a man of sordid reputation. Said I couldn't have a man like that under my employ."

"I did," Buckman said. "What of him?"

"He's riding here with the Sioux prisoner as we speak. I need Waite to turn that prisoner over to me before he gets here."

"Why?"

"Crook won't lift a finger to help us. Unless we force him to. This Indian prince may know something about Red Cloud but most likely doesn't. Crook'll keep him in cell doing no good at all. Him dying at the hands of a white man, though—that should stir things up, get this damn war on and over with."

"You sure Sioux on the warpath is what you want, boss?" McDermitt asked.

"We need the Sioux gone once and for all, can't keep livin' like this, always watchin' over our shoulders for raids. This guerilla back and forth will go on for years. Maybe this helps speed things up, maybe it don't, but it's time to take matters into our own hands."

"You want me to take on Waite for the boy?" Buckman asked.

"I can't have anything to do with killin' a federal marshal," Alvord said. "Easier to buy him anyway."

"You can try," Buckman confirmed. "Hardly need me for that, and much as I like workin' for you, Mr. Alvord, I won't ride alongside Waite."

"He's that bad an apple?"

Buckman's face contorted. "He perjured himself before Judge Watkins over a shooting outside Rapid City. We had three men in custody, two of which were instrumental in a case against a corrupt congressman. One got loose, came at Waite with a shovel. Waite, angry and lazy, killed all three but told it like the others were coming at him. Case fell apart. Disillusioned me something fierce, ended up tossing my badge over Father Waite."

"Father?"

"He shot up a church in Mexico posing as a priest." Buckman crossed himself. "Lord knows how many he killed just to collect on one reward. They called it the Bloody Baptism. Man's a loose cannon if ever there was one. Only law he cares about is his own."

"Jesus," Alvord said. "Well, he's the one got this Sioux boy." He sat in silence a moment, then turned his head back to the Fort. "Think I got an idea."

25. Apologies.

PAULA TOLD WAITE WHAT HAPPENED in the river, the mountains and the panhandling camp. It was late in the night, probably closer to morning. They'd stopped to rest and water the exhausted horses.

There'd been no camp made, no sleep, and there wouldn't be. Paula's anxiety of being caught kept her restless anyhow.

For a girl who hadn't even met many folk in her life, it startled her to think back on all the enemies she'd made in the past few days. Vance and his men, townsfolk in Little Holstein, the marauders in the plains, a camp of panhandlers and a Sioux hunting party. Not to mention the most notorious gang in the territory.

She didn't include, Misun, of course. Even now, after she'd denied him his chance at freedom, she knew the boy wouldn't count her among his enemies. And she hated herself for it. The guilt grew worse with every mile that brought them closer to Fort Laramie. Every rest stop she contemplated telling Waite they couldn't go through with it, or at least loosening Misun's restraints enough for him to slip away.

But every rest stop she continued on with the boy tied on her horse.

"Best not lose any sleep over them goldbricks, lil' partner," Waite said as he stuffed his mouth with food from Alvord's men. "Expect that the Sioux party trailing us will stumble across their little operation, won't leave 'em be like before. They'll get what's comin'. Might be dead already."

Paula blinked, realizing how tired she was as she tried to summon her voice. She didn't argue that the panhandlers weren't all bad, that they hardly deserved slaughter. She was too consumed in her own worry to spare concern for them. Instead she rubbed her eyes. "Hard to lose sleep if you aren't getting any in the first place."

Waite laughed then scarfed down the rest of his biscuit. He rose from his sitting rock to relieve himself away from camp in the stream. "That's why I like this girl, Ritter," he called downstream. Alvord's men knelt on the bank splashing water on their faces, recoiling as they saw him. "And why I like you less and less."

Ritter said nothing, barely even looked Waite's way.

With the men occupied, Paula walked to Misun. He lay on the grass behind her horse. He twitched, as if aware she hovered over him. She held back tears but couldn't hold her words. "I want you to hate me," she whispered.

He didn't whisper anything back. Didn't move.

She knelt at his side. "I promise I'll try to get you back to your people after the Army talks to you. I'll tell them how you saved me. I won't let them…" She couldn't make that promise and they both knew it. "I'm sorry."

Still he was silent, as if he'd learned to speak English and forgotten just as fast. "Do you want me to help you? Just say something. Please."

"I do not hate you." He was almost inaudible.

She knelt over him another minute, wanting to pull down his blindfold.

"Let's move!" Waite called from the water. "Best be out of the mountains by sunrise."

Paula swallowed hard. With Waite's help, she got Misun back to his feet and sat him ahead of her on the horse.

✦ ✦ ✦

Waite was disappointed with their pace. They couldn't make much headway over treacherous terrain in the dark, but even as the morning cast light over the rocky fringe of the mountains, they couldn't drive the horses any harder. Paula's fought her most of the time. Waite's in particular neared collapse, seemingly as old as Waite himself. They proceeded down a slope of thin trees and stacked boulders made smooth over time.

Ritter rode at the head of the column with his men close behind. Eventually Paula remembered them as Teddy Smokes' son, Robert, and a cowboy named Jenner. Paula rode with Misun in the middle with Waite bringing up the rear. They found the main road that led to Gentry, but it wouldn't widen until they emerged into the plains.

When they came to a wide, crater-like depression devoid of vegetation, Ritter ordered Robert ahead to look about. Paula couldn't help glowering as she caught up and matched Ritter's pace. He raised an eyebrow when he caught her staring. "Can I help you?" he asked, swatting at an insect.

"You still haven't apologized," she said, her voice as dry as the sandy depression around them.

"What would I apologize for?"

Paula's huff was loud. She turned her gaze forward. "You'll be plenty remorseful when Marshal Waite brings you in on charges."

Ritter stifled a laugh. "How about instead of an apology I tell you a secret," he began. "Your friend back there, Waite? He ain't your friend. He only gives a shit now because you're a meal ticket. He's like me—just needs to get paid."

"Bullshit," Paula snapped. Her mouth tingled as the word escaped, as if the simple syllables coursed with power, earning her the right to ride alongside any of the men there. "You don't know him. You didn't even know who he was before yesterday."

"I know him a lot better than you, kid. Loyalty and love do not abide in that man. He's only got himself."

"Would a man like that stand up to eight guns by the river? Would he rip through three marauders in the mountains to save me? Would he still be ridin' a prisoner in with half the world chasin' him?"

"Loyalty and fire are two different things. Killin' comes second nature to some. As simple as drawin' breath. You can see it in his eyes."

"You haven't seen his eyes when he speaks his heart," Paula countered.

"When's that, when he's halfway through a bottle?" Ritter asked, pointing.

Paula turned to see Waite tilting a bottle perpendicular to the ground, smacking his lips when he emptied it and tossed it on the trail. Paula turned away when Waite's eyes met hers. "He's crass," she admitted softly. "Don't mean he's discompassionate. I know what I know. He won't let anyone hurt me. You least of all."

This time Ritter's laugh bit. "You have a champion now. We'll see how long that lasts once your reward gets doled out. The second Alvord's pocketbook dries up I'll be gone. He ain't no different."

Paula flashed with anger. "If you're so apathetic to your boss' well-being then why did you kill my Pa for nothin'?!" she bellowed. When his smile turned malicious another voice soared.

"Keep your mouth shut, Ritter," Waite barked, galloping between he and the girl. "Get up with your men. Not another word to her."

Ritter's grin remained. "You're in charge, marshal," he said, still looking at Paula.

Waite sighed and turned to his partner, panting and flushed red as she watched the gunman ride ahead. "Best keep your voice down, Maddox," Waite said, glancing behind them. "We'll be free of the reprobates soon enough. Just keep focused on your prisoner. Don't need him runnin' again before—"

"Why, Paula Maddox!" a voice called from ahead.

Ritter and Jenner came to a halt. Robert was still off behind the rocks to the right, out of view—the voice wasn't his. Waite reached for Paula's reins with one hand while he pulled his revolver with the other. Paula's heart dropped when horses emerged from behind the rocks ahead.

"I'd know that pretty, vengeful voice anywhere," said Roderick Crowe, is smile wide.

26. Convergence.

When Waite tossed a rope into her lap, Paula jumped as if she'd heard a first shot. "Tie a noose around the boy's neck, fasten it to the saddle," Waite said in a hushed hurry.

Paula stared as if she hadn't heard him. She opened her mouth to protest but he cut her off.

"Just do it. Quick and quiet." Paula obeyed, praying he knew what he was doing. If the rope wasn't so coarse, she'd have dropped it from the sweat on her hands.

She glanced at the Sibling Gang lining up in front of her, blocking the way ahead. Paula counted six horses rather than eight and whispered so to Waite.

"Unless they lost a few they've got sharpshooters in position somewhere," he confirmed without breaking his gaze from Crowe. His voice was cold. When she glanced his way to gauge if this was the end, she noted his fearsome focus from Little Holstein. The vicious intent from the forested bowl in the mountains. The indomitable will when he waited for Vance at the river. Paula's heart raced but found strength in his maddening courage.

He wasn't going to back down.

Whoever ended up with Misun, either Waite or Crowe was about to die.

Crowe's smile broadened when he stopped his advance. He nodded to Waite and the other three but kept his eyes on Paula. "You look well, Miss

Maddox," he called. "A might trail-worn but still in one piece. Even with your spirit I wouldn't have bet on that. But here you are with a hogtied prisoner ready for delivery. With a posse, to boot."

"I'm who you're talkin' to, Crowe," Waite replied on her behalf.

"You're no fun, Waite," he said with a dismissive gesture. "Paula here is more interesting."

"I ain't interested in talk with a murderer," Paula shouted, to Waite's chagrin.

Crowe's smile morphed into a melodramatic scowl. "You wound me. Don't you want to know how it is we came to be here waiting for you? I—"

"My business ain't with you yet, Crowe," Waite interrupted, taking back control. "Give us the road and I'll let you have a few days head start a'fore I come after you."

Crowe's grin returned. "Mighty generous, but so long as you got that there Indian I got business with you." Crowe titled his head as if amused. "He's not much bigger than you, is he, Paula?"

"You can't have him," she said, angry at the sound of her voice shaking.

"I appreciate all the work you done to get him this far for me, Paula, but I do have to take him off your hands."

"If you shoot us off our horses, they'll run and Misun will die," Paula said hurriedly, proud to have put together the marshal's plan despite how it made her feel. She lifted the rope around his neck.

Crowe's expression teased. "Misun, huh? Mighty friendly."

Paula blushed at her slip.

"I don't want the boy dead any more than you do," Crowe said. "No reason we can't all profit from our meeting today. Tell you what. I don't know what General Crook might offer for this boy but I'll offer you twice what I did at Little Holstein." He reached into a saddlebag and pulled out a bound stack of green bills. "Four hundred dollars, Paula. All you have to do is hand the boy over and head home to your momma and sisters. You're out here for the money. Take it."

Paula felt Waite's eyes on her. When she glanced at the marshal, Crowe's smirk grew. "Don't worry about grayhead, he'll find some other bounty to ride in, the old mercenary. Maybe it'll even be me. Take the money, Paula. I'll deliver Misun there alive and unharmed to the Fort. You got my word on that."

Waite kept his gaze on Paula, as if allowing her permission to consider the offer. Her heart pounded, desperate to take the noose from Misun's neck. Even so, taking it off condemned him just the same—Crowe wouldn't appeal for the boy's life at the Fort.

She held firm.

A tear ran down her cheek, but the fire in her eyes told Crowe and Waite her answer.

It was Waite's turn to smile. "Tell you what, Crowe," Waite interjected again. "We'll give him to you for free. All you have to do is best me for him. One-on-one. Your boys stand by, so do mine. Just you and me."

Crowe tucked the money in his jacket pocket, his disappointment authentic. "Well that sounds mighty sportsmanlike, Father. Unfortunately, I was in Omaha when you picked off Joe Ziegler and that big German brother of his. Gotta be fast to best two fast Germans at once."

"Gotta be fast to head up an outfit like yours," Waite countered.

Crowe scoffed. "Hell, Reece is faster than me. I'd need a death wish to draw on you without the boys. Thankfully my ego affords me no illusions. I think we'll just insist you give up the boy as a group." Crowe turned his attention back to the girl. "Last chance, Paula. I don't want to hurt you."

"Your sister deserves what she's gettin'," she said, still shaking.

Crowe stared her down a long moment, as if admiring. He sighed and reached for his gun, as did the others. Waite did the same, queuing Ritter, Jenner and Robert.

No one fired.

"Your sharpshooter may drop me, Crowe, and one or two of your boys may well walk outta here with this Indian, but whoever dies here, you'll be among 'em," Waite said.

Crowe smiled.

Paula doubted she'd ever see something so threatening the rest of her days.

"My sharpshooter is smarter than you think, Waite." Crowe raised his hands and made a tugging motion as if pulling something that wasn't there.

Paula heard the zip of the bullet before she heard the return of the rifle. The shot tore through the rope in her hand, severing its anchor to the saddle.

Then, an eruption. It sounded like Waite got the first shot off but Jenner and Robert dropped from their horses first, closest to Reece at the end of the gang's line. Paula's horse took off on its own, nearly bucking her and Misun off in its panic. She heaved on the reins to direct the animal toward the largest rock column. Whether by Crowe's order or good fortune, no shots seemed to come her way.

Paula retreated behind an outcropping of granite. Only now did she remember she wasn't carrying a weapon. She peeked out and saw Waite fall from his horse. "Waite!" she screamed.

He managed to kick away from his animal quick enough, having already gunned down three of the six horsemen. Crowe included.

The bandit's dark stallion was already running away without him while he writhed on the rock, his gambler's hat knocked free. Reece galloped to his boss, leaping off the horse to pick him up. One of the gang exchanged fire with Ritter, somewhere out of sight past the rocks. The remaining two charged at Waite.

"Is Waite dead?" Misun asked from the horse.

"I... no, hold on," Paula said, kicking forward.

Waite had taken cover in a divot of rock but he wouldn't last long. He'd either broken or sprained something judging from his hobble, and he was struggling to reload as the Mexican advanced on him.

Paula shouted to get the Mexican's attention as she galloped toward him, then threw her canteen at him. When he pointed his gun her way his head emptied from Waite's shot.

"Hurry!" Waite said, already hobbling for the added cover of the tree line behind them.

Paula followed as shots sailed her way. She looked back once they were behind another group of trees, finding Crowe on his feet beside Jimmy Reece. The other rider retreated, either killed or abandoning pursuit of Ritter. Paula grimaced at the thought of Alvord's killer abandoning them.

The shots stopped as Crowe remounted. Regrouped, the four remaining riders approached the tree line where Waite had dug in behind a thick trunk. The marshal directed Paula away toward another rock column.

"Paula!" Crowe shouted, his voice hoarse. "Even Waite can't protect you one on five! Give up that boy and this foolish pride! All you have to do is take the money, it's still yours. Don't die out here for no reason."

Waite winced as he hobbled, breathing hard. He stared at her.

"I don't want you to die," Paula said to him.

"Ain't gonna. But… Got a life ahead of you, lil' partner. Maybe it's time you got home."

Again Paula wanted to move, to turn and run or charge into Crowe, but again she remained where she was. "Misun…" she said to the boy. "I…"

Misun turned his head as if to speak but they both paused when they heard the distant gunshots and screams. Crowe turned as well.

"Shit," Waite said.

"You must go," Misun said to Paula. "They are here." She didn't have to ask who. She heard the thunder of hooves approaching.

"Make sure that horse is hidden back there," Waite said, finishing the reload of his revolver. "Don't make a sound once it's over."

"When what's over?" Paula asked.

They came so fast. Six of them. One of the warriors leapt off his horse onto Reece. Paula closed her eyes when she saw Reece's poncho and chest split down the middle.

"You must go," Misun said louder.

"Too late for that," Waite said.

Paula watched Crowe and his two remaining men retreat east where Ritter had escaped. The Sioux trailed with guns and war cries filling the turbulent air. Paula locked eyes with Misun—giving him permission to go. To rush for them. He didn't budge. Maybe knowing Waite would gun him down, maybe knowing if his kin saw her they'd kill her.

Waite spun around when he heard a horse approaching from behind. He nearly fired but held when he made out the rider.

"Jesus, point that thing someplace else," Ritter said, peering past the trees at the Sioux. "Time to go."

Waite didn't have to think twice, heaving himself onto Ritter's horse.

Ritter threw a rag from his saddle at Paula. "Gag him before he gives us away."

Paula wasn't sure he would but did as she was told, knowing Ritter would incapacitate Misun with force if she didn't. They backed away slowly then made their way around the battlefield at a guarded pace. Paula looked back to catch a final glimpse of Jimmy Reece, his poncho soaked red.

27. Reckoning.

THEY FOUND ONE OF THE SIBLING GANG's runaway horses a few miles up the trail. Waite took it. He was slower to mount this time, dazed.

He'd cut his head in the fall from his horse. Blood leaked from the cut near his temple into his ear, giving him vertigo for the first miles of the ride. It didn't look like his leg was broken, more likely a sprained ankle, but it was cut up and bleeding.

After the fall to the rocks, not to mention facing down two lines of gunmen in superior numbers within three days, it was a miracle he still drew breath.

Waite maintained the greater miracle was that they'd slipped by the Sioux. Even with the Sibling Gang to distract them, escape over Sioux ground with a prisoner and wounded hadn't been likely. They weren't out yet, of course.

Ritter took a moment to bind Misun's hands himself while Waite situated. Paula expected the boy to resist, to break away, but he held still. Much to Ritter's annoyance, Paula removed Misun's gag and allowed him to sit upright behind her. "All you had to do was call out to them and you'd have been safe," she said quietly.

"You would not be safe," he replied. "I promised."

Paula doubted if she'd be able to ride him any further to the Fort—if she'd even have the resolve to take him to Gentry. All she knew was every step closer to the Fort was a betrayal of something inside her. Though letting him loose would surely be an equal betrayal.

"No time to dawdle," Waite managed. "Won't take them Sioux long to find sign and start after us. Even if Crowe managed to kill the bulk of 'em, this is still a race to the finish."

"You're in no shape to be racing anywhere," Ritter said. "You'll need stitches on both of those scrapes."

"Can't stitch a scalp back on if I lose that," he returned. Waite didn't say anything about Misun riding freely with Paula. She wondered how much he gathered from their exchange. She wasn't sure what there was to gather, of course.

Paula sighed in relief when the plains opened up before them. Ritter insisted they wean their gallop to a steady trot or risk Waite bleeding out.

"I may be pale but hardly inept," the marshal insisted.

"We'll be able to spot any Sioux on our tail now that we're out in the open," Ritter maintained. "We made it, most of them are dead. Whatever aren't would have caught up by now if they found sign."

"Sioux can sneak up on you even on open ground," Waite said, reaching for the canteen that came with his new horse. "Ain't that right, boy?"

Paula looked to Misun. It was the first time the marshal had ever spoken to him, seriously anyway. Misun only offered the lawman an empty expression.

They rode at an easier pace until the last of the rocky terrain turned to grass. Ritter paused briefly at a stream to water his horse and refill the canteens. Waite remained on his horse. Paula couldn't tell what was in his head, maybe just dizziness, but he looked... off. So did Ritter. She hadn't expected him to keep such a close eye on the marshal. "Go on, I'll form up the rear," Ritter said as he mounted.

Paula started forward to lead but paused when she heard Ritter's voice again.

"Somethin' on your mind?"

She looked back to see both he and Waite at a standstill by the creek.

"Why don't you take lead, Ritter?" Waite asked.

"And leave a lovestruck girl or a half-bled old timer to keep an eye on the rear horizon?" he scoffed. "Don't think so."

"Shut up," Paula shouted.

The marshal's revolver angled to Ritter's chest.

"The hell are you doin'?" Ritter asked, his voice biting.

"Preemptin'," Waite said. "Pretty keen to fall in line behind us, ain't ya, Ritter."

"Think I'm gonna shoot you out of your saddle?" Ritter barked. "In the back?"

"I think you aim to collect on this boy on your lonesome. I've known enough men to spot the shifty ones when I see 'em."

"I came back for you, you stubborn sonofabitch!" Ritter shouted. "Could have—should have—left you to them Sioux. Instead here I am lookin' after you while you accuse me."

"Maddox," Waite called. "You figure Ritter here for the sort to look after anyone he don't stand to profit from?"

Paula wasn't sure what to say. As much as she hated Ritter, he'd saved them. That made twice as it concerned her. Was the marshal growing paranoid as they grew closer to the Fort? "I... Just ride in front, Ritter," she said.

"Too late for that, lil' partner," Waite said. "I don't pull my gun unless I aim to use it."

"I don't give two shits about your reward, Waite," Ritter snapped. "I make ten times your salary."

"And this benefactor a'yours has you ridin' through badlands purely to see justice done and this boy safely delivered, is that right?"

"I told you, Mr. Alvord wants the Indians gone. If this boy can help—"

"This boy could give up Red Cloud himself and it wouldn't change Crook's mind about where to deploy. Not while gold is comin' out of them hills in Dakota. If your boss is so damn smart he'd know that."

Waite paused but pressed on before Ritter could defend himself. "But you're smart too, ain't you, Ritter? Your ears pricked when you heard Maddox reveal this boy's family. He's important somehow. Wouldn't be a hunting party tearing through them mountains after him if he wasn't. This one might be worth plenty more than Alvord figured. Might even be a good bargaining chip on the trail if a raidin' party comes callin'. Alvord would pay plenty more than Crook for something to ransom to Red Cloud, I bet."

Paula wasn't even sure if Waite believed what he was saying, much less if she did.

"You must have hit your head harder than I thought," Ritter said, his voice dripping with acid. "Sioux don't stop to negotiate, no matter who that boy is."

Waite nodded, his face halfway to believing him. Only halfway. "But Alvord will still pay on the off chance, is that it?"

Ritter's exasperation brought a vein to his neck. "He's payin' me to ride this boy to the Fort, you miserable old—"

"Don't really matter what you intend on, I suppose," Waite said, still calm and collected. "Whether you mean to kill us to take the boy to Crook or Alvord, the fact is you mean to kill us. And after all the horseshit my partner and I have been through I ain't inclined to let you. So, I tell you what, Ritter. On the slim chance I'm wrong and you are just a loyal asshole rather than a low-down, back-shootin' sonofabitch, I'll let you turn about and head back to Alvord now. We'll clear this up, along with the death of Maddox's Pa, when I ride her back to Carbon."

"We had a deal!" Ritter shouted, spit flying from his lip. "You'd both be dead twice over if not for me!"

"And it was damn smart of you to keep us around so long as Crowe and the Sioux were at your back," Waite said. "Looks like you don't much need us anymore. We return the sentiment."

Ritter flung his arm at Paula, his face red. "Are you just gonna sit here and let him spout this bullshit? Use logic, for Christ's sake!"

"Do what I do for long enough, Ritter, and logic becomes your gut," Waite answered for her. "In the end I can only guess at why you're fixin' to kill us, but you ain't gonna."

Ritter's fury subsided some in the moments to follow. Waite's expression didn't change, and Ritter seemed to accept it. "I ain't one to forget when a man points his piece at me," Ritter said, low and menacing. "Marshal or not, we got business when you get to Carbon. Or you could holster that piece and skin it again, save me the anticipation."

Waite allowed a thin smile. "Takin' advantage of a man when he's dizzied and bled-out?" he asked.

"Would that deter a man like you?" Ritter asked. Their gazes didn't break.

Paula spoke when Waite slowly holstered his revolver. "Hold on," she said, seeing no sense in either of them getting shot up. Especially Waite—maybe he wasn't thinking clear with his wound. Surely he—

Paula jumped as the shots cut through the breezy air on the plains. Wisps of smoke escaped both Waite and Ritter's barrels, but only Ritter spit up blood. He slowly hunched over and fell off the horse, landing with a loud thud in the grass. Paula quickly dismounted to check on him. He was still alive, already rising to his knees as he groaned and clutched the wound in his gut.

"Pick up his gun, Maddox," Waite said, holstering his.

Paula stopped in her tracks.

"What?" she asked.

"Go on," he coached her, almost gently.

She did as she was instructed.

Ritter watched her pick it up, not bothering to fight for it. He already looked paler than Waite.

Paula offered the weapon to Waite but he shook his head and gestured to Ritter. "He ain't mine to kill."

Paula blinked, slowly shifting her gaze to Ritter. He stared up through his wheezing, the hand over his wound now soaked. His perpetual smirk was erased. For all the apathy the man put out, a very real terror had taken hold in his eyes. It looked as though the thought of dying out here had never even occurred to him.

"Please," Ritter managed, the blood in his mouth muddling the word. "I saved you."

Paula desperately grasped for her rage, for her sorrow. "I wouldn't be out here if it weren't for you." She said it softly. The scorn and vengeance still burned hot, but something else threatened to drown it out even as she raised the gun to Ritter's chest. It wasn't pity. Even as the man faced the unexpected realization of his mortality, even as he bled and slobbered in the dirt, she knew it was what he deserved. How many other families has this man destroyed before hers? Surely more than a single bullet, a single death, could rectify.

It wasn't some moral conundrum, either. She paid no thought to what Pa would want or not want her to do. He was dead. This man killed him.

She looked up at Waite. His eyes gave her permission. He must have known as well as Paula that some judge would let Ritter and Alvord off the hook for Pa's murder. Waite had given her justice the only way he could.

And yet...

Paula glanced back to Misun. He stared at her with anxious eyes. They didn't tell her anything he hadn't already said. *You will not hurt me.* His words by the fire that night were the grease around her rage, making it impossible to grasp.

Waite didn't say anything more. He didn't remind her this man killed her father, didn't tell her it would be easy or that Ritter had it coming.

Paula focused on the sound of the gunshot that tore into her father, the feeling of his hand suddenly going limp on Red's table. Her hand shook as her breathing quickened. Ritter was speaking again, but Paula didn't hear him. The world beyond her barrel disappeared.

Her finger tightened on the trigger... but Paula realized she'd failed to cock the weapon.

She lowered the gun, then dropped it. She stood there a long moment staring at her feet, then walked back to her horse without looking at any of them. She tried not to let them hear her cry.

She didn't jump at the second shot or the sound of Ritter hitting the dirt. She wouldn't spare the gunman any sympathy. Still she cried. The marshal walked his horse past her. "Come on, lil' partner," he called softly. "Almost there."

She swallowed what emotion she could before mounting behind Misun. The boy didn't say anything as they started after Waite, but his expression looked relieved.

28. Familiar Faces.

GENTRY WAS SMALLER THAN CARBON, so far from the railroad. It might as well have been New York when Paula saw it on the horizon, desperate as she was for the safety of civilization. Waite wasn't so optimistic. On the way in he told her he'd opt to bypass the town altogether if they could. He wasn't in the mood for any more surprises or run-ins with trouble. The Fort was only half a day away but he needed a stitch or two and they were all out of food.

"And everyone after us is probably dead," Paula reminded him, surprising even herself at how somber she sounded.

"There's always somethin' else waitin', lil' partner," he said. "Though I reckon that convergence of interests back in the mountains turned out plenty fortuitous." He tried a smile as he reached out to pat her back. "Maybe our luck is finally turnin' around."

Paula looked to Misun. She supposed that all depended on perspective.

People on the street gazed at the bloodied marshal as he rode into town with the girl and a bound heathen sharing a horse behind him. A few mutterings echoed from storefronts and doorways. A sheriff, from the look of him, came out to meet Waite as he dismounted and hitched outside a doc's office. "The hell happened to you, Waite?" he asked, glancing at the mismatched youths behind him.

"Trouble," the marshal returned. "Doc in?"

"Not sure. Any of that trouble on your heels?"

"Trouble's all dead," he returned, winking at Paula.

She didn't return the gesture.

"What about the Injun?" the sheriff asked.

"Our guide through the mountains," Waite lied. "Got things handled here, Schmidt."

The sheriff huffed and turned to leave. "Stay away from the saloon," he said.

Waite was already inside the doc's, beckoning for Paula and Misun to follow.

A woman in a dress too long for her legs met them when they entered. From the frown on her face, Paula could tell the woman had met Waite before. Whatever she was about to say caught in her mouth when she noticed Misun. Waite raised a hand defensively. "He's friendly."

"Nice to know at least one of you is," she said, though hardly convinced. "What happened?"

"Got bushwhacked in the mountains. Where's the doc?"

"My husband is away at Fort Laramie. He's helping with an amputation, he won't be back until this evening."

"You can get me patched well enough," he said, tossing his hat to a nearby chair.

Her frown deepened but she held her tongue upon seeing Paula. "Are you alright, dear?" the woman asked. "That cut on your face looks inflamed."

"Marshal's hurt worse than I am," Paula offered. "Maybe I could just wash up somewhere?"

"Of course, there's water in the back. I can heat some up and—"

"No time," Waite said. "Need to get to the Fort ourselves. Just patch me up so I don't bleed-out and make sure my partner here doesn't have anything infected. She's tough as a mule, she'll be fine otherwise."

The doc's wife looked doubtful but hustled him to an operating table. He poked his head out to Paula and Misun before sitting down. "Maddox, go fetch us food and drink after you clean up," he said. "Try the outfit across the street first. Tell 'em Waite's here and good for it. If you get any trouble about debts just show your teeth, they scare easy enough. Misun stays here where I can see him."

Paula and Misun exchanged uncertain glances. The boy remained in the foyer while Paula found her way to a washroom complete with a pump outside. The water on her face felt good but she wished she had soap. Time enough for that later, she supposed.

She glanced in the mirror on the wall and saw her face for the first time since Carbon. Dirt smeared her cheeks. Scrapes everywhere. Misun had washed most of the blood from her cut in the river, but her forehead and hand would surely scar. Her clothes were beyond filthy. She could see the trail of soot behind her where she'd walked in.

She paused when she saw Misun's reflection in the mirror. Staring at her from the center of the foyer. She walked to him and whispered, "You're finally goin'. Aren't you."

"I am sorry."

She felt something release in her, then shook her head. "I'll get by. I... I don't want you to die."

Misun said nothing.

She considered reaching for him, even to touch his shoulder, or maybe his hand, but stopped when she heard Waite grunt from the next room. "There are too many people here, someone will see. Wait until we're back on the trail. I'll hold a gun on him, or... I don't know, I'll come up with something. Just let me think. I'll be right back. You won't leave, will you?"

"He knows you will not hurt him, Paula."

"Just wait," she told him, turning for her partner in the next room, raising her voice. "I'll see about supplies."

"Make it snappy, lil' partner," Waite called after a wince of pain. "Fixin' to flee before Mrs. Everdine puts me on a stretchin' rack," to which the woman released a huff.

Paula regarded him on the way out. His pant leg was rolled up so the doc's wife could scrub the cut along his calf. She half expected him to have found a bottle or asked her to fetch him one, but he sat empty-handed. Focused, like at the river.

Misun was right—even if she got the drop on Waite, he'd know she wouldn't harm him. Maybe she could plead with Waite, honestly. Implore him to let Misun go, then go back to find Crowe's body for the reward. It would be dangerous with the Sioux still about, but he had warmed to her. Maybe she could talk him into it.

The general store was busy. A handful of cowboys picked through the shelves for sugar and coffee. A herd was probably passing out on the plain. Paula wasn't sure where to start and decided to ask the storekeeper about Waite's dubious credit before she initiated a spree. The man behind the counter rolled his eyes when he heard the name, his expression as dour as the doc's wife.

With basket in hand, Paula wandered the shelves for several minutes. She only needed a little food for the trail but her mind was already rehearsing how she would approach Waite with her new proposal. She doubted he'd take it well—probably erupt in the poor lady's house.

Paula passed over hardtack for a bag full of ready-made biscuits, then picked up four cans of beans. Surely they'd resupply for the return journey to Carbon. Getting in line to claim her items, Paula spotted a colorful jar sitting on the counter. Candy, swirled white and red over long sticks. She reached in for three sticks, setting them on a napkin on top of the beans and biscuits. "That all?" the shopkeeper asked, as if expecting far more from Waite.

Paula glanced back into the shop. It got plenty cold at night and she was without a blanket. "I'll be right back," she returned, hustling to an aisle with clothes and tent supplies. The blankets were on the top shelf. She reached on her tiptoes but came just short.

Sighing, she looked around for something to stand on. A crate full of kettles rested on the bottom shelf, so she reached to pull a box out. She stopped when another man grabbed it first. He quickly withdrew his hand and turned to apologize but she beat him to it.

"I'm sorry, I…" They'd been standing together in the store for several minutes but never really looked at each other until that instant. Both were dirty from the trail, but with full view of each others' faces their eyes went wide.

"Paula Maddox?" said Alvord, incredulous.

Paula didn't say anything, caught between shock and terror. She took a step back, otherwise unsure what to do. She could see his thoughts rushing together as his eyes glanced around the shop, searching for who she could be with.

"What are you doing here?"

Her silence seemed to tell him enough.

"It was you? You rode that Sioux out here?" A disbelieving smile spread over his face. "Where is Marshal Waite?"

Paula's surprise betrayed her. How could he know about Waite? What else did he know?

Alvord put his basket of items on the floor and extended a hand for her. "Paula, I can help you. Tell me where the marshal and the Indian are."

She turned and ran for the door, leaving her goods on the counter.

29. Bought and Paid For.

"Waite!" Paula yelled the moment she stepped into the doc's.

He burst out of the procedural room with his head stitched up but his pant leg still rolled. His gun was already in hand, reading the panic in her voice.

"Alvord! He's next door! He knows about us. He wants Misun!"

The boy took position at her side, his expression resolute.

"Slow down, Maddox. You saw Alvord here?"

Paula turned to point at the general store. Her heart raced when she saw Alvord emerge from the front door, staring at the doc's from across the street. "That's him," she said. "He mentioned you by name and asked me where to find Misun."

"Who's he with?" Waite asked, glancing down the length of the street through a window.

"I don't know, I didn't see anyone else I recognized," she said. "But he has to have men with him. A lot. He never goes anywhere without them."

"What's all this about?" the doc's wife asked. "I'm not done with your leg."

"You are now," he returned. "Get me my boot."

When the doc's wife hesitated, obviously confused, Paula ran to fetch it for him. He pulled it on while scanning the street. Alvord had left the store and walked into a livery a few buildings east. "Whoever he's got with him is on the way. Best we get gone. Might be a sprint to the finish line after all."

"Do you think he wants to kill Misun?" Paula asked.

"Ritter would have let that big golder do the job when he found you if that's all he was after. Alvord wants the boy for himself."

Waite rose and glanced outside from the corner of a window toward the livery. "Appreciate the help, Mrs. Everdine," he said to the doc's wife. "I'll have to owe you."

"You shouldn't be riding," she returned, folding her arms. "Neither should the girl. Not if it means putting her at risk."

"She's my partner," Waite declared.

Somehow Paula felt taller.

"Maddox, you keep tight hold over the boy. We're gonna mount and veer behind this building, swing south out of Alvord's vision. He'll try to head us off at the Fort but we'll worry about that once—"

"Jeffrey Waite!" a shout came from outside.

Waite turned back to the window and scowled. "Christ," he said, gritting his teeth,

"Who is it?" Paula asked.

He waved her to the window. Five men had assembled down the street. Alvord was among them on the right. The other four wore duster jackets. All looked armed.

"Buckman," Waite said, seething. He pointed to Alvord. "That's your man?"

"That's Alvord," she confirmed. "Who are the others?"

"Horses of the same color," Waite said, grabbing his hat from the chair and tugging it over his balding head. "Used to be law, just hired guns now. Must be workin' with Alvord. Buckman must be holdin' a grudge. Stay inside with the boy, Maddox. I'll handle this."

"There are five of them!" Paula exclaimed.

"They ain't gonna unload on law with Schmidt and half a town in plain view. And if they do, I'll kill 'em."

When Waite took a step toward the door Paula latched onto his arm with both hands. "Please," she said. "You can't die. Not now."

He huffed but ended up smiling. "Don't fret, lil' partner. Just gonna kill two birds with one stone. Stay put now, ya hear? Keep Misun close."

She held her grip on his arm a long moment but eventually nodded and released him, stepping back by Mrs. Everdine.

"Don't you dare start a fight at my home, Waite!" the woman said. He only tipped his hat as he walked onto the porch. Ignoring Mrs. Everdine's protests, Paula and Misun positioned themselves by the window.

Waite folded his arms and stared down the group in the street. They took a few steps closer, the man in the middle coming closest. His frame was tall and his features long. His face was cleanly shaven and there didn't appear to be hair of any kind under his hat.

"Buckman," said Waite.

"Waite," said Buckman.

Silence hung over the town for a moment, the few people on the street sensing something explosive in the air. Most backed away. Eventually Waite smiled when he saw Buckman hang his hand loose by his side. Ready.

"I see that pole is still firmly wedged up your ass," Waite said from the porch.

"Not very amiable talk for two colleagues in the middle of town," Buckman said.

"Colleague? Funny, I don't see a badge. Thought you lost it after your paragon pissy-fit in front of Judge Watkins. How's the beacon of truth routine worked out for ya?" Buckman prepared to lash back but Waite cut him short. "You fixin' to introduce your benefactor?"

"There's no need for unpleasantries, Marshal Waite," Alvord said from the line. "I'm here to make you money, not take it from you."

"Not interested," Waite said. "Though I'm sure Judge Parker will be interested to hear how a former marshal who festooned his honesty for the pleasure of the court has taken up as a gunhand and impeding a federal agent in his business. Might just have to investigate that on my way back to Carbon."

"Funny you should mention Parker, Waite," Buckman said. "I just got back from a drive in Nebraska. Did you know Morgan Ziegler survived? He's a talkative one despite taking a bullet to the throat. Wonder how long it'll be before Parker orders you back to Omaha for deposition in the of the murder of Ziegler's brother."

"The Ziegler case is closed," Waite said flatly.

"You killed that man in cold blood, Waite," Buckman said. "You'll lose your badge this time, and I—"

"I ain't interested in that," Alvord cut in, angrily hushing his man. "Not when we all stand to benefit. Waite, I know you have the army's Sioux prisoner with you. I've already spoken to General Crook on this matter. He ain't offering a reward for the boy, only orders to bring him in. Simple fact is, Crook is focused exclusively to the north. He ain't gonna help us clear out the savages in the plains, we have to do that ourselves."

"Bullshit, no reward," Waite snapped. "I've got a high priority prisoner with tactical information about the enemy. Crook'll pay hand over fist for him."

Alvord slowly raised his hand, holding a piece of paper. "This is a copy of open bounties as of this morning. Took it straight from the Fort. Here."

Waite didn't respond for a moment, then told the rancher to come up slow. He did. Waite snatched the paper from his hands, reading it over.

Paula watched him, his expression unyielding.

"The hell do you want anyway, rancher?" Waite asked as he read. "To gut this boy and leave him on Red Cloud's front door? Stir a hornet's nest big enough to garner Crook's notice, is that it?"

Alvord stepped closer. "Look at all the damage this one savage did just by bein' here. High time we—"

"He ain't done nothin' but get captured, we're the ones doin' this to *him*!" Paula shouted, stepping into the doorframe.

Waite tensed and motioned for her to move back inside. When she stood her ground the marshal ignored her and turned back. "Why should I believe this horseshit? I don't see any boys in blue, just you and a gaggle of mercenaries."

"How long do we go back, Waite?" Buckman asked. "When have you known me to lie? There's no army reward. I was at the Fort too. They're waiting for you to show up then show you the door. Unless there are fresh orders from Judge Parker recalling you to Nebraska."

Waite nearly snarled something but Alvord cut back in. "Unlike Crook, I'm still willing to pay for help eliminating this scourge from the Laramie Plains." He took a step closer, his voice softer. "All you have to do is hand over the boy. Report you lost him, then ride him back to my ranch. I'm sure you're as unappreciated as my friend Buckman. I appreciate my associates plenty."

Alvord set his eyes on Paula. "Dear, I'm sorry about your Pa. Was never my intention for that to happen. If you're lookin' for compensation, I owe it. Just give up this prisoner and I'll take care of you and your family, be it on your ranch or setting you up somewhere else. Got my word on that."

Paula only glared at him, waiting for Waite to cut the rancher off with a snide remark or a gunshot as he'd done with Ritter—she didn't really care which at this point. Instead, the marshal red over the paper again.

"Let me help you, Waite," Alvord said. "Take a minute, think about your situation."

Waite passed over Buckman and the others in the road, hands still close to their weapons. "Get back inside, Maddox," he said.

She couldn't see his eyes but could guess what was in them when she saw Alvord's panic. Her breath quickened, anticipating the vindicating rub of metal on leather, of the five blistering shots that would drop Alvord, Buckman and the deputies before they could even pull their guns.

The seconds drew on like hours, but eventually Waite turned. To her. She expected vengeance, the icy focus, even something righteous in his eyes. Instead there was something foreign. Compassion.

Paula's mouth slipped open, as if what she was seeing was impossible. It felt like he'd turned his gun to her when he said it. "We need to talk, lil' partner."

Paula took a step back, hitting the doorframe with her back. "You're not actually thinking about it, are you?" she asked in a harsh whisper. She balled her fists. "Are you crazy?!"

"Paula. You set out on this trip—we both did—for the reward. There ain't none," he said, offering her the paper. "Least not at the Fort. Misun ain't here. Maybe we squeak somethin' out of Crook but… This rancher may be a prick and but he's the only one offerin' what we both need. What we deserve. What you need for your family, what I need to get out of here and hang these guns up for good. Crowe is long dead, his body gone. This is our best bet."

He saw the betrayal on her face. Saw the anger on Misun's close behind her.

Paula didn't take the paper, just stared at him.

"I don't know what happened out there between you and the boy but Alvord's right about that much. Boy's just a savage, they all are. This land'll never be safe so long as they're out there terrorizing it. If it wasn't Ritter who shot your Pa it might have been that boy."

"I... you..." Paula felt short of breath.

When Waite approached to put a hand on her shoulder she wheeled back. "You *idiot*!" she bellowed. "Did you not hear what Alvord said? He's talking about murder. War! That ain't what we agreed! Waite... please... You can't do this."

He looked more wounded in that moment than he had getting shot or falling from his horse. "Paula, I've been in war before," he said softly. "I lost everything. Union soldiers burned my family's house to the ground. I know what it's like to lose your Pa, all that you have. But terrible as it was, that war was the only thing that could ever have changed things for the better. Just like things have to change out here. Sometimes that's the only way to clear a path to the future. Ain't fair, but that's what this place is."

"You don't believe that," Paula said, tears welling. "You're a good person. You said you'd protect me."

"And I will," he avowed, as adamant as she'd heard him. "I will get you home safe and I will make sure your family gets to wherever you want to go. But Maddox, I'm destitute. I don't own a thing 'cept this gun, and one way or another some judge is about to take even that from me." The gentleness and sympathy hardened into resolve. "I have given up too much for too long to pass on what might be my last chance for a few damn years of peace. It's time I took the best deal I can. It's time we both did."

"No," Paula said, shaking her head. She turned and saw Misun close behind her, tense. Ready. She positioned herself between him and Waite. "No. Misun doesn't deserve this. Alvord deserves justice."

"What about me, Paula?" he asked, striking his chest. "What about you and those sisters a'yours? This is the only way you can take care of them. This is the only way I can help you. I promise I will. You're just a girl, you have to... I'm asking you to trust that I know what's best for you."

"I ain't just a girl, I'm your partner!" she cried. "You're supposed to do what's right. This ain't it. This ain't it, Waite!"

Alvord signaled something to Buckman as he shooed away onlookers then came closer, but Waite put up his hand to hold him back. "There ain't right or wrong for folks out here, Paula," he said. "Sometimes it's about the best a man can do. The best anyone can do. I've been tellin' you that. It's time you learned. Now come on out from there."

Paula backed into the doc's house. Waite saw her eyes darting between Buckman and his deputies. When he turned to shout for them to get back, that he'd handle her, she slammed the doc's front door. "Run," she told Misun, already pushing him away.

His eyes were alight like she'd seen Waite's before gunfights. He grabbed her hand and pulled her after him as he bolted past Mrs. Everdine for the back door, pushing through at top speed. Paula heard the sound of shouting and footsteps behind them in the house and around it but kept running.

Gunshots blasted their way as the youths ran between the buildings and into a house half framed on the west side of town. "Dammit, not when he's got the girl!" Paula heard Waite shout. Another shot ricocheted off a wheelbarrow to their left. More fire erupted behind them. Paula turned to see Waite gun down at least two of the deputies before she disappeared into a post office through the back door. "*Not at the girl!*"

Paula guessed Misun was leading her back toward their horses or to others he'd seen hitched in town. "Hey there!" a man's voice shouted from inside. Someone tried to reach for Paula while another tried to tackle Misun. The boy threw his shoulder down and plowed past the would-be rescuers with reserves of strength Paula didn't expect.

No gunfire emerged when they tore back onto main street, but Paula could hear footsteps racing behind them—one of the gunhands and another two men who had joined the chase. It was Buckman himself that reached them, racing from behind another building to cut them off. He flew into Paula, ripping her away from the boy. Misun's roar was murderous but Buckman met his charge with the butt of his revolver. Paula felt the thud pound through her as if he'd struck her as well.

"Stop it!" she yelled as one of the men chasing them caught up and sent his boot to Misun's middle. They didn't relent until she attacked, clawing at the remaining deputy. Paula wasn't sure what struck her but it landed just above her temple. She remembered hearing Waite shouting as she hit the dirt beside Misun, feeling the boy grasp at her hair.

Another shot flew and a body dropped beside her. "Goddammit, Waite, those are innocent men!" Alvord called.

"Innocent don't mean assaulting a 15-year-old girl where I'm from," he recoiled, out of breath. There were no more shots but Waite threw a fist at his old acquaintance, hard enough to knock Buckman back several paces. "Everdine!" Waite shouted. "She needs help!"

The last thing Paula remembered before passing out was Waite carrying her back down main street to the doc's.

30. Survivors.

Paula

I am sorry things came to a head between us. I never intended harm to your person or your heart. Those shots at you were not mine. By the time you wake I will likely be gone. I will ensure Alvord pays your family what he owes. I intend to leave the territory once I have payment. I do not expect you will desire my company henceforth so I will not offer to return and escort you home. Alvord will send a man to do that. Mister and Missus Everdine are a good sort, you can trust them. Forget about the boy. I will see he meets whatever fate quickly.

Jeffrey Postlewaite

Paula found the note on the table beside her bed. She read it several times. It felt like the man's boorish handwriting, but she strained to hear the words from his mouth. The blank space covering most of the paper suggested intent to say more.

She set the letter in her lap for a minute, as if waiting for the words to sink in. He was gone. She tried to hate the marshal, telling herself to crumple his note and burn it with the candle at her bedside. Instead she left it where she'd found it. There wasn't time for hatred.

From the look of the room (and the hint in the letter) Paula guessed she was still at the doc's office. Her head felt like she'd smashed against another boulder in the Laramie River. There was no bandage but she could tell a cut had been cleaned.

No clock offered time on the walls, but the window was heavy with the dark of deep night. She looked around for her boots and found them beside her bed. Quietly, she slipped her legs from under the sheet and pulled the shoes on. Paula crept to the door to see if either of the Everdines were awake. Before her hand touched the doorknob she paused.

Independence gripped Paula like Misun had clung to her that afternoon. Working the window open, she slid out onto the dirt, thankful they'd left her on the first floor. She skirted the buildings to the main road. Her horse was gone. Only the saloon at the end of the road shone light from its windows.

She stood alone in the center of town for several long moments before her panic gave way to sorrow. After everything, it was suddenly just... over. On one hand she knew she should be grateful. She believed that Waite would get money from Alvord to Ma. That was why she'd set out from the ranch with Misun, after all. She wondered what Alvord had in store for the boy. Perhaps he'd be kept as a bargaining chip. More likely his head would decorate a stick somewhere to provoke.

Either way, Misun would die at Alvord's hands.

Paula felt the need to sit. She nearly took to her knees in the road but looked back toward the Everdines' porch. She could still slip back into her room to bed. She had nowhere else to go. Nothing else to do.

Even if she found the sand to steal a horse, even if she made it to the mountains in the dark, even if she navigated her way alone without running into Sioux, the panhandlers, mountain lions or brigands, even if she made it back to Alvord's before they killed Misun, she wouldn't be able to save him.

Paula wandered to the edge of town, staring into the darkness. Eventually she made for the saloon. She pushed open the swinging doors and took a seat at an open table, not caring if anyone saw.

No one seemed to notice her. Only a few guests sat drinking. A circle of men played cards at a table in the corner. A pair of girls sat with a man by the stairs. None of them looked in their right minds, absently staring at shot glasses while one of the women stacked glasses into a pyramid. Another man stood at the bar sipping whiskey. The barkeep cleaned a glass, watching a clock, willing it to strike the closing hour, no doubt.

Paula folded her arms over the table and hid her face in them when she felt tears rising. The same crippling helplessness that ensnared her in the days, weeks and months before Pa's death reared its head. It stung all the worse after her brief stint as the master of her own fate. Of all her lamentations—that her friend would be sacrificed, that her champion had deserted her, that she'd never fully avenge Pa—perhaps the most painful was the realization that she may never again hold the keys to her future.

Pa would have been proud to see her carve her own path, if only for a moment. She liked to hope so, anyway.

Paula sat in relative silence for another few minutes, deciding she'd wait to return to the Everdines' until the saloon closed or someone threw her out. It turned out she wasn't the one who needed throwing out. She looked up when she heard raised voices at the bar. The man who'd been drinking alone looked to be in a tiff with the barkeep. "I hate to break it to you but this whiskey is dog piss in the first place," the man said.

"Dog piss or not, it costs money," returned the barkeep. "I'll be seeing some before you see another glass."

"You already have."

"I've seen enough for two drinks, you're on your sixth." The man raised an arm and took a step back from the bar as if to show the barkeep something. Paula found herself fixed on the man, knowing she'd seen him before. Maybe a trader from Carbon?

"Mister, I've been shot, which I assure you is the only reason I'm in this shit-piss town. But like your doc up at the Fort, your banker ain't here either. Not at this hour. When he wakes and opens up I'll get you paid, so—"

"If you had money I'd suggest you save it for the doc, but since you don't I suggest you get out before I add another hole in your side," said the barkeep.

The man released a long sigh, staring the barkeep down. "Mighty hospitable around here," he said, putting on his coat. The barkeep only turned to resume his cleaning, likely to grab a closed sign or a gun. With the barkeep's back turned the man reached for the bottle on the other side, taking a defiant or drunken swig. The barkeep heard and sent a fist across the counter to the man's face. The drinker landed on his backside along with the bottle.

Paula's eyes went wide when she saw the man's face. Determined to stop him from pulling the gun he reached for, she bolted to him. The barkeep pulled free a sawed-off scattergun from behind the counter, making his way around for the main floor. The card players turned to the scene as well, bracing for trouble.

Paula precluded it when she knelt at the man's side in the spilled liquor. "Pa, that's enough," she said, setting her hands on his shoulders and shaking him. "Time you got home. Ma's going to be worried."

The barkeep lowered his weapon. He raised an eyebrow as Paula struggled to lift the man. "This your Pa, miss?" he asked.

Paula nodded. "Yes. I'm sorry, he... lost someone today. Can you help me get him up?" The barkeep huffed but set his gun on the bar. He leaned over and pulled the man to his feet. The man looked dazed, fixed on Paula as if seeing a ghost. He said nothing.

"You have horses outside?" the barkeep asked.

"Yes, but would you mind getting some water for him first so he can sober up? I don't want him to fall off and break his neck." Paula tried to look her most sympathetic.

The barkeep didn't seem to care, tilting his head. "Aren't you the girl who got into it with Marshal Waite today?" he asked.

Paula's heart skipped a beat but she kept focused. Like Waite. "Yes. I ran away. This is my father come to fetch me," she said. "Can you please help him? I'm sorry for the trouble."

The barkeep glanced between the two of them and then over to the cardplayers, turning back to their game. The barkeep seated them at Paula's table. When he returned with water he told them to be gone soon.

Paula stared at the man across from her, waiting for him to speak first. Eventually his open mouth closed into a smile, though his incredulity remained. "You are no ordinary rancher's girl, are you, Paula Maddox?"

"You are no ordinary train robber, are you Roderick Crowe?" She peered down the length of his jacket to search for the wound he'd shown the barkeep. "Are you alright?"

He followed her eyes and pulled open his jacket. The bloodstains were already dry and crusty. "Alive," he answered. "More than you expected,

I see."

"Do you need the doc? His wife is here, at least. She can patch you up."

"Already did that myself," he said. "His holiness shot me in the gut but it didn't do all that much damage." He reached into his pocket and pulled out a destroyed watch, nearly shattered. "'Cept to my timepiece. Probably saved my life. Had to dig out a few pieces though, wasn't too pleasurable."

"Lucky," she said.

His smile grew. "Seems to be my day for luck," he affirmed. "Why did you do that?"

Paula kept her gaze on him but took a moment to respond. "I don't know. I guess because… you're the only person I know here."

He tilted his head. "Where's the good Father?" he asked.

Paula took a long breath, trying to condense everything. "Alvord bought Waite. Misun is an important person in the tribe. Alvord will kill him to rile up the Sioux and force the Army to fight in the plains. Doubt it will work, but there it is."

Crowe stared at her as if he hadn't heard right, then shook his head. He took a long drink of his water. "And they call Virginia a fiend," he said mostly to himself. He looked at her and saw the grief, the tear stains still moist on her cheeks. "Well I told you so, Paula Maddox. I told you Father Waite was no holy man. Sorry you had to find out the hard way."

She didn't respond, not sure if she should defend him or not. "How did you survive the Sioux?"

He made a face like he wasn't sure himself. "Circumstances like that call for a reciprocal mind-set," he answered. "Savagery for savagery."

"Tell me," she said.

"Not a very polite story."

"Tell me," she insisted.

He nodded. "Not a very polite place, I suppose. Well, not much to it. Piano Bill and I were alone and running. One group caught us, we took two, they got Bill. Was down to knives and fists after that. I heard more coming and hid in shrubs. Can't sneak up on a Sioux but you can wait 'em out. Did just that. One came lookin' for me, I slit his throat and stole his horse."

He paused to gauge her lack of reaction. "Tale like that would have left you shuddering when first we met. You must have seen more on the trail with Waite than I figured."

"Yes," she said simply. "So what are you doing here?"

He shrugged. "I was drinking whiskey," he said. "Now I'm drinking water. Got you to thank for that, I suppose."

"You're giving up?" she asked.

"On what? Virginia? She's probably dead by now. Probably was when we were still back in Carbon. Now your prisoner is Waite's prisoner, and I have no Sibling Gang. Doesn't leave me in much of a sister rescuin' position, does it?"

"What will you do now?" she asked.

"No idea."

She fell quiet, as if the notion depressed her.

He leaned forward on the table, wincing from whatever wound the gunshot left. "What about you, Miss Maddox? Did that bunko lawman drop you at the saloon or are you just a night owl?"

"I…"

He continued while she searched for words. "Misun was more to you than a meal ticket, wasn't he?" he asked.

Paula tensed to rebuff the notion but found no point. She didn't know how she felt. "He's a good person," she said. "Not a savage. He doesn't deserve what he'll get."

Crowe nodded slowly, waiting for more. When she didn't offer any he leaned back, folding his arms. "Best do something about it, then," he said. She narrowed her eyes with resentment but he continued. "You can't do it alone, of course. Waite's damn proficient with a firearm, my timepiece is proof of that. I'll go with you."

She stared at him blankly.

"What, think you'd be better off alone? I'll sober up soon."

"Don't jerk me around," she said.

"I'm done with that. You're not somebody I'd want to cross later on. I know that now."

"I'm serious," she said, flashing anger.

"So am I," he said, matching her volume. "I'll go with you. I may not be in great shape or particularly useful without my outfit, but I wager I can get you back through the mountains, at least."

She stared at him, her distrust lingering. "Why would you help me?" she asked. "Don't tell me it's because I saved you just now."

"I suppose that could be a reason. But, Paula, I just like you. Have from the first minute I laid eyes on you. You're not just a passenger."

"What does that mean?"

"Means you got balls, kid. More than most men."

"You don't know anything about me."

"I know you stood up to Jimmy Reece. I know you stole that boy away from me and recruited a crusty old lawman to ride him through badlands to Fort Laramie. I know you think quick and act quicker. You take what you want. I respect that."

The hesitance in Paula's eyes morphed to vulnerability, as if at odds with what the outlaw was saying. "I… don't even know if…"

"If you want to go?" he finished for her. "Course you do. It's the right thing."

She scoffed. "What would Roderick Crowe know about the right thing?"

"Everyone knows what the right thing is," he said. "Trouble is it's different for everyone. The important thing is having the stomach to do it."

Paula pushed back from the table, shaking her head. "You must know it's impossible. Waite alone would stop us. He's with a former marshal and Alvord's gunhands. There's no way past them."

"My sister and I have broken out of places plenty more guarded than some big augur's ranch," Crowe said. "There'll be a way."

"Suppose Misun is already dead," she said.

"Suppose he is."

"I don't see how you can tell me not to give up on Misun when you're giving up on your sister," she said.

Crowe nodded slowly and stared off into space. "Truth is I gave up on Virginia a long time ago. She's not who she once was. But she's still blood. I was obliged to try."

"Suppose we do get Misun back," Paula said. "Would you just steal him from me to trade for your sister if she's still alive?"

He shrugged. "That would run a bit counter to our current aims, wouldn't it?"

"That wasn't a 'no'," she said.

He grinned. "It wasn't, was it?"

Paula frowned but set his flippancy aside. Her heart beat fast, fueled with purpose. "So what now?" she asked.

"Well, best hurry, whatever we do," he said. "Saw plenty more Sioux in those mountains. I speak a little of their language from captivity. They're definitely on the hunt for someone. If Misun is this important they'll find him eventually, maybe even ride up here and to Carbon in force. Waite probably went around the mountains this time to be safe. We could beat him back to Alvord's if we take the western pass."

Paula gulped at the notion but pushed back from the table and rose. "What are we waiting for then?" she asked.

Crowe grinned but reached for his water. "Me to sober up, mostly."

31. Common Denominator.

PAULA WAS SICK OF SO MANY new horses. All of them seemed obstinate, as if the only riders they took seriously were fat men loaded with supplies. She wondered what had become of Jessamine. The old girl was probably one of Alvord's by now. She wished she could at least whisper a quick goodbye to her old friend. Perhaps she'd get the chance at Alvord's ranch.

Crowe saw her struggling to keep her new steed at pace with his and turned with a grin. "Shoulda snatched some spurs with that saddle," he said.

The look she gave him was hard boiled. "It's bad enough you stole this horse—did you have to take the saddle too?"

"I didn't take you for a barebacker," he returned.

"I could have made do with a blanket or the old, busted rig at the stable. This looks like it cost more than the horse."

"Must have—that beast looks dumb as the shoes on its feet."

She looked away.

Crowe slowed his pace to match hers and help coo her animal forward. "I never understood guilt," he said. "Life's too short for it."

"Even though what you do makes lives shorter?" she snapped.

"You may not believe this, Miss Maddox, but I don't just ride around shooting anyone who looks at me funny. I picked that saddle you're on for a reason. Your comfort wasn't it."

"What do you mean?" she asked.

"Who do you think treasures his saddle more? The man with an expensive rig trimmed with color and linens, or the man with a rig falling apart at the seams?"

She only blinked.

"Whoever owned that there rig has plenty enough money to buy a new one without batting an eye, Paula. Whoever had the busted rig barely had a pot to piss in. If you got to take, take from he who has plenty."

"You didn't have to take anything," she said.

Crowe looked ahead but held his smile, as if aware what her tune would be after three days with no saddle at all.

Paula let the silence hang another few hours. It had been nearly a day since Gentry. Back in the mountains, Paula could hear the roar of the Laramie River just ahead. She remembered the cold, forceful rapids pressing against her. She clutched the saddle tighter.

Crowe led her on a different course, to the western bridge. The rocks and pines all felt eerily familiar. If she'd never seen these woods again she'd have been the better for it, but every second mattered.

The western bridge was a sturdier breed than its deposed brother. Wide tresses kept it safely in place rather than heavy rope. They walked its length atop their horses, though Paula refused to look down even for a moment.

Finding their way back to a familiar trail, she felt upside down at how utterly her situation had changed. After everything it took to get Misun though the mountains to the Fort, here she was chasing him back the way she'd come. She'd thrown down Waite's shield for Crowe's sword, yet even as she'd traded a marshal for an outlaw, she'd recused herself from executioner to become liberator.

Everything felt so convoluted. Whatever was right in all this had been lost. The only constants were Misun's innocence and Alvord's guilt. Evidently that was enough.

✦ ✦ ✦

Rigby and his wife were nowhere to be found at their cottage in the mountains. Crowe helped himself to supplies anyway, smashing in through a backdoor to raid beans and dried meat. Thankfully he restrained himself only to what they'd need for the next few days.

Paula frowned at the notion of robbing the Rigbys both ways, but their betrayal at the bridge mitigated her sympathy.

That evening, they stopped to rest in the trees. "How did you know to wait for us on the trail?" Paula asked as she scooped into a can of warmed beans.

Crowe raised up the meat in his hand after tearing a piece off. "The generous benefactor of our meal," he said. "Ran into good Mr. Rigby and his blushing bride retreating to Gentry. After we caught the train and found you conspicuously absent, I rode the boys north around the mountains straight for Gentry. Might not have caught you if you'd ripped through the mountains, but apparently Waite decided to take his sweet time."

Paula didn't mention the delays of Misun's escape and falling into the river. "Did you kill the Rigbys?" she asked, bracing herself.

"Had to," Crowe answered, his mouth full.

Paula felt her heart drop. "Why?"

"Rigby told us what he'd done, how he misled you and Waite to the wrong bridge. I can't abide liars."

"Even though his lie ended up helping you?"

"Truth be told, wasn't so much lies that brought down Ben Rigby as his pretty wife," he returned. He saw Paula's confusion and elaborated. "Killing her was a kindness compared to what the boys would have done with her otherwise."

"You're sick," she snarled, remembering Mrs. Rigby's fragile face, along with the faceless women from the plains.

"Maybe, but leading an outfit like that takes a certain sickness," Crowe said. "That's the thing about mad dogs. If you don't throw them a bone every so often they'll break their chains and maul you instead. Even so, I don't allow that sort of thing to befall women."

Paula felt sick. She saw his eyes, though. There was a heaviness to them. Regret.

"Best I get some sleep," he said, turning over. "You won't mind taking first watch, of course."

Paula considered shooting him in the back as he snored. Instead she tucked herself under a blanket and said a prayer for the Rigbys.

✦ ✦ ✦

"How did you get to be boss in the first place?" Paula asked the next day as they rode. "You don't seem like they were. The rest of your gang, I mean."

Crowe shrugged. "Virginia pulled those boys together over the years," he answered. "I was just along for the ride at first. I seemed to end up doing most of the talking after a while, and Virginia trusted me to handle things when she was gone. Said I was the only one with restraint." A dry chuckle escaped.

She turned to him with a puzzled look. "You said you gave up on your sister a long time ago," she recalled from the saloon.

He looked exposed like she hadn't seen before. "She was a gentle child, if you can believe it. Played with a doll, chased me around a field. Then we were orphaned. Parents shot down in the house. Never knew by whom. She's older than me by two years. She took care of me while we wandered, scraped by. Protected me. She was fierce when someone came at us, but never cruel. Somewhere along the way that changed."

"What happened?" Paula pressed.

From the look on his face, Paula wasn't sure if he'd ever talked about his sister in this way. At least for a long time.

"Wasn't any one thing, Paula. Kick some dogs long enough and they cower, lie down to die. Kick others and they bite, even get a taste for blood. Virginia's first few killings were to keep us alive. Then she had something to prove to the world. Those were the best days. We had plenty as we started robbing uptight assholes, but it wasn't enough for her."

He paused. "Then we held up a train car from Denver. Already cleared out everyone's pockets, but she emptied both revolvers into folks where they sat. Reloaded and kept firing even as they ran from the car into the trees. Like it was open season on pheasant. I'd never heard her laugh that way before."

He glanced back to Paula to gauge her reaction. The girl looked like she didn't understand. "I don't know that she gets any joy from heists anymore. From anything, really. 'Cept watching things burn." He smiled, tipping up Paula's hat to focus her. "But she's family, right? She may be a monster but she's my monster."

"Does she feel the same about you? She even look at you like a brother anymore?"

He laughed. "Perhaps too much for anyone's good. She once took off for Powder City with a degenerate named Higgins to hide out after a railroad job. Blood was still wet on her face when we parted but she made sure to kiss my cheek and wish me well before she rode off. She shot Goyle dead for laughing."

"She sounds completely insane," Paula said.

He nodded. "Reckon you're right. But we all have to anchor ourselves to something. Virginia's all I got."

Crowe offered nothing else and Paula didn't ask. They kept riding until they hit the plains at nightfall.

✦ ✦ ✦

"So why are *you* the way you are?" she asked as they sat round their fire. "So Virginia was crazy. What about you?"

He stared at her a long moment, as if deciphering what she wanted to hear and how he could impart it. "It's man's nature to take what he wants," he said at last.

"And you want money," she said. "Killing."

"I want freedom, Paula. That's what this land is. It won't be here forever. The more rail lines get laid the farther freedom flees to the west until it eventually hits the ocean and flitters off to the heavens. I happened to be born at a fortuitous, if not fleeting, time. That's all."

"The whole country's free," she said.

"Even a rancher's daughter from a flea-bit town in the Wyoming territory knows better than that. Were you free, Paula? Was your Pa? Or were you under this big rancher's boot? If Alvord hadn't shot your pappy down would you have ever—"

"Shut up," Paula said, more tired than angry. "Just shut up, Crowe."

"You were the one who asked." He paused for a moment, still watching her. "Why are you the way you are, then?"

Paula gave him a befuddled look. "What do you mean?"

"Brave. Stubborn. Adventurous." He snickered. "Good."

"I'm not any of those things," she retorted as if they were as a mockery. "This all just… happened."

"Nothing just happens. You made it happen."

"You and Waite are the ones who ride at fearful odds in gunfights," she reminded him. "I still flinch when I hear a pistol cock."

"A fear of death has no bearing on bravery, Paula. Waite rides headfirst into trouble because that's all he knows—because he knows he'll come out on top of most trouble. You run into trouble knowing you probably won't come out of it. You run in because it feels right to you. That's bravery."

"And why do you run into trouble?" she pressed. "Do you just get thrills from it like your sister?"

"I hope I don't come across as mad as my dear sister, but I'd be lying if I said I didn't enjoy my work," he said. "But I also plunder and rob and steal because some people deserve to be stolen from. A man, or a girl for that matter, shouldn't have to live confined. We're not born subordinate, why live that way if you don't have to?"

"You're trying to tell me you only rip off the Alvords of the world?" Paula asked. "What about all the people in the mines waitin' on the payroll you stole off the trains?"

"Federally insured money, but that's not the point," Crowe said, waving it off with his hand and leaning forward.

She didn't let him continue. "Yes it is! You think you're some kind of Robin Hood but you're just stealing for yourself! You're hurting or killing people along the way. You're no better than Alvord. Don't you see?"

"I have a code. More than your friend Waite has, anyway. I still want to know why you choose to be such a paragon."

"I don't know that word," she said flatly.

"I'm asking if you're really this bent on delivering justice to Alvord or if you're just infatuated with a savage," he said.

Paula nearly snapped at him again but held her temper. "Someone needs to give them both what they deserve," she said. "That's all. No one else seems to care. I'm sick of it." She stared him down, determined to stamp out any doubt in his mind. "Do I look like I enjoy any of this? Does it look like I've done this before? Waite was right. I don't belong out here. I've almost died more times than I can count since I left Carbon."

202 ◆ Tyler Tullis

"I don't believe that for one second," he rebuffed. "You were born for this place. You have a taste for it now. For action—doing something. You won't be able to live without it. Out here is the edge. The only place people like you and me are really alive. You and I aren't so different, Paula Maddox."

"You're a murderer."

"You wouldn't kill Alvord if you had the chance?" he asked. "You know that's what's coming, right?"

She paused, her anger subsiding as she thought back to Ritter bleeding on his knees, her barrel extended to his head.

"I'm not like you," was all she said.

He shrugged. "You're more like me than my own sister, at least."

32. Waiting for Waite.

PAULA AND CROWE ARRIVED AT ALVORD'S ranch well ahead of its owner. Crowe insisted they ride the wee morning through the last stretch of the plains to make good time. By this point Paula was conditioned to the lack of sleep. Her body ached as she struggled to keep from falling off the horse, though the sensation stemmed primarily from the constant rush of adrenaline as they neared the ranch.

They arrived on the outskirts at dawn. Shadows danced across lights in the main house. One rider mounted to head for the southern perimeter, maybe for Carbon, but otherwise the place looked deserted.

"Alvord employs more security than the railroad," Paula commented. "The place usually has a man for every cow."

"Well there aren't any cows that I can see, and my gang thinned out whoever remained before tracking you to Little Holstein."

Paula noted the fresh mounds protruding from the ground to the south.

Leaving their horses within a light thicket, the two jogged almost a mile to the ranch and hopped the fence. Paula pointed out the barn ahead. "That's where I hid the night they killed my Pa, where I found Misun," she whispered.

"Alvord will probably throw him back in there once he arrives," Crowe said. "Might as well be inside waiting for him."

They rushed to the barn in a low crouch. Paula was dizzy with irony— where she'd snuck onto the ranch before to kill, now she was here to rescue.

Crowe had other notions in mind. "You're not getting that boy out of here so long as Waite is alive," he told her once they situated in the barn's loft, the same corner Paula had used for cover. Crowe sat on a hay bale counting ammo for his single revolver. He set it and his thick knife over the hay. "You know that, right?"

"Wasn't nothin' said about killin' Waite," Paula whispered.

"He betrayed you," Crowe reminded her, not bothering to conceal his volume. There was no one around that they could see.

"He... That's not what he thinks about it," she returned meekly.

"Don't," Crowe said sharply. "Don't try for one minute to make his holiness out to be some hero deep down. I told you before. He's a murderer, same as me, but a hell of a lot colder 'bout it."

"He's a marshal," Paula insisted.

"And I'm an outlaw. But here you are with me looking to rescue this boy. Nominal roles don't count for much when things start to slide, do they?"

"Why do you want to kill him so bad?"

"I already told you. We'll never get away, certainly not far, at least, so long as he's still around. I can hold my own in a fight but few can stand up to Waite. Sonofabitch sold his soul to the devil for that speed of his."

Paula stared at him, studying his eyes. "You two go back farther than this business with Misun, don't you?"

Crowe raised an eyebrow. "We do," he admitted. "No burning vendetta, though, if that's what you're thinking. He was on our trail once before but we slipped him easy enough. I just don't like him, that's all."

"Do you always kill people you don't like?"

"Only the ones with no code."

Paula scoffed. "What is your code, exactly, Roderick Crowe?"

This time Crowe scoffed. "Nothing I could impart concisely enough to satisfy you."

Paula glanced out at the empty ranch through the loft door then back at him. "Not like we got a whole lot to do right now."

He sighed. "Any code worth its salt is one you act on, not explain."

"So I should judge you for all the trains you've robbed? All the people you've killed?"

"You've never seen me rob a train, nor the manner in which rob it."

"I've seen the manner in which you kill."

Crowe went silent at this, staring out to the horizon where the riders were sure to eventually appear. "Don't get me wrong, Miss Maddox. I don't fancy myself an estranged folk hero. I'm bound for hell on a runaway freight train for the judgement I've dealt. But even bad men love their sisters."

Paula thought about challenging him further but stopped short. He wouldn't have been there if he didn't believe in something. She supposed it didn't matter what.

✦ ✦ ✦

A few hours later, probably around ten o'clock by Paula's guess, Alvord, Buckman, two gunmen and one other rode onto the ranch from the north. Misun rode with a bag over his head beside Waite. Behind him was another man with a bagged head, as if they'd picked up another prisoner somewhere on the trail. Crowe only recognized the marshal (and former marshal) but he didn't have a very good view without a spyglass.

Paula released an audible groan when they threw Misun and the other prisoner into a barracks between the house and the barn where Alvord's men slept between drives. Crowe shot her a look to say he could do without her theatrics, that the barn had still been their best bet. Alvord galloped straight for the house ahead of the column, running up the porch stairs. Two men met him but he raced past.

The scream was distant but it still made Paula jump. The sound of a grown man crying, wailing, wasn't something she'd heard before. Even from Pa. It filled the air for several minutes. Buckman and one of the others rushed into the house immediately while Waite and another man spoke in front of the barracks.

"I guess Mrs. Alvord died," Paula said after a moment.

She blushed when Crowe looked at her, surprised at how callous she'd sounded.

"Good for Misun, at least," he said.

"What does that mean?"

"It's unfortunate about the Missus. But it's a welcome distraction.

Alvord'll be too busy diggin' a grave to worry about killing our boy. Waite won't let his guard down, of course, but the rest will."

"So what do we do now?" she asked.

"Wait for an opportunity," he said cautiously, watching Waite amble to the house with the other man.

Half an hour passed until Alvord emerged with a shovel. Paula recognized his son Jacob behind him. She and Crowe watched Alvord walk from the house up to a hillside. He started digging while the boy watched. Buckman emerged for a moment to speak to one of the men outside. Eventually he went up the hill alongside Alvord while three men walked into the barracks with the prisoners. One other, a maid from the look of it, went out to pump some water and take it in the house.

"There's our window," said Crowe.

"What?"

"That'll be for Waite. Probably taking a bath, at very least washing up. With Buckman up on the hill and the others watching Misun this is the best shot we're likely to get." He turned to check his revolver a final time then thrust it into Paula's hands.

"What are you doing?" she asked.

"We'll make a dash for the house along the creek and those weeds. Not much cover but we can dip into the water if need be. I'll slip into the house for Waite, you'll stay outside to warn me if anybody comes in after me. Once he's dead we'll get the boy and slip out down the creek. We'll have to circle back for the horses."

"You think you can get past whoever's in there and get the jump on Waite?"

He grinned. "Virginia and I have broken out of and into worse places. If we get out of this, remind me to tell you about El Presidio. It involved a cannon and mule. That was quite the distraction."

Paula forced herself to say what she'd been thinking all morning. "I don't want you to kill Waite."

His smile vanished. "We've been over this."

"Why can't we just get Misun first? Waite'll be none the wiser, same as Alvord and Buckman."

"Do you know why they call him Father Waite?"

She looked down.

"You do, don't you? Those Mexicans he gunned down in that church were just people. Women and children who knew the kingpin Waite was after. Lord knows how many others he's killed for less. And as long as he lives, he won't stop comin' for us. His pay depends on it."

Paula swallowed hard, silent.

"I'll take that as your permission. If so, follow me now. If not, well, you have the gun. Use it on anyone you see fit."

"You're not taking it inside?" she pressed as he made his way for the ladder to the ground level.

He smiled and tapped the knife on his belt, then began climbing down. "Gun wouldn't do me any good against Waite."

33. Knife to a Gunfight.

PAULA HELD HER BREATH AS she descended the ladder, praying no one would slip by a window in the house. Her boots made what seemed like a colossal sound when she slid to the dirt, running low after Crowe. The creek bed lay thirty feet or so from the barn. It felt like the distance to Carbon in the open.

When Crowe slid into the weeds, Paula attempted to do the same. She winced at noise from rock sliding. The grass and willows grew from the edge of the creek but were sparse. The creek itself hung a few feet to their left but wasn't deep enough to conceal them. It was their best approach but a poor excuse for cover if anyone took an intentional look around.

The pair had nearly reached the house when a man stepped out of the barracks. Crowe quickly seized Paula and pulled her lower into the ditch, pushing her flat on the slope. Paula nearly dropped the gun, scrambling for it in the dirt. She convinced herself the man at the barracks couldn't have heard them over the breeze and the babbling water. Crowe kept perfectly still beside her, his grip tight on her forearm.

The man outside the barracks cursed as he fumbled with his trouser buttons and sucked a finger at the same time. It looked like he'd been cut—blood dripped from his hand while he used the other to relieve himself. Paula looked away but Crowe's eyes darted across the ranch from the grave site to the house. "You know how to bird call?" he asked in a hush.

"Not very good," she admitted.

"Well make it convincing because lives will depend on it, yours included. Provided the bleeder there heads back into the barracks, I'll slip into the house 'round the back. If anybody comes outside who could see me when I rush back here to you, or if Alvord comes back down from the hill, whistle once, then again when the coast is clear."

"What if the coast doesn't clear?"

"Then you won't whistle again, will you? If anybody comes into the house though, whistle twice. I'll need to find a hiding place. You got that?"

"Yes." She paused. "You're just going to stab him?"

"Gun would be a little loud, don't you think?"

"You're going to slit his throat?"

Crowe's brow furrowed. "Tell me you aren't entertaining any notions of blowing this whole thing to save him—because that will end very poorly for you either way."

"Just go," Paula said, looking away.

He sighed and pat her shoulder twice. "I should be back quick. If I'm not, you can retreat to the barn the same way easily enough. Try again later without me if you want. Just don't use that unless you absolutely have to," he said, pointing to the gun.

"I've never even shot a pistol before," she said. "I don't plan to now."

"Remember that if Alvord strolls down here with his back to you. We'll fetch your Indian once I'm done, alright?"

She nodded once, trembling. "Just... be careful."

He flashed his roguish smile before scurrying up from the brush and darting to the west corner of the house past the porch.

Paula couldn't see him or anyone else through the windows in the minutes that passed. Perhaps Waite was talking to someone or at least in someone's sight. Crowe would wait him out. She panicked, wondering how long this would take. Alvord would return for water or his wife's body eventually. Someone would ride up from town, see her in the creek. She'd never felt so vulnerable nor anxious.

Paula's attention slipped from the house to the barracks when she heard muffled screams. Something slid about on the floor, banged against a wooden frame. She tensed her grip on the gun, wondering what they were doing to Misun. Surely they wouldn't torture him—what reason would they have? Then she remembered Cliff Ritter and the type of man he was. Alvord must have had more like him.

More minutes slipped by with no sign of Crowe. No activity. Just the muffled voices and jostling from inside the barracks. Paula looked around her on all sides. Alvord continued digging as his son and Buckman looked on. Silence from the house, struggling from the barracks.

Before she knew it Paula was on her feet sprinting from the weeds to the barracks, pressing her back against its main door. She'd still be invisible to Alvord but windows from the house stared her way. With her ear to the door, Paula heard grunting peppered with the occasional laugh. She tried to peer in through what space remained between the double doors but couldn't make anything out.

She glanced to the house and the horizon. Still nothing. Crowe would be fine without guard for a moment. Gently pushing the door at a snail's pace to mitigate any sound from the hinges, she spied an empty bunk and rushed toward it out of view from the main corridor. Glancing up past a mattress, she saw Misun tied to one of the bunks across from her. He remained hooded.

Down the length of the bunks were three men. A woman was on the ground in front of them. One of them held her down with a knee on her back while another pressed her head to the floorboards. Her hands were tied behind her back. The third man stood over her and puffed from a cigar.

"My brother was on that train you shot up," the smoker said. "18 years old."

The woman said nothing, already severely beaten, but she screamed when the smoker drove the ashes of his cigar into her shoulder. She thrashed but the men held her in place.

Paula acted without thinking, as if the woman under the three men was the same one from the Laramie Plains. As if she were Mrs. Rigby. The men turned when they heard her gun cock. None of them moved for a moment.

"Step back from her," Paula said.

They exchanged glances as if deciding whether someone was playing a joke.

"Now!" Her gun extended straight to the man in the middle—they opted not to test her further and spread with hands up. The woman on the floor recoiled from them. When one of the men inched away Paula realized there was another door in the back from which he could escape.

"One more step and I kill all three of you," she whispered. "Untie her. Now."

"Alright," the one in the middle said. "No need for the gun, little miss. I know you from town. I—"

"I swear to God I will kill you if you say another word. Cut her loose."

The man swallowed loudly. He pointed to a knife hilt protruding from his boot. She gave him permission with a gesture of her gun. The other two didn't look armed, but a gun belt sat on a nearby bunk. Paula watched without blinking as the center man leaned down for his blade. He cut the woman's ropes.

"Help her up," Paula said.

He didn't have time. Before he knew what hit him the woman wrenched his knife from him and plunged it into his chest. She ripped it out just as fast, slicing the back of another man's leg from the floor. The man with the hole in his chest hadn't even fallen by the time she heaved his blade into the last man's neck, even as he took hold of the gun on the bed.

Paula kept her gun outstretched but her face went white as the woman furiously stabbed and slashed at all three of the downed men. Paula feared their screams would attract attention, but they were short-lived.

The woman kept hold of the knife as she pushed up from the bodies. She pulled one of their jackets on then leaned against a bunk, panting and bleeding. Blood dripped from her lips, though it didn't look like hers from the smear marks. Paula remembered one of the men bleeding from before. Sure enough, one of the downed men had a terrible bite on his hand.

The woman eventually looked Paula's way, taking in the terrified girl. "Put your pistol down," she said.

Paula was slow to come back to her senses, having thought nothing would haunt her more than Waite's attack on the marauders in the mountains. She lowered Crowe's revolver and went to Misun to start untying him. "Can I… do anything for you?" she asked, gently.

The woman shook her head, studying the girl. "No," she said, reaching for a pillowcase on an adjacent bunk. She pulled it off the pillow and wiped herself down, smearing the blood. "Who are you?" the woman asked.

"Paula Maddox," she returned mechanically. "Who are you?"

The woman paused, throwing the soiled pillowcase away. "Call me

Ginny," she returned. "You live out here, Paula Maddox?"

"No. Well, yes. Another ranch nearby."

"Just out on patrol looking for damsels in distress?" Ginny asked, strapping the free gun belt around her waist.

Paula pulled off Misun's hood and helped him up. "I'm here for him," she said. "He's my friend."

Ginny collected her messy brown hair behind her to make a loose ponytail. "Looks like you're a good friend to have. Where am I?"

"A ranch outside of Carbon. Wyoming. It belongs to a man named Alvord. Do you know him?"

"Never heard of him before a few days ago," she said. "Sprung me from jail, rode me here. Guess I'd have been better off in the cell."

Paula paused, staring at the woman harder. Something was off about her. Familiar. Her nose was formed a certain way, her hair was colored like...

Paula titled her head as if seeing a ghost.

Ginny's eyes narrowed. "You alright, kid?" she asked. "Don't go limp on me now, I need to know how many others are out there, what the place looks like. How many more men does this Alvord have?"

"He... There are..."

Misun sensed Paula's shock and eyed Ginny suspiciously. He'd received a few fresh hits but he looked mobile enough.

"I'm here with your brother," Paula said at last. "He's in a house next door about to kill Marshal Waite. Alvord has another three men nearby, maybe more."

"Wait," Ginny said, holding up a hand. "My brother? You don't even know me."

"You're Virginia Crowe," Paula said. "Roderick and I came here to free this boy. Your brother is about to kill Marshal Waite in a house out yonder."

Ginny didn't bother to hide her skepticism. "Why would Roderick want to save some Injun boy? Where are his men?"

"Dead," Paula returned. "Waite and a party of Sioux killed them in the mountains a few days ago. Crowe... Roderick, that is, he aimed to trade my friend for you at Fort Laramie. But... you're here."

Paula figured that Alvord must have paid off a judge or a jailer to free

Ginny. Maybe he wanted revenge on her for all the stalled payroll. More likely he wanted a bargaining chip against the Sibling Gang the same as he wanted Misun to use against the Sioux. Waite must have told him the Siblings were destroyed, but whatever the reason, here stood their leader, covered in blood and dirt.

"You can help him," Paula said. "We could—"

"Hold on," Ginny said, coming closer. "I'm still not sure I believe any of this. Did my brother know I was here?"

"No," Paula said. "But he's been trying to save you for weeks. He'll be happy to see you, I know it."

Ginny looked to have another question ready but paused to study the gun in Paula's hands. She reached for it, plucking it from the girl's grasp without a second thought. She looked over the hilt and barrel.

"Sonofabitch," Ginny whispered. "He is here." She kept the gun but sized up the two youths before her. "Well I can tell you right now I'm not stopping anyone from killing that old cur Waite. Take me to my brother and we can talk about this Alvord. I'd be more than happy to kill him after all this hospitality he's extended."

Paula felt a dark joy take root before Misun grasped her wrist. There was a caution in his eyes as if to ward her from Ginny. Paula nearly told him everything would be fine. That's when they heard the gunshot.

34. Siblings.

THE SHOT WAS MUFFLED, CLEARLY from inside the house. A shout rang out from somewhere, then a woman's scream. Paula heard footsteps, both close and far away, rushing closer. She, Misun and Ginny ran to the front of the barracks, peering through the cracked door outside. Alvord and Buckman were halfway to the house. Jacob remained on the hillside where they'd likely told him to stay. Another man on a horse raced from the ranch's south side. The maid ran out the back of the house, shouting Alvord's name.

Paula's heart dropped when she saw a body come flying out the front door, tumbling down the steps of Alvord's porch. She turned to gauge Ginny's reaction upon seeing her brother bloodied in the dust. He'd been shot in his right shoulder. Ginny looked tense but didn't move.

Waite emerged from the door. His face was wet, half covered in shaving cream. A towel hung over one shoulder. His gun rest comfortably in the holster along his waist. The marshal stared the outlaw down from the porch with a satisfied grin spreading his mustached lip wide. He let Crowe push himself up, clutching at his bloody shoulder as he rose full length.

Ginny made her way to the opposite side of the barracks. "What are you doing?" Paula whispered frantically.

"Leavin'," Ginny answered.

Paula grabbed her forearm and pulled the woman around with all her strength. "That's your brother!"

Ginny slapped Paula's face with the back of her hand. Misun tensed but Paula held him back. "And that's Marshal Waite, plus two other guns at least," Ginny returned. "Rod's dead. No one's faster than Waite. He'll want to kill me in front of my brother or the other way 'round. Goddamn sadist. Ain't stayin' to find out."

"He's your brother," Paula repeated. "He rode across the territory for you."

"With seven killers at his back. I got a baby and an Injun. Nothin' I can do for him."

Paula's jaw slipped as Ginny turned and hurried for the back door. "I wish they'd just got on with it and hung you," Paula said through clenched teeth.

Ginny looked back from the doorway. "Why the hell do you care?" she asked.

Paula had nothing to say.

Ginny rolled her eyes. She took two pistols from the men she'd killed then tossed Paula her brother's gun. "Good luck." Then Virginia Crowe slipped out the back in the low run to the south.

Paula stood silent, a tear moistening her cheek as it slowly dripped down. She wasn't sure why it hurt so much—perhaps it was just the terrible symmetry of it all. When she turned for the front of the barracks, Misun touched her shoulder.

"We must go," he said. "I left sign for my people in the mountains. They have found it by now. They will come. They will kill everyone. Even Waite. Even you."

Paula swallowed hard but walked past him for the front. "Go if you want," she said.

He didn't, following her to the door.

"You!" the shout shattered the afternoon air as had the gunshot. Alvord ran headlong from the hill, his eyes fire as his burly form closed the gap to the outlaw. The rancher's punch was muted by the breeze but Paula felt it all the same. Crowe sailed backward, tumbling over the dirt. Alvord pressed on like a runaway freight train, sending his boot to Crowe's middle, then his face. Paula turned breathlessly to Misun who looked on with a blank expression.

It was Buckman who pulled Alvord back, lest he cleave Crowe's head in.

"She'd still be alive if not for you!" Alvord bellowed as Buckman and another man restrained him. "You brought this violence on us, you goddamned cur!"

Crowe was slower to rise this time, only making it to his knees. Alvord commanded a gun from Buckman. "You can't just gun him down, Curtis," the former marshal implored.

"I'll do whatever I damn well please with this filth," Alvord barked. "Waite, your gun!"

Waite didn't move. Didn't take his eyes from Crowe.

"Do you want to be paid or not?"

"Don't you threaten me, you infestuous bastard," Waite shouted. "You're paying for services already rendered—you're here with your prisoner alive. You'll not be shooting this man, he's worth more still breathing."

"He killed my wife!" Alvord exclaimed.

"Ain't what Maddox told me," Waite returned, his impatience on display. "Your man Vance did that, and I've done for him. Roderick Crowe is mine."

"Whatever the reward on him alive I'll double for him dead," Alvord said.

Waite finally turned his gaze to the irate rancher and released an irritated huff. "Maddox was right about you, Alvord," he said. "You know that?"

Alvord glared at the marshal but said nothing.

"Fine." Waite walked back into the house then reemerged with a second pistol. He threw it to Crowe's feet. "Looks like you pissed off the wrong man this time, Crowe. But I'll give you a sportin' chance."

Crowe glanced to the revolver in the dirt before him. He spit blood and possibly a tooth to the side. "How generous," he said. His voice sounded like his face looked.

"I had to go for your man Reece first, last time," Waite said. "He was always the fastest of you. Maybe you care to prove me wrong."

Crowe managed his smile, revealing bloody teeth. "Not especially," he returned. "Hence sneaking up on you with a knife."

"That's the problem, Crowe—you didn't sneak up on me."

"You've got a squeaky floorboard and lady luck to thank for that,

Holy Father."

The silence hung while the marshal waited for his opponent to reach for the weapon, but Alvord broke it.

"Hold on," he said, then turned to march toward the barracks. Something dark and vengeful powered his heavy strides.

Paula's heart beat fast.

He was coming for Ginny. He wanted to kill the Siblings together.

Misun grabbed Paula, leading her out the back, but she held firm. She raised Crowe's gun to the doorway, pointing it at the door.

Alvord threw open the doors and found her there with the gun aimed at his forehead. The color drained from his face. He said nothing, his jaw slack.

This time, it wasn't about Pa. It was for Misun. Even Waite.

The shot knocked Alvord down, blood and dust spraying from his side. Paula nearly fell over as well, nearly as shocked as Alvord she'd fired.

"Paula?" Waite shouted from the porch, leaping down the steps two at a time. "Paula!" He kicked the gun away from Crowe to Buckman, dashing for the girl before Alvord tried anything.

The rancher pushed up, holding his side where he'd been shot. His face warping with fury, he rose and kept coming, pulling his revolver. Shocked, Paula fumbled with Crowe's gun. Misun intercepted the rancher, heaving his gun up and away. A shot blasted through the barrack's roof. Waite arrived to push Paula away and point his gun at Misun.

"Don't!" Paula cried.

Misun hesitated with another gun in his face so Alvord delivered a blow to the boy's gut, doubling him over.

Paula rushed to Misun's side. "Stop it! Waite, don't do this!"

He lowered his gun from her. "The hell are you doin' here, Maddox?" He pulled her up and off the boy even as she struggled. He pushed her outside the barracks as one of Alvord's men rushed in to subdue Misun. Waite grabbed her shoulder. "Paula, this is over. Let the boy go."

"You're disgusting!" Paula shouted through her tears. "How can you be so selfish?! You're killing for *him*?!" She threw her hand toward Alvord. "He's going to start a war, and for what? To save some money?"

"You're as foolish as your father was," Alvord lambasted, his temper slipped. "I'm trying to protect this country, to protect you! My wife—"

"Louis Vance killed your wife!" Paula screamed. "Your man! Not the Sioux!"

"Paula, you are too young to understand what needs to be done here," Waite interjected, motioning for Alvord to back off as Buckman helped him, calling for the maid to bring bandages.

"You're going to kill an innocent boy. You're going to use his death to kill hundreds more. And you're doing it because you want to get paid. I'm not too young to understand that."

Waite seemed to harden, shaking his head. "Ain't no one innocent, only naive," he said. "Like you. I'm done tryin' to explain that. Go home, Maddox." He walked past her, making his way back to Crowe.

The man who tied Misun came to her next, binding her hands and feet then picking her up to load her onto a wagon. Paula cried and screamed to no avail.

Waite resumed his position in front of Crowe, again tossing a firearm in front of him. "Get up, Crowe."

"Wait until the girl leaves at least," Crowe said.

"Get up. Now."

Crowe sighed and shot Paula an apologetic glance. Paula watched through her tears as the outlaw struggled to push himself up on his knee, leaning over for the gun. He held his weapon but his stance was all wrong— even for being shot and beat to hell, Paula could tell he wasn't going to fight. "I'll shoot you where you stand either way, Crowe," Waite said. "Don't make me count to three."

Crowe said nothing.

"Fine. One... two..."

Paula grimaced as two shots filled the air.

But Crowe didn't drop.

Waite did.

The marshal stumbled then fell to a knee in the dust. He opened his coat and dabbed at blood from his side. He dropped his gun, panting.

Crowe only smiled that damn smile, teeth red with blood. "I like this," he said. "That you'll die wondering if I got fast or if you got slow." He pointed his gun to finish Waite off, but the next shot didn't come from either of the duelists.

Paula saw the smoke from Buckman's gun. The shot pierced Crowe's chest. He fell at once, blood pooling around him. Crowe's smile finally faded.

She felt fresh tears but she didn't cry out. No one spoke for a moment. Neither Buckman nor Alvord offered Waite assistance as he collected his gun and pushed himself back up. His clothes were wet with blood to his waist. He looked stunned, sweeping his gaze between Crowe's body and Paula.

Paula watched Waite start back for the house before she heard it. They all did. Rumbling in the distance. Paula followed Waite's eyes to the north behind the house as riders appeared on the horizon. Then came the battle cries.

"Jesus Christ," she heard one of the men behind her say, backing away before he finished binding Paula.

"Get inside!" Buckman bellowed as the Sioux hunting party raced over the northern expanse of the ranch. At least twenty, maybe more. All on horseback. Bursts of smoke peppered the horizon followed by the whiz and ricochets of slugs against the wagon. It felt like being in the river rapids again. Facing impending death.

Paula frantically pulled at the ropes on her wrists, burning her skin as she rolled over in the wagon. Then she felt a knife slide along her skin to severe the bonds. She recognized the strong pull of hands heaving her up. Waite pulled her toward the house as he unloaded at the charging line of hostiles. Hearing shouting behind her, Paula saw Alvord retreating to the closer structure—the barracks.

"Misun!" Paula shouted at Waite. When he didn't stop she pulled against him, planting her feet.

"Goddammit, Paula, not now!" he shouted.

Yanking hard enough to rip her sleeve, Paula spun from Waite amid the incoming gunfire. Waite didn't come after her this time, hobbling up the steps to the house for the cover of indoors. He collapsed at the door, pulling himself inside.

Paula ran to the wagon first. Buckman and another man were pinned there, rifling through supplies for ammo. Buckman tried to shove Paula under the wagon to hide as the Sioux made it to the house, firing into the windows. She fought from his grip as the former marshal's head snapped back. He fell beside her with a gaping hole in his forehead. Paula felt her courage slipping. A fresh stream of firepower from inside the house seemed to draw the raiders' attention. Waite had likely found a gun safe or a collection. It gave Paula the seconds she needed.

Sprinting, she cleared the twenty-some paces from the wagon to the barracks. Only one bullet streaked her way. The door was closed but she threw herself into it, desperate for the safety of cover. She looked up when she heard the scuffle on one of the bunks. Alvord had a bloody arm around Misun's neck. "Get away from the door!" Alvord shouted.

"Just let him go!" Paula wished she'd grabbed Buckman's gun.

"He's our only chance to get out of this—if we let him go we'll have no leverage. He'll tell them to kill us."

"If you don't let him go they'll kill us anyway! He's my friend, he'll protect us."

"You maybe," Alvord said, his voice quaking.

"Your son is out there!" Paula cried. "If you don't give them what they want—"

"Shut up!" Alvord whispered harshly, setting his gun on Paula. "If you give us away we won't be—"

Misun twisted out of the big man's grip in a sudden push downward. Before Alvord could get a shot off Misun leap up to jab his thumb into the rancher's right eye. Alvord howled and staggered back as he bled. Misun rushed forward as he fell, grabbing a metal pail beside a bed. He struck the rancher over the head with it, disorienting him.

Paula stood speechless while Misun immediately leapt aside and rushed for the door. "Stay here," said the boy.

"Misun, wait!"

He didn't look back on his way out.

Paula found Crowe's gun on the floor and tucked it into her trousers. She heard fresh gunfire erupt, peppering the side of the barracks. Hoofbeats and shouts came her way. She smelled smoke—somehow the building had caught fire.

Alvord sluggishly pushed himself back up but Paula didn't wait for him. The coast looked clear when she emerged from the back of the burning barracks. She ran hard for the barn and a horse, praying the Sioux wouldn't notice with so many other targets at the house, that Misun could soothe their rage. It didn't sound like it from the flurry of gunshots behind her.

Paula stopped running when she saw smoke rise from the barn as well. Fire emerged from the loft, engulfing the hay. Two warriors rode from the rising pyre, coming her way. She watched the tussle between Alvord's last man and the warrior. The warrior's blade flashed red.

She sat on her knees, not bothering to lift Crowe's gun.

She couldn't take this anymore. Death had chased her, grazed her, tricked her, so many times. No more.

Paula closed her eyes as hoofbeats encircled her, as a warrior dropped from a horse and strode to her. She shrieked at his touch but no blade pierced her, no bullet tore into her. Only a tight squeeze on her shoulder and the warmth of someone close. She opened her eyes and found Misun there, arms outstretched as he spoke a flurry of words she didn't understand to his kin. There looked to be some debate exchanged among the Sioux, but ultimately the six or seven riders fell quiet.

"Misun?" she said, barely audible as he left her and pulled himself onto a blanketed horse.

He stared at her a lingering moment but said nothing, his face sad but hard. Then he turned and regrouped with the other riders at the house. They departed as a group to the north.

✦ ✦ ✦

Paula couldn't find the strength to stand until she saw smoke begin to rise from the house as well. She wandered there. Alvord lay outside with his head caved in. She felt nothing.

The man often seen with Buckman lay next to his boss, riddled with bullet holes.

She searched the burning house. Papers wafted from Alvord's office as a cabinet collapsed in flame. They might have been dollar bills. She found Waite's body hanging out a back window. He'd been shot a second time, this time in the neck. She stared at him until the heat and the smoke drove her from the house. She wouldn't have been strong enough to move him.

Paula wandered up the hill and shouted for Alvord's son. There was no body. Perhaps he'd made his way off the ranch in the chaos. Perhaps he was hidden somewhere and too scared to come out. More likely he'd been kidnapped or killed.

She was the only one left on the ranch.

She returned to Crowe's body. She didn't cry. For a moment she considered taking his remains up the hill and burying them where Alvord had intended to place his wife. It didn't seem right. Not because he was a thief and murderer, but because things were already convoluted enough. Plus, she still needed him.

Paula was able to find one horse still on the southern side of the ranch. Buckman's, from the look of it. It would have been easier to heave Crowe's body into the wagon but the one in the field was shot half to hell. It probably wouldn't get far. With all her strength she wrapped the outlaw's body in two blankets then tied it behind the horse. She started for Carbon's sheriff office.

35. Tall Tales.

PAULA CRINGED WHEN THE TRAIN came to a halt, knowing it would wake Hannah. Her sister's cries were immediately followed by sighs and groans down the length of the car. Hannah had never even been off the ranch. After three days on the train, the baby's demeanor was less than pleasant.

Paula lowered her head as she jostled their two cases of luggage from the seats. The conductor glared at the Maddox family as they stepped out of the car ahead of the others. The pestering man had tried to relocate them three times, once to a cargo car, but Paula refused to move. She'd bought the tickets herself, and Hannah was entitled to cry. She didn't know it but her father had just died.

Elizabeth gripped Paula's hand as they stepped onto the station floor. Both sisters' heads gradually angled upward as they caught view of the entire building, seeming to arch like a great stone cathedral. Neither of the sisters had ever seen so many people—there weren't as many residents in Carbon as there were train go-ers on the first platform.

Paula expected to be ogled like a lost cow ambling down main street. They stuck out plenty, Ma and the girls. They were in ranch clothes, for one thing. The coal residue of Carbon and the dust of Cheyenne still clung to their faces. But no one seemed to pay them any mind, content to bustle and jostle toward their trains.

They hadn't brought much with them from the ranch. They could afford to buy new things, after all. Ma stored cash within her dress to protect against pickpockets through the many stations.

Paula looked to her mother as she stepped off the train, cradling Hannah and cooing whispers of comfort. She looked nearly as tired as the baby. Her eyes swept through the churning crowds. Ma's smile widened when she caught sight of a group by a newspaper stand.

"Come on, girls," she said, beckoning for Paula and Elizabeth to follow.

Paula guessed her grandfather in the crowd from his relieved smile. He was a tall man, dressed in a short coat with a black vest underneath. He stared at Ma for a lingering moment as they came face-to-face, then opened his arms. Paula looked over the faces of the others. A couple, a separate man and four children around Elizabeth's age. The rest of her family, she supposed.

Sadie was crying when she withdrew from her father, offering the baby to the woman Paula guessed to be her aunt. "Thank you, father," Paula heard her say.

"I'm glad that you've come home, dear," he said. "I'm sorry for your loss."

Sadie nodded but quickly turned to the girls standing behind her. "Girls, meet your Grandfather Reginald," she said, motioning for them to approach.

Reginald called a man to take the bags from Paula. She was hesitant to let go but Ma flashed her a strenuous look. Reginald bent over and smiled. "Paula," her grandfather said, offering his hand to her first. "Hello."

"Hello," she returned.

His smile seemed to widen at the firmness of her handshake. "And Elizabeth," he said, touching her shoulder.

Elizabeth blushed brightly.

"I'm very happy to finally meet you both. I'm sure you don't remember, Paula, but I did visit you once many years ago in Rock Springs when you were a baby."

"Ma told me that," she confirmed blankly. Perhaps she was tired, maybe disappointed, but in what she couldn't say.

A silent chuckle escaped from Reginald, as if letting something slide. "Well, you're very brave, Paula. Coming here with your mother and sisters. I know what you've been through."

"Oh."

"You've got your mother's free spirit, no doubt of that," Reginald said as he stood up. "She ran away once when she was a girl. Three days out at the lake. Your grandmother, rest her soul, was beside herself. I can't imagine what your absence for a week must have done to your mother. You won't be running away anymore, now, will you?"

Paula remained blank. "No," she said.

Reginald smiled. "You may call me sir or grandfather."

"Yes, sir."

Reginald gestured to the rest of the family, introducing them.

Sadie had an older sister and a younger brother. The sister was there with her family, all four of the children hers. Paula's uncle was a soldier and single—the man from whom she'd taken her name. Paul. She knew from Pa that he'd been promoted to an officer's rank after sustaining an injury to his arm. The empty shirt sleeve told her they'd had to amputate. Given his full-dress uniform she supposed he remained a soldier, decorated at that.

One of Paula's younger cousins—Danton, if she remembered— approached after introductions. "Did you really spend a week in a barn and see a real shootout?" he asked.

Paula's aunt quickly slapped his wrist and told him to mind his manners. Paula said nothing.

Back in Carbon, Paula had tried telling her story to the interim sheriff, a man appointed by the Union Pacific from the Cullen Mine. He told Paula she was in enough trouble without telling lies to the law. Paula told her mother the truth as well when they reunited, but Sadie cut her off before she even got to the part about meeting Marshal Waite. "Paula, this isn't one of your adventures from the professor's books or a tall tale from those dime novels—you scared me to death running off like that. Now tell this man the truth about how you found Roderick Crowe."

Paula gave up after that, knowing she could offer no proof of all that had happened. Waite, Crowe, Alvord, Ritter, Buckman, the panhandlers— everyone was dead. She might be able to wire for the rail house operator in Little Holstein, even to Clementine or Wauldruff, but why bother? It was over anyway. All that mattered was the thousand-dollar reward for Crowe— alive or dead.

Instead of the truth, Paula told the sheriff she'd ridden to Alvord's ranch that night to confront him about shooting her father. When she heard he was gone she'd stowed away in the barn loft, too upset about Pa to come home. A week later she said Waite rode into the ranch with Alvord but was confronted by Crowe and a raiding party of Sioux. Everyone was killed, as a ride to the ranch confirmed, but Paula told them she'd helped the late Marshal Waite hold a gun on Crowe when she came down from the barn to investigate the commotion, just before the Sioux attacked. Said she ended up shooting him before he could escape.

She figured they wouldn't give her any reward if she hadn't contributed something.

Hauling the body back as proof, her false account turned out to be enough to earn her the reward. The Union Pacific was just happy to see Crowe and his gang destroyed. Paula was surprised that the railroad man, Owen Rudolph, who personally paid Sadie the reward money, didn't refute the story, knowing at least part of the truth. Paula guessed he didn't want his name being dragged through the mud with Vance's, having played a part in the death of Mrs. Alvord.

Paula said nothing of Misun.

She could tell that Red, who rushed to her when she rode into town after a week's absence, suspected something more at play. He might have believed her story, she thought, but by the time he inspected her injuries she'd lost interest in the truth.

The Maddox family departed Carbon for good a few days after Paula's return, leaving almost everything behind. Pa had already been buried at the Carbon cemetery. Paula cried when she saw the grave, wanting him to have been buried on the ranch he'd died for. They couldn't afford a tombstone at the time so they'd opted for a wooden plank in the shape of a cross with his name etched in. Paula tried to spend some of the reward on a tombstone but Ma wouldn't let her until they'd safely reached Chicago and their financial future was guaranteed. Paula was furious.

"The tombstone," she said before Reginald could lead them out of the station to a car.

Everyone paused and looked at her.

Ma released a huff and leaned in to tell Paula now wasn't the time.

Paula ignored her. "My Pa was buried in Carbon. Ma said you'd help us pay for a tombstone. Will you? Sir?"

Reginald raised an eyebrow then glanced to Sadie, an apologetic and hopeless look on her face. "We'll discuss this matter another time," Reginald said.

"I want to know now, sir," she returned.

"You will not speak to your grandfather this way," Ma told her sternly, hands on her hips.

"It's alright, dear," Reginald said with a defensive gesture. "Paula has been through much in the past week and isn't yet familiar with our ways. She will learn, but I can promise her now that I will see to a tombstone for her father."

Paula swallowed hard, relief coursing through her. She found her eyes tearing. "Thank you," she said.

The group proceeded up and out of the station for the street. It was noisy unlike anything Paula had ever heard. While they waited for a carriage to swing around and pick them up, one of the older cousins tapped Paula's shoulder. Maxwell, a boy her age. "What is the west like?" he asked, hopeful.

Paula didn't say anything.

36. Lost in the Wilderness.

MA AND THE GIRLS LIVED in Reginald's townhouse. He had been alone there after his wife passed away a few years before Sadie ran west with Art. The townhouse felt like a castle to Paula and Elizabeth. Their bedroom alone was bigger than any room in the ranch house. The house had its own library. Everything was ornate, or at least polished. Paula's entrancement only lasted so long, beset by melancholy as she wandered the long hallways and staircases.

The family, including Paula's aunt, uncles and cousins, met regularly there for tea, neighborhood social hours and discussions after church. Paula enjoyed none of it. Her aunt was pretentious. She knew little more of the world than her own children, despite her opinions otherwise. Sadie's brother Paul kept to himself, as if being there was as much a chore for him as it was for Paula.

The cousins, Danton, Maxwell, Sophia and Josephine, were mechanical in their decorum, expressing few independent thoughts or questions in the presence of adults. In private they asked Paula and Elizabeth all sorts of things about Wyoming for the first few weeks. The rift between cousins grew as it became apparent they had nothing in common.

Paula's discomfort socializing with family was plain to see. When asked to speak she often offended someone with candid observation interpreted as flippancy. She tried fitting in, exhibiting the behavior of her peers, if only for Ma to save face, but Paula increasingly felt like she'd never fit the role of a dignified young lady.

She finally had the dresses she'd once craved, but she felt out of place in them. She felt out of place around a table with teacups in hand. She felt out of place at the piano or in a sewing circle with Elizabeth, Sophia and Josephine. She felt out of place around girls who would likely never see a cow. She felt out of place in a city where smoke was more plentiful than clouds.

Paula hated having her entire day scheduled weeks in advance. On the ranch she'd tended to the work that needed doing because their livelihood depended on it. So long as she completed the day's work before sundown, she could usually do things at her own pace. Art let her decide what they'd tackle first. He let her wander, read, or play as soon as her chores were done. At her grandfather's insistence, Ma kept the girls to a strict timetable. Study, etiquette, athletics, cooking, piano, sewing, table talk—each allocated at designated times throughout the day.

Reginald could sense his eldest granddaughter's deflated but defiant spirit. To her dismay, he seemed proficient in breaking it as she'd seen stallions broken back home. He never raised his voice to her, but his will in the house was absolute. The consequences for disobedience or deviation from the schedule meant more study, no dinner and confinement to the bedroom or library. It also made her mother sulk, and Paula had seen enough of that to last her several years.

Ma was quiet around the house, tending only to the baby most of the time. She relayed the girls' agenda each day, accompanied them shopping for clothes and school supplies, sat with them at dinner, but showed little interest in speaking about the life they'd left or the new one they'd arrived in. Paula could see the defeat hanging in her mother's eyes at every turn. She recognized it all too well—it was the final look in her father's eyes.

Things began to feel normal, or at least regular, once school began. Both sisters were enrolled at a private academy for girls, the same that Sadie and her sister had once attended. Elizabeth seemed to make friends easily enough.

Paula was a different story. Girls made fun of her under their breath for her boyish mannerisms. The way she sat at her desk or walked. The way she sneezed or loudly blew her nose. The way she shoveled food into her mouth. Being a Catholic school, Paula sometimes skipped class to explore the massive cathedral next door. She felt equally out of place there.

She wasn't sure if she believed in God anymore, or at least that divine reach extended as far as it was billed.

Paula sometimes wondered if Margaret Vance would have trouble making friends too. She wondered what had become of her. She'd never been fond of Margaret, but they had more in common than she'd ever appreciated. Including losing their fathers. Paula wondered what she'd say if she ever saw Margaret again. She hadn't killed Louis Vance, but had she not recruited Waite, the shopkeeper would likely still be alive.

Memories of Waite were bittersweet. She wondered how different things might have been had he chosen a different path that day in Gentry. She wished she could have been there with him at his ignominious end, to have resolved things between them. Life didn't always tidy up so nicely, she supposed. Misun was proof of that.

Misun. Paula thought about him most of all. He'd just… left, that day. Without a word. After all they'd been through. At one point she'd been convinced he cared about her in a way no one else ever had, as if they'd shared some sort of unbreakable bond. She wasn't sure what she'd been expecting to happen.

Everything ended so quickly in those final moments on Alvord's ranch. The independence she'd mustered, the respect she'd earned, the wherewithal she'd built, the bonds she'd forged, all snuffed out along with the men she'd ridden beside. She returned to Carbon not as the partner of Marshal Waite or Roderick Crowe, but as the meek rancher's daughter who'd run off to hide in a loft.

Paula often wondered if that week on the trail had built callouses or just bruised her.

Paula was always the first up to read the newspaper when the Great Sioux War broke out in 1876. The concentrated fighting seemed to be in Dakota. She wasn't sure what had triggered the hostilities but remembered what Waite once told her. If enough gold was in the Black Hills, the Indians would eventually have to be cleared out. Perhaps General Crook had grown tired of waiting.

Things got worse after a Lieutenant led his men to slaughter by a river called Little Big Horn. People in the west were scared, people in the east enraged. The paper called the Indians savages, animals, barbarians. Crook got reinforcements. Bloody headlines dragged on for over a year, accompanied by pictures of victorious cavalry and dead Indians scattered and bloated over wet fields. The man they called Red Cloud was captured, but still the Indians rallied behind Crazy Horse. Paula always expected to one day see Misun's face among the dead or captured in a newspaper, but she never did.

Then, in 1877, it was over. Crazy Horse was stabbed by a soldier's bayonet trying to escape custody in Camp Robinson. Sitting Bull and the Lakota fled to Canada. Settlers and panhandlers flocked to the Black Hills and further west along the Union Pacific, the Indian threat all but neutralized. Their way of life, destroyed.

Reginald said "Good riddance," at breakfast, and Paula, typically quiet, asked him in with striking volume what in the hell he knew about Sioux or any people who had been on that land longer than he. People just trying to protect their lives and what was theirs the same as she'd tried to protect her ranch. Reginald sent her to her room, and on the way up the stairs, Paula heard her mother quietly appologizing. "Civilization will sort her out."

Paula continued to read news hoping she'd find Misun alive on one of the steamboats relocating his people south to reservations. She would never see him again. She would, however see Virginia Crowe. Paula continued to find the outlaw's name in headlines from time to time, having held up another train or eluded the law after shooting up some town. Reginald scolded Paula when he found entire papers with Ginny's wanted image ripped up and thrown away. Paula kept ripping them up.

37. Inevitability.

At 19, Paula filled in dresses but still felt awkward in them. She wore makeup regularly, let her hair grow long and braided it.

Never so flamboyantly as today, though.

She stood alone by a window, having excused herself from the party to get away from Sophia and Josephine. Sophia was listless as usual, never one to muster excitement for anything, but Josephine had become a positive boar over the last few years. Paula forced herself not to cringe as she heard her cousin's laugh echo from the ballroom to the vestibule where she stood, threatening to crack the stained glass throughout the ornate halls of the church antechamber.

"You mustn't leave me with them," Elizabeth whispered, appearing behind Paula.

Paula didn't look away from the window, staring at the city skyline. "I thought you were off with Jean Claude," Paula said, mustering a soft smile.

Elizabeth reddened. "His name is Jacque," she spurted. "And no, grandfather doesn't like me to be alone with him. You know he doesn't approve."

"Neither do you," Paula reminded her. "You're only keeping him around to stick it in grandfather's craw."

Elizabeth couldn't help her smile. Her sister was right, but more than anything, she liked to hear idioms from their old life fall from Paula's lips. They seemed to come so rarely anymore, certainly not around Reginald.

"Colin is looking for you," Elizabeth said, revealing why she'd really come.

Paula didn't react.

"Grandfather favors him, you know."

"Grandfather's last chore before the cough takes him is to marry us off," Paula remarked.

"Don't say that. He's going to be fine."

"He's dying, Beth. He smokes more than the factories. You're going to have to let him go."

"He isn't all bad, you know," Elizabeth said, staring out the window as well. "He took care of us."

"And will long after he's gone," Paula confirmed.

"Will you still go to university if he passes?" Elizabeth asked in a conspiratorial whisper.

"It can't be any worse than staying here waiting to be married off to some dolt," Paula said.

Elizabeth looked into the ballroom through the open doors. Their mother danced with her new husband to the half symphony Reginald arranged. "Do you hate him?" she asked. "Or do you just hate that he isn't Pa?"

"I hate that she married him because grandfather told her to."

Elizabeth's eyes fell to the floor and her right hand came up to grasp her left elbow.

"What's wrong?" Paula asked.

"Sometimes I worry that you hate me too," Elizabeth said.

Paula reached over to hug her little sister, leaning her head against hers and gently rocking. "I love you, Beth." She felt Elizabeth return the hug. "And I don't hate them. I just… don't understand them."

"What's not to understand?"

"Somewhere along the line Ma lost her sand. Like she's a penitent child paying for running away all those years ago."

"She just wants what's best for us. So does grandfather."

"They want what they think is best for us."

"What do you want?"

Paula gradually let her sister go. "I don't know."

They stood there for a long moment until another of Josephine's cackles bombarded the air. Paula couldn't mask her grunt, and when she found Elizabeth smiling, a laugh found its way free as well. They both tried stifling their giggles as guests walked out of the ballroom.

"The only reason anyone talks to her is her family name or her cleavage," Elizabeth said. Paula shot her a look of shock but Elizabeth only shrugged. "It's true."

Paula grinned. She gazed at the party, beginning to lose steam as the night wore on. "We should go back in. We'll be missed. And I don't want Ma's feelings hurt."

"She knows how much Pa meant to you," Elizabeth confirmed as they made their way for the door. "She knows you're never going to be like Josephine. She wants you to go to university more than anyone so you can get away. No woman in our family has ever gone to university before. I bet you'll like it."

"I hope so," Paula said blankly. "Will you write me?"

"Every day. But only if you write back..." She trailed off when Colin appeared in the doorway.

Elizabeth blushed and curtseyed. "Hello, Colin," she said.

He tipped his head. "Miss Elizabeth," he returned. "Would you mind if I spoke to your sister a moment?"

Elizabeth took her leave, shooting Paula a coy glance through the door that only flustered her sister more.

Colin's smile was nervous. He looked into the ballroom as well. "A beautiful wedding. I am happy for your mother. And you, of course."

"Thank you, Colin," Paula said.

"Might we walk together?" he asked.

She nodded and turned to follow him into the illustrious hallways away from the ballroom.

Paula met Colin in her second year at school. He had graduated from a boy's academy further north, but their families were friends and often brought them together for social events. Reginald was a former business partner with Colin's grandfather in some financial enterprise Paula didn't bother to inquire about. Colin was nice enough, occasionally making her laugh. He gave her gifts on occasion. Lately he seemed all the more determined to spend time with her before she left for university. He was about to finish his time there, set to follow in his father's footsteps as a financier. Reginald adored the boy.

Paula saw the way her grandfather pat Colin's back when he welcomed him into the house, heard the way he lauded Colin's academic achievements at dinner even when he wasn't present. Paula knew this was the man Reginald intended her to marry one day.

"What do you imagine you'll study at university?" he asked as they walked to the largest window overlooking the city.

"I'm not sure yet. I thought about history, but truth be told I'd rather apprentice with a carpenter somewhere. Do something instead of sit at a desk all day."

Colin smiled. "I might have guessed you'd say something like that."

When he paused to look at her fondly, she raised a skeptical eyebrow. "You're not going to get sappy on me, are you?"

"I'm just going to miss you, is all," he said. "When you get back... well... I'll want to talk to you."

"Who the hell else is there to have interesting conversation with around here?" she said. They both smiled.

"That's exactly why, you know. I admire that you speak your mind. That you are determined to become your own person. You deserve someone who respects you for your determination, for your aptitudes. Someone who recognizes what makes you happy and can provide it."

"I don't even know what makes me happy, Colin," she said.

"You love the outdoors. You should have a house outside the city. With horses and a garden to tend. Anything you want."

Paula sighed. "We'll probably be the next couple in there getting married, Colin, you don't have to try so hard." She didn't mean it to sound abrasive and felt guilty.

Colin seemed disappointed but blushed all the same. "I know you may not... love me, Paula," he admitted softly. "But we enjoy each other's company, do we not? Surely that's something. You and I aren't so different."

Paula nearly offered a sigh of surrender to the seemingly inevitable union she'd share with the young man. Then a memory flashed to mind. A conversation she hadn't thought of for years.

You and I aren't so different, Paula Maddox.

Paula's eyes glazed as she stared out the window, gazing west. At first she could only visualize the fire, its embers dancing up to the trees in the darkness. She remembered the disgust, the resentment and the fear that she felt in that moment across from Roderick Crowe. She hadn't thought about him nearly as much as Misun or Waite, even Alvord, but suddenly his voice carried clear as a bell in her mind.

You were born for this place. You have a taste for it, now. For action—doing something. You won't be able to live without it. Out here is the edge—the only place people like you and me are really alive. You and I aren't so different, Paula Maddox.

"Paula?" Colin asked, seeing her slip into what must have looked like a trance. "Did I offend you?"

Paula blinked, shaking her head. "No," she said softly, her heart beating faster. She looked at Colin, then down the hallway to the ballroom, then back to Colin. She smiled, her mouth opening wider as she breathed excitedly.

"What did I say?" he asked, puzzled.

"It's not what you said," she returned. She took his hand, shaking it.

"What's this?" he asked with a tickled smile.

"My gratitude," she said. "You've been a good friend, Colin. You'll make someone a good husband someday, I'm sure of that."

His smiled waned. "But not you," he said more than he asked.

"You'll provide for someone, Colin. I'm through being provided for. Pa, Waite, Misun, Crowe, Reginald... I'm done with that now. I'm leaving."

Colin had no idea what she was talking about but could tell from the strange confidence in her voice she wasn't talking about university. "Where are you going?" he asked.

Paula glanced to the ballroom again, feeling the tug to her mother and sisters. She should tell them what she was about to do so they wouldn't worry. They'd only try to stop her, of course, probably succeed once Reginald heard. No, the time was now. Elizabeth would take it hard at first but understand later. Paula would still write. They'd see each other again.

Paula turned back to Colin, staring dumbfounded. "I'm going home," she answered.

38. The Chicago Sentinel.

Paula made it to Omaha in two days. It didn't take her long to gather what few things she needed from Grandfather's townhouse. A bag of clothes, a little food and the money she'd been allowed to keep from Roderick Crowe's reward. It wasn't much, but it was plenty to get her by for a few months, maybe even years. She tucked Crowe's revolver into her pack, having kept it hidden all these years, even from Elizabeth. Paula bought a few more supplies in Omaha, including a riding hat, tall boots and long jacket. It would be winter on the plains soon. No place for a dress.

She rode the train past Cheyenne and Carbon without debarking. Both towns were barely recognizable with all the new buildings and roads. Her destination, Evanston, lay on the westernmost edge of the Wyoming territory. Where Virginia Crowe had been sighted a few weeks back, the latest newspaper story claimed.

With her bag slung over her shoulder, Paula walked to the sheriff's station to make her inquiry.

"Bullshit," the sheriff said of the newspaper story. "Haven't seen Virginia Crowe here in months. Must be halfway to Mexico, this time a'year. She always goes south in the winter."

The sheriff told her about a card dealer at the saloon who'd supposedly run into her and her gang in Sheridan a few months back. The barkeep barked at her to get out when she marched into the saloon but she ignored him, sitting at the dealer's table. A pair of Irishmen stared at her from the nearest table with dishonorable intentions in their smirks. Paula kept

Crowe's revolver tightly in hand under her coat.

"Don't see this everyday," the dealer said, leaning back with hands on his belt.

"I'm not here to play," Paula returned as he sat.

"How ominous. Especially from a woman."

"It's a woman I'm looking for," Paula said, grabbing the wanted poster from her coat pocket and unfolding it. The dealer's playful expression dissipated.

"Let me guess—an admirer?" he asked.

"Sheriff said you ran into her up north. Any idea where she might be?"

"I just played a hand at her table," the dealer said. "Not exactly simpático with killers."

"She didn't say anything?"

"What, about her hideout? Wouldn't be very smart if she did."

Paula realized too late she should have just played cards and worked her question in innocuously. The shouts of the barkeep and stares of the Irishmen prompted her to keep going as quickly as possible. "Sheriff told it like you had more of story," she pressed.

"Not everyday you run into a woman wanted for more money than you've ever seen, much less play cards with one."

"She have a gang with her?" Paula asked.

"Couldn't say," the dealer returned, growing impatient. "One's a bit preoccupied sitting next to Virginia Crowe."

"Sounds more like you're the admirer," Paula said as she stood, aware no fruit would grow from such obstinance.

She made it halfway to the door before the dealer shouted to her. "Gold," he said.

She turned back. "What do you mean?"

"She flashed some on the table. Said she'd just come into a lot of it."

Paula gave a single nod and walked back to the train station on the main road. She kept her hand on the gun in case the Irishmen cared to follow.

✦ ✦ ✦

Paula arrived in Sheridan a few days later. It would be a costly mistake if the dealer had been wrong or lying, but she figured it was a better lead than "south for the winter." Sheridan was nestled into the southern range of the Black Hills, not as brimming with settlers as Deadwood, but busy enough.

The paper reported a private stagecoach had recently been robbed by parties unknown. It wasn't linked to Crowe but she'd been spotted here in recent months.

Again she paid the sheriff the first visit. A former Chicago copper come west, by his accent and clothes. Stone, was his name, though Paula suspected it was actually something decidedly more Italian.

"About three months ago," Stone said when Paula asked the last time Crowe had been sighted. "She's smart enough not to walk into the saloon anymore but she held up a stagecoach carrying ore bound for the Fort outside town. Whole damn caravan of Pinkertons couldn't hold her off. Not sure how she does it."

"Plenty of dynamite and sharpshooters, I reckon," a deputy called from another room.

The sheriff rolled his eyes. "Marshal McCatheryn is after her gang but they've probably split up after a haul like that, headed south. What's your interest, anyway?"

"I'm a reporter for the Chicago Sentinel," Paula lied, reaching for the pencil and paper in her bag as if all the proof she'd need.

Sheriff Stone looked her up and down again as if she didn't look the part, or any, for that matter. "Well apart from Higgins, only McCathryn knew the latest. Expect you'll want to track the marshal down. He was headed for Denver, last I heard."

"Who's Higgins?" Paula asked.

"One of her boys. He got hit by a Pinkerton and she left him to die. 'Cept he didn't. Not 'til we fixed a rope around his neck. Just stretched him a week ago."

Paula raised an eyebrow. "You couldn't get him to give up anything?" she asked.

The sheriff's brow furrowed. "Sounds like Higgins thought Crowe was comin' to rescue him right up 'til the end, 'coordin' to Shorty. Didn't say a thing other than that."

"Shorty?"

"One of our regulars. Got a court date with Judge Casternack Friday, this time on murder charges."

"Can I speak to him?" Paula asked. "I'd like to talk to anyone who was up close with Crowe or her gang."

"You plannin' to write me and Sheridan into your paper Stone asked.

"I can, depending on what I learn here," she answered.

The sheriff beckoned her back to the jail cells in another room. "Wouldn't expect much from Shorty. Mean but stupid. Usually in here for assault and deviance in public."

Paula found the man curled into a corner of the darkened cell, rubbing a finger along one of the rugged bricks. "Thank you, sheriff," Paula said as if to dismiss him.

Stone hesitated but left her to conduct her interview, warning her not to get too close to the bars. She could see why when Shorty caught sight of her. He slid to the bars with voracious eyes.

"Never seen you before," he said.

"I'm writing a story for the Chicago Sentinel. Can you tell me anything about the man you were jailed with? Higgins?"

"What kind of story?" he asked.

"About Virginia Crowe and her gang. If you can tell me anything that helps me find them, I can cite you in my article."

"You barely look twenty," he said.

"Do you know anything?"

"I do."

Paula waited. "Tell me."

"Unbutton that shirt and I'll tell you."

"I'm serious," she said, trying not to snap.

"So am I."

"That's not the deal."

"It is if you want to know what I know."

Paula couldn't mask her contempt as she stared him down. She walked closer to the bars, reaching up to the top button of her shirt. Shorty's eyes widened when it came loose, when her fingers dropped to the next button.

She watched him salivate, watched his knuckles go white on the bars.

Then he tensed, feeling the cold steel even through the fabric of his shirt. He looked down and saw the gun pressed to his stomach in Paula's free hand. "I'm not a reporter and I'm not going to open my shirt. What I am going to do is blow your fucking guts onto the wall if you don't tell me where Crowe is."

She saw Shorty think about calling for help but he held fast when she pushed the gun harder.

"I don't know," he said.

"What do you know?"

"Just that Higgins thought she was comin' to save him. Kept braggin' about it, about how he'd slept with her and how he was the brains after her brother died. He was always braggin'... That's it."

"He didn't say anything about where they bed down, where they were supposed to meet up?"

"South, that's all I know. Didn't say where."

Paula grimaced. "Thanks for nothin'." She pulled up her gun and slammed Shorty on the forehead between the bars. He fell back shouting and cursing but Paula was already out of the room refastening her buttons.

39. Virginia Crowe.

PAULA FOUND HERSELF AT A DEAD end until she remembered why the name Higgins sounded so familiar. Roderick Crowe had mentioned it in a story about his sister while he traveled with Paula through the Laramie Mountains. Said she ran off with Higgins to a place called Powder City.

Sheriff Stone told her where to find it. Turned out he'd been sheriff there before the city fell to ruin. Once a promising mining camp, Powder City was quickly deserted as larger strikes were reported from Deadwood and the camps further north. A post office and general store that doubled as a saloon were the only buildings that showed any sign of life as Paula rode into town. A hotel stood beside three houses and a sheriff's office, occupied solely by spiders and their cobwebs.

Stone told Paula to find Sheriff Teague when she arrived. He'd lazily served under Stone as a deputy years prior and inherited Stone's role for lack of competition. Paula found the flabby lawman asleep in the post office. Apparently the Powder City sheriff's office had never been completed and the temporary roofing collapsed last winter.

Teague didn't know Higgins but the postmaster did. The outlaw had lived in Powder City for almost two years before he got mixed up in some gang robbing prospectors. A gullible man, it was said, boisterous and quick to emotion. Liked to get in scrapes.

The postmaster didn't know where Higgins called home but guessed one of the old prospector's cabins left in the woods outside town. He didn't recommend Paula go out there alone. She insisted she'd be fine, that she was Higgin's sister come to collect his things since he'd been hanged. The postmaster offered his condolences.

Sheriff Teague went back to sleep.

Paula rode out with Crowe's revolver close. She stumbled upon two cabins along a narrow creek, both occupied. The first group, a haggard looking family with children, pointed her toward a cabin higher in the hills. The second group were two men who looked outside their minds with boredom. She decided not to bother with them, backing her horse into the trees slowly.

She found the last cabin up a winding trail in the dense trees, well off from the creek. Paula studied it for a long moment, observing no movement or light behind the closed windows. She dismounted quietly, sneaking from tree to tree until she came to the porch. No sound. Pulling the window shutter open with the tip of her firearm, Paula braced for shouts or gunfire. None came.

The cabin was empty but someone had been there recently. The smell of coals in the fire made that much clear. A bed with messily strewn sheets was damp on one side. Paula rummaged around for any sign of Ginny. Paula wasn't sure what she was looking for other than women's clothes, but whatever it was she didn't find it. For all she knew the cabin belonged to a curmudgeon digger who still believed the southern Black Hills offered greater riches than the north. The cabin certainly smelled like a filthy old man.

Snow penetrated the treetops as Paula rode back to Powder City, dancing around her as if gleeful she'd come up empty handed. Paula gripped the reins tightly. She should have listened to the sheriff in Evanston in the first place. Ginny was probably drinking tequila in Arizona or Mexico.

Paula wondered if it was worth going all the way to Denver. She was already months behind Marshal McCatheryn. Ginny was probably long gone. She'd be back, surely. Perhaps Paula should just wait her out rather than burning what remained of her money on train tickets. Maybe it was time to cut her losses. She had enough money left to make it to Utah or California and get her start on a ranch. She could save enough to start her own someday, somewhere far where no one could find her until she wanted them to. Reward money for Ginny would have made things easier, but finding the outlaw had always been a long shot.

Paula shook her head. The money had always been secondary. It was about justice. Ginny was the embodiment of the wanton greed that had destroyed so many lives. Monsters like her eroded the resolve of men like Waite, besmirched the memory of men like Roderick Crowe. They brought out the worst in men like Alvord and made men like Vance desperate. The thought of Ginny riding free, laughing as she gunned down innocent folk, kept Paula awake at night.

Paula had hoped killing Virginia Crowe would mark the end of the nightmares and regrets from her ordeal, and in turn, mark the beginning of her new life. Marching out of the church that day, Paula had promised herself she would never be passive again. Her decision to return west would be meaningless if she hadn't at least tried bringing Ginny to justice.

But she'd failed.

The wind bit at Paula on the final stretch to town. It was already late afternoon. No sense in riding for Rapid City until morning. Wondering if she'd be able to find lodging in the livery, she made her way to the post office to ask. The postmaster and Teague were gone, either closed or across the street at the saloon. Paula hitched up there and pulled her coat tight on the way up the steps.

She checked over her pistol before going inside. The owner would probably leave her be, but she was more worried about lonely men like the Irishmen in Evanston.

She glanced through a saloon window for anyone she'd want to keep clear of. Two men sat at the bar, while another four sat around a table. The group looked to be playing dice and throwing back shots. Three empty bottles already decorated the table, and the barkeep walked a fourth over.

The sole woman at the table swiped the bottle from him.

Paula's heart skipped a beat.

It was her.

Virginia Crowe.

Ginny.

She looked older than Paula remembered, with paler skin and a grisly scar cutting from her forehead into her scalp.

Paula felt her heart racing like it hadn't since the Sioux attack at Alvord's ranch. She knew she should back away from the window before someone saw her staring, but she couldn't bring herself to move. After all the enemies Ginny had made, all the people hunting her, all the reward she was worth, there she sat by a window in a rundown bar.

Maybe this was the safest place for her—where no one would think to look. Maybe her notoriety wasn't what it once was since the death of her brother and the Sibling Gang. Maybe she just didn't care.

Whether by arrogance or apathy, there she was.

Paula reached for Roderick Crowe's revolver and realized it was already in hand. She thought about taking aim through the window, of swinging around the doorway and blasting. Ginny looked drunk enough that she probably wouldn't present a challenge in a straight fight. The men with her must have been her new gang, but none of them looked sober either.

Judging if she could confront so many even in their current state, Paula thought back to Misun.

You will not hurt me. You will not hurt anyone.

Had she really changed in the last four years? Paula felt something rise in her throat as she lowered her gun. She watched Ginny throw back another shot, listened to her cackle as one of her cohort fell from his chair, passed out. Past the malicious eyes, Paula saw Roderick Crowe in her face. Then she saw Louis Vance. Private Delsman. Mrs. Alvord. The Dunlaps. The Rigbys. Waite. Pa. All the people who'd been pulled into that wave of destruction. All the untold souls whose lives had been destroyed to the sound of callous laughter.

Paula walked into the bar.

She was surprised how fast Ginny recognized her. The moment Paula planted her feet beside Ginny's chair, the outlaw's eyes fixed on her as if staring down a long-forgotten ghost come back from the ether. Ginny didn't notice Paula's weapon, but she seemed to know what was going to happen.

Paula didn't wait. She had no interest in reminding Ginny how she'd left her brother to die or how much pain she'd dispersed. She only raised Crowe's pistol and fired.

Paula flinched as blood spattered onto her cheek while it exploded onto the shattered window behind her. Ginny slumped over slowly, then fell out of the chair as had her drunk companion.

The other two men she'd been playing with didn't raise their guns or fly out of their chairs. One of them stared slack jawed at Ginny's body before turning to the girl who'd killed her. The other looked near passed out himself. When Paula turned her gun to them, they raised their hands, slowly pushing back from the table.

"What the hell are you doing?" one of the men from the bar called. It was Sheriff Teague, more horrified than angry. He rushed over, reaching for his gun. Paula kept hers tight in one hand, but with the other produced a wanted poster from her coat pocket. The picture depicted the recently deceased prior to her scar, but Teague recognized her, a look of shock and dread spreading across his face. He said nothing else as Paula dragged Ginny outside, into the falling snow. Everyone in the bar followed.

"Any of you know which is her horse?" Paula asked the small crowd.

One of the men she'd been drinking with pointed it out along the hitching post.

Paula asked the barkeep to help her heave the body over the saddle, flashing him a dollar. He did, wordlessly. Paula mounted her own horse. She reached into her coat for several more dollars and handed them to the barkeep as she rode by, apologizing for the window and the mess. Teague and the rest watched as the girl made her way to the southern edge of town on the road to Rapid City, undeterred by the snow and cold.

The End

Afterword

This book is part of a revised and rereleased collection from Tyler Tullis, representing his published work between 2012 and 2021.

The books include:

The Broken Afterlife
Originally published 2012

Assassin's Echo
Originally published 2014

Killing Virginia Crowe
Originally published 2015

The Park Ranger
Originally published 2018

Twenty-Six Trillion and One
Originally published 2021

An interview with the author.

Why revisit these books?

These five stories follow my evolution as a creative writer. Looking back at the earlier novels especially, I saw the need for a fresh coat of paint. What started as a technical chore quickly became a joyous resurrection of old friends, and I felt the urge to share them anew.

They're different genres. What unifies them as a collection?

These standalone books share a central storytelling mechanic. Each focuses on two central protagonists whose shared journey and dialogue volleys help them reckon with their pasts and prepare them for their futures. These pairings are often built on conflict and competing moral codes. Characters are constantly asking "can I trust you" or "how can I convince you to help me," creating dynamics in which protagonists challenge and build each other up. I think it underscores how life is a team sport—no Frodo gets very far without a Sam.

These main characters often come from different worlds (figuratively or literally), which creates interesting opportunities for fish-out-of-water interplay, and occasionally to explore seemingly incompatible romantic tension. The stories mostly pick up late in characters' journeys, almost like epilogues to past traumas. Often the reader is piecing together backstory, uncovering obscured pasts. Given so many structural similarities, grouping the books as a collection made sense to me.

What sort of changes did you make?

Mostly technical editing, but I also stripped out some overblown plot and bloated description. If you read the books in order of original release, you'll notice they generally get shorter. I like stories that are paced quickly, so I've learned to write more concisely. You also see my affinity for character dialogue increase book after book. I tend to focus on those interactions—I'm considerably less interested in choreographed action sequences.

I completely reimagined a few scenes in The Broken Afterlife and Killing Virginia Crowe, an undertaking I wasn't expecting. I generally don't believe in changing art once it's released to the world, but in this case, I felt I could take liberties to make a few scenes more urgent or less convoluted. It's less director's cut, more repair job.

As a male, why do you write so many female characters?

I'm mindful that all the main character pairings feature a man and a woman. I suspect this is reflective of my own lived experience, being a man who has learned from so many talented, resolute, resourceful and self-aware women. That's how I've tried to write female characters—as the smartest, funniest and most interesting people in their respective stories, typically as authorities and moral anchors. Adelaide, Cami, Paula, Naomi and Beck—none of them are damsels in distress.

Do you have a favorite among these books?

I have a favorite attribute of each book.

- I'm a fan of The Broken Afterlife's plot and worldbuilding. It's a little John Constantine, a little Robert Langdon, but the nature of this book's divine conspiracy is unique to anything I've encountered in the genre. I also enjoy how the mystery continues to unravel right to the final chapter. This book underwent the biggest transformation for the better.

- Assassin's Echo is pretty dense with plot, but it resolves in an unexpected way. Hopefully readers can see how much fun I had playing in this sandbox—I woke up every morning feeling like Jason Bourne when writing this.

- Killing Virginia Crowe leans into western tropes, but each of its flawed characters feels decadent within that world. The tension Paula experiences in her calculus of how to treat Misun is perhaps the most urgent drama I've written. I love this climax and the resolution to Paula's arc.

- With The Park Ranger, the relationship and dialogue between Naomi and Baird is special. They both drew so much on feelings I was grappling with at that point in my life. I think it helps ground and add weight to the protagonist-stalked-in-the-wild setup.

- In Twenty-Six Trillion and One, I'm cooking a full course meal with only a few ingredients, which felt gratifying as a writer. It's my biggest story in terms of scale and stakes, but the smallest in terms of length and how focused it stays on its two protagonists. Ultimately it's a book about an alien visitor, but its emphasis stays on that character's "humanity" over his god-like power. That's something I wasn't mature enough to accomplish in earlier stories.

Any self-reflection to share with readers?

It's been said all fiction, to a degree, is autobiographical. I can attest to that. You empty a lot of yourself onto these pages, be it in the way dialogue is constructed, beliefs certain characters hold, even describing the way something looks or smells.

For me, there's more to be said and revealed in one work of fiction released every decade than daily social media posts over the same time horizon. That's why it means so much to me when someone reads one of these books. I understand the reader is making an emotional investment of time and extending their own vulnerability to explore a distilled snapshot of someone else's mind. It's an honor I don't take lightly.

Though, I feel it's important to acknowledge, I once did. From fantasy and science-fiction trilogies I wrote as a kid to earlier versions of these books in need of polish, I've independently published a lot I'm not proud of. I was overzealous and impatient in my youth. My writing and storytelling abilities just weren't there yet, and I wish I'd had someone look me in the eye and tell me so. With the release of this collection, I've made peace with how my journey brought me to this point. As a mentor of mine says, always forward, never straight.

What does the future hold?

I will continue writing, but with far less frequency. Creative writing demands more time and emotional stamina than I have to give amid other priorities in my life. I've also closed shop on my business, ended my digital presence and downshifted my audience to friends and family. Knowing the people who matter most to me are enjoying these stories and viewing this side of me is its own reward.

In the meantime, thank you so much for reading any or all of the books in this collection of fiction. I sincerely hope you enjoy them.

About the Author

Tyler Tullis is an independent fiction writer. He primarily works in organizational communications strategy. When he isn't writing fiction or comms plans, he is reading, paddleboarding, golfing, playing video games, responsibly traveling, volunteering and advocating for climate policy. He is married and lives in the Pacific Northwest of the United States.

At the time of this publishing, Tyler recommends:

- The video game *The Legend of Zelda: Tears of the Kingdom*
- The novel *The Past is Red* by Catherynne M. Valente
- Progressive metal band Periphery
- The podcast The Ezra Klein Show
- *The Expanse* novels by James S.A. Corey
- Comedy rock band Ninja Sex Party
- The book *What We Owe the Future* by William MacAskill
- The show *Attack on Titan* originally written by Hajime Isayama
- Stand up paddleboarding whenever one can
- So bad they're good '90s movies *Point Break* and *Robin Hood: Prince of Thieves*

www.ingramcontent.com/pod-product-compliance
Lightning Source LLC
Chambersburg PA
CBHW020551180626
46810CB00007B/2459